Praise for *North of Foothill*

"Buckle up as Orlando Davidson and Homicide Detective Jimmy Sommes drive you, tires squealing, into the dark underbelly of Southern California. Sommes is drawn into a deadly game of betrayal and redemption where bullets fly and old friends become dangerous foes. This is a high stakes, low morals game, and a cat-and-mouse caper you won't soon forget."

~ Ed Davis, author of *The Last Professional*

Other Books by Orlando Davidson

A Jimmy Sommes Investigation

Baseline Road

NORTH OF FOOTHILL

A JIMMY SOMMES INVESTIGATION

By

Orlando Davidson

ISBN: 978-1-963832-44-0 (paperback)
ISBN: 978-1-963832-63-1 (ebook)
LCCN: 2025951372

Printed in the United States of America.

Artemesia Publishing
9 Mockingbird Hill Rd
Tijeras, New Mexico 87059
www.apbooks.net
info@artemesiapublishing.com

Content Notice: This book contains descriptions of drug use, pornography, mental illness, police actions, and physical assault and trauma that may be disturbing to some people. The book also uses racial slurs and derogatory terms that were in use at the time that this book is set. We have kept this language to reflect its usage at the time, but the author and the publisher condemn the usage of such language whether it was used in the past or today.

To my children Daniel and Shannon Davidson, again and always; and also to my wonderful new friends in Charbonneau, Oregon who have provided a fresh dose of inspiration.

FOREWORD

Songwriters used to treat New York City as the center of the universe, citing the 59th Street Bridge, 110th Street, 42nd Street and every last borough, as if we all lived there or ought to.

Mysteries are also rooted in place, whether it's Raymond Chandler's Los Angeles, Dashiell Hammett's San Francisco or John D. MacDonald's Fort Lauderdale. And the riches have been more widely dispersed in recent years.

Like a Chuck Berry song, noir anthologies have name-checked and embraced cities across the U.S. Those titles are sometimes inevitable – *Brooklyn Noir, Detroit Noir, New Orleans Noir* – and sometimes unlikely: *Cape Cod Noir, Milwaukee Noir* and, mining the Buckeye State for unexpected criminality, both *Columbus Noir* and *Cleveland Noir*.

Claremont is an even more unexpected setting for mystery stories, but it's happened. Kem Nunn's *Pomona Queen* touches on Claremont while largely taking place in the gritty city next door, the yin to Claremont's yang, while Sue Grafton's *A is for Alibi* briefly stops in Claremont before moving on.

Still, no mystery writer made extensive use of Claremont (pop. 37,000), a tidy college town on the border of California's Los Angeles County and the Inland Empire, until Orlando Davidson thought to do so in *Baseline Road*.

Speaking as a later-day Claremont resident, as well as a chronicler of the region, I can assure you, the reading public, that the streets of the so-called City of Trees and Ph.D.s are clean, not mean. Traditionally, the joke was that the sidewalks rolled up early. It's still a town where people prize their 40 winks.

Davidson was a college student here in the 1970s, the period when his protagonist, Sgt. Jimmy Sommes, is chasing down leads. In *Baseline Road* and again in *North of Foothill,* Davidson evokes the Claremont and environs that he knew.

He namedrops real-life places of the era: watering hole Bodene's, prime rib specialist Lord Charley's, roadside steakhouse Sycamore Inn. The freeways flow freely enough that characters drive up to Barstow without a second thought. There are cop bars, wide open spaces and a vaguely frontier spirit, a sense that the characters are navigating a zone where city rules don't extend.

Yet the menace here is far from the rain-soaked streets of Chicago or NYC. A dirty cop lives in a nondescript apartment in suburban Upland, near a Mexican fast food spot. (It's based on the locally beloved, but long gone, Mi Taco.) That cop tests Jimmy's scruples over combo plates at Bob's Big Boy.

The favorite meeting place of Jimmy and pal Carol Loomis is not a shadowy parking garage or neon-drenched tavern but the absolutely normal Marie Callender's. Apparently it made a potent margarita.

Do the place names matter to the rest of you? Not really. *North of Foothill* is a work of fiction: funny, tragic and absurd, exciting, violent and sexy. But for those of us who live here now, and those who lived here in the 1970s, the details add another layer: of authenticity, of nostalgia, of memory.

Who needs Sunset Boulevard, Pacific Coast Highway or Mulholland Drive? Jimmy Sommes has Foothill Boulevard, Mission Boulevard and Sierra Avenue. Orlando Davidson brings them to life.

David Allen
Claremont, Calif.
Columnist, *Inland Valley Daily Bulletin*

CHAPTER ONE

May 9, 1974

I WAS OFF-DUTY BUT ARMED, my Smith and Wesson service revolver tucked into a shoulder holster hidden under my light blue sports coat. Billy, the assistant manager at Mister Louie's, a dive bar/club on the south, funkier, side of Foothill Blvd, had called me for a favor. Since he also booked the musical acts for the club, I'd agreed, even though my band, Salton Sea, was on hiatus. Our dipshit singer/rhythm guitar player was in "anger management" therapy, which left the rest of us, even his backup singer/girlfriend, managing our anger with him. He'd wept uncontrollably while singing the Rolling Stones "Wild Horses" at our last gig in La Verne a month and a half ago—and then he'd attacked the drum kit. We needed his voice, so the rest of the band had agreed to be patient with our problem child. Supposedly, he was doing better. Thus, staying in good graces with folks like Billy remained important. I told him we'd be playing again soon.

Billy had told me that everything about the new management at Mister Louie's gave him the creeps, even scared him. There were lots of guns, lots of drugs. He'd asked me to check it out on this quiet Thursday night. He was there but agreed to stay clear of me. Every band I knew, including ours, had played at Mister Louie's, often for mostly friends and family. It was a small joint.

So I guess I was "semi-off-duty," the phrase my good buddy, Detective Carol Loomis, had used when introducing herself to Annie Hoover, now the love of her life, at a legal clinic in Claremont two years ago. It had been at the beginning of the "Claremont bombing" case—the one that almost cost Carol her life.

It was during the same case that my outfit, the San Bernardino Sheriff's Department, working in concert with the LA County Sheriff's Department, managed to shut down a drug gang and solve an old murder. Carol had moved on, leaving the Claremont Police Department, and already was the best private investigator in Pomona Valley, even without having her full license yet. Meanwhile, I'd stayed put, still serving as a San Bernardino County homicide detective.

It was May, my favorite month of the year in Southern California, and today had been beautiful—low seventies, blue skies as far as the eye could see. Earlier this morning I had wandered around Palmer Canyon, where I live, mulling over a possible job change. San Bernardino County Undersheriff Sam Fuller, my boss and mentor in the law enforcement business, wanted to promote me to lieutenant, move me to the San Bernardino headquarters, and give me a fancy title: Supervisor Major Crimes Division. It came with a private office, a secretary, and a substantial raise. All the homicide investigators in our entire county would report to me, and I in turn would report to Sam.

"I'm not going to be here forever, Jimmy," Sam had told me, "and you don't have the political savvy to do my job. Not that you'd want to. But this new position I'm creating will allow you to keep whoever replaces me from completely screwing everything up. Plus, you can cherry-pick, assign the really juicy cases, which you know you love, to yourself and your new eager beaver partner."

I was skeptical. I envisioned spreadsheets, budget reports, disciplinary matters, and other crap landing on my desk. Hell, I was accustomed to being the cop in trouble with superiors for my occasionally unorthodox crime-solving methods. Could I really see myself being the grown-up in the room, doling out warnings and punishment? My mother, of course, loved the idea of this promotion. "You're thirty-seven years old and there's hope for you yet," she'd said.

Even Carol Loomis, not a bureaucratic type, told me it was a "pretty big deal." Of course I liked the money part of it. Who wouldn't? Everything cost more these days with all the inflation. But I just wanted to be Sergeant Jimmy Sommes, work out of the Alta Loma substation, wear blue jeans, let my hair grow down to my collar, and do battle with the bad guys. Sure, I could tell Sam no. But the Sheriff's Department was like the military. If you said no to anything, you were pretty much screwed and got passed over from then on. I didn't want to end up back in Yucaipa where I'd started, pulling the weekend duty.

The part about my new eager partner was true. Jim Kreuger had transferred down from Portland late last year. I met JK, as we called him, during that same 1972 bombing case. He helped me save Carol's life after a desperate chase through Portland on a dark night that resulted in Mark Collins, the shadowy ex-CIA hitman, dying from the two bullets I fired into his chest. I've never regretted it, not for one waking moment, although my dreams haven't always quite matched this level of certainty. Taking a life sticks with you, for keeps. Forget all that nonsense on television, where lawmen routinely gun people down with big smiles on their faces. Nevertheless, up there in Portland, it was an easy call, the hitman or Carol.

JK was learning that there seemed to be more bad guys in wild San "Berdoo" County than in the entire city of Portland. While still technically a patrol officer while all the paperwork caught up with reality, JK served as my partner. He was diligent and good at his job. I was leaning on him too much these days as I brooded about various facets of my life and drank too much in the process. Damn, this might have been part of Sam Fuller's master plan. Let JK handle Alta Loma when I moved to headquarters and got motivated again. I tried to put such thoughts aside for the evening. Carol had reminded me more than once that complaining too much about a possible big promotion made me sound like a spoiled baby. She always managed to cut right to the heart of the matter.

Time to focus on Mister Louie's and my surveillance gig. The club was located half a mile or so east of the venerable Sycamore Inn in a small shopping center and sandwiched in between a good, cheap Mexican restaurant and a beauty parlor. Foothill Blvd was part of the old now-decommissioned Route 66, but few made the connection. I thought that bit of trivia was cool, but nobody asked me about it so I never got to share my local's knowledge. Mister Louie's was in San Bernardino Sheriff's Department jurisdiction, right on my Alta Loma/Etiwanda/Cucamonga beat. I loved the sound of that tri-city rhyme, but the times they were a-changing. All these small county cities were growing like crazy and community movers and shakers and politicians were pushing for the creation of a brand new city to be called "Rancho Cucamonga" that would swallow them all up. It was in the name of progress, and there was nothing I could do about it. I hung on to the past as best I could, both as a lawman and a temporarily unemployed fiddle player.

I ordered a beer and potato chips while I eyeballed Mister Louie's. On impulse, I added a shot of Wild Turkey to my order. I toasted President Richard Nixon as I downed the shot. They were planning to impeach that crooked son-of-a-bitch. It was starting up in Washington. Good riddance. I hadn't voted in the 1972 presidential election, a first for me. McGovern was too liberal; Nixon was too creepy.

Tonight was mostly about the music. A group of talented Claremont musicians—not really a band—were playing country rock tunes, probably just to keep up their chops. These guys made any kind of music sound good. I knew them all except the bass player, a skinny, long-haired dude wearing a Moby Grape T-shirt who looked barely old enough to order a beer. The other fellows, seasoned vets, knew me on account of my fiddle playing for Salton Sea, but these guys were the real thing—coming out of bands that had recorded albums and backed up singers like Linda Ronstadt and Jackson Browne. Sometimes we drank together at the nearby

Midway Bar, but never far from the surface was the fact that I was a cop, not the ideal companion for a musician in this day and age. They had the courtesy to smoke their joints in the parking lot before ordering their beer inside.

Bob, the lead singer and rhythm guitar player for this assemblage, had passed me on his way to the small stage. "This place is getting fucking weird," he murmured, "but they paid in advance, even overpaid." He patted the pocket of his jean jacket. Without any talk or fanfare, the group started cranking out tunes. Merle Haggard's "Mama Tried" was first. Dylan, Burrito Bros, and Johnny Cash songs all followed, music that was near and dear to my heart.

I was sitting in a booth to the far left of the small stage, nursing my Budweiser. It was a good vantage point to watch both the band and the rest of the club. The red Naugahyde stuck to my jeans. Did they ever clean this place? About five songs in, I saw two men enter the club in the dim light and stop to talk to the bartender, a new guy I'd never met. These characters were acting like they owned the joint, laughing and talking too loud, oblivious to the music. Very rude. The bartender handed them a bottle of clear liquid and two glasses, and they each poured themselves a couple of shots. Probably tequila or mezcal. No money changed hands. The three men shared some sort of noisy joke. What Carol Loomis called my "cop radar" began to ping. They looked like extras from a New York City crime movie and certainly weren't local. Why bad guys self-identify themselves remained a mystery to us in law enforcement, but it made our job easier. These guys looked young and stupid, even from a distance.

Something *had* gone wrong with this club. Who the hell was this bartender? It didn't feel like the friendly little joint I was used to. I surmised that these new characters were either LA or Vegas mob. Bad guys were growing like weeds these days, not to mention the Mexican drug cartels. I would advise the young assistant manager to find another job before things went completely haywire here. Still, since nobody was breaking any laws, I turned my attention back to the music. The band was giving Dylan's "It Takes a Lot to Laugh, It Takes a Train to Cry" a fine, stretched out treatment with the slide guitar putting you on that same mail train with Bob. I was knocked out, as always, by this music and thinking about ordering another glass of Wild Turkey.

That's when the shots rang out, multiple shooters, very loud—likely .357 Magnum handguns—but not in the main area of the club, thank goodness. The sounds came from somewhere behind the stage, maybe the back room. The smell of exploding gunpowder quickly reached all of us. *Fuck!* I jumped on the stage yelling at the musicians, "Get out, front entrance, now, leave your stuff." The small crowd was doing the same. Pulling my revolver, and likely outnumbered and outgunned, I went in the other direction toward an opening at the back of the stage, not having any idea what was on the other side. Except that they had big guns. I was on full alert, worried about getting my head blown off.

The back room was to my right. I knew from our gigs it was for storage, not a place the musicians normally went. The door was half-open, blocked by a body, with another prone body not far from it. The coppery scent of blood was overwhelming, mixed with the unmistakable stench of violence. The cool evening air helped some, coming from a concrete loading bay directly in front of me that fronted a small parking area. A car engine blasted to life. It was a big, dark sedan. I ran toward the opening, wanting to get the license plate. I saw two men in the car. Or was it three? I got a fleeting image of what may have been a person in the back seat. The driver hit the headlights, momentarily blinding me, and then made a left turn toward the driveway. I could see again. The car was a dark blue, late model Lincoln Continental. The passenger in the front seat was big and bald and had a crazed look to him. He stared at me, raised his weapon, and fired in my direction as I hit the deck. At least one of the bullets hit the wooden roof above my head. With no angle and a less powerful weapon, I returned fire toward the Lincoln, three shots from my revolver, if only to keep the guy off me. Then I heard a cackling laugh and the passenger yelled, "Get us the hell out of here, Monk." Burning rubber like a race car, the Lincoln headed toward Foothill, took a wild, screeching, fishtailing left turn, and was gone. I saw a flash of a California license plate, but I couldn't get the number.

The sirens started. I pulled out my sheriff's badge and holstered my gun. Within a minute, two Cucamonga patrol cars pulled into the parking lot, shotguns pointed in my direction. *Don't shoot me, you assholes.* There was lots of commotion, me yelling, "Cop, cop, cop," at the top of my lungs, my badge held high. They finally got it and stood down, lowering their weapons. I filled them in on the Lincoln and told them to call it in ASAP. I proceeded to the back room, my .38 drawn again. It was empty except for two dead bodies: the hoods I'd seen at the bar inside the club. What the hell. Was this a mob hit gone very wrong? From the location of the bodies, I could see they'd barely made it inside the back room before getting shot. There were no weapons to be seen. The guys that fled must have scooped them up.

The crime scene techs and medical examiner would have to figure that out. The room was dimly lit, but I could see an empty Jack Daniel's bottle, crumpled up In-N-Out Burger wrappers, and three lines of white powder spread on a small table, ready to snort. There was a considerable amount of blood spatter on the wall behind the table, on the other side of the room from the dead guys. It appeared somebody else had gotten shot too. Was it the third man I thought I saw in the back seat?

Christ! I needed to find that blood trail before the patrol guys trampled all over the evidence. "Stay clear, now," I barked. "This entire area, including the loading bay and the parking lot, is a crime scene. And please contact the San Bernardino Sheriff's Department. You know the number. We'll need the works."

A Cucamonga patrol sergeant showed up, flashlight in hand, watching his step. I knew him by sight. "I'm Sommes,

San Bernardino Sheriff's Homicide. I just happened to be here for the show. We've got a double homicide in that back room," I said, gesturing toward the reeking mess. "The shooters got away. They shot at me on the way out, from a dark blue Lincoln, California plates. I returned fire to no effect. There may be bullets lodged in the roof above the loading bay. Tape this room up and don't let anybody in there until the crime scene team shows up." I sprinted back into the club.

Where's the goddamn bartender?

CHAPTER TWO

May 3 – Glen Alpine, North Carolina

P*ETE GILES WOKE WITH A* start. That damn Civil War dream again. It was a movie that never changed: seeing his ancestor, Josiah Giles, die bravely at the Battle of Shiloh but not before first losing his nerve (and his rifle) and then engaging in heroics and killing a bunch of Yankees with the reclaimed rifle. As usual, the dream was so vivid that Pete could feel and even smell the muck and gore of the battlefield. He was sweating.

It had really happened and was akin to religion for the five generations of Giles men that followed. The story was told at family gatherings, particularly when the ladies had left the table and the men smoked their cigars and drank their bourbon. Confederate Captain Cole, his ancestor's commanding officer, had written to Josiah Giles's widow later in 1862, saying that her husband had acquitted himself well at Shiloh and had even passed something the commander had invented on the battlefield that very day that he called the "True Giles Test." It had to do with a mistake or failure of nerve, followed by a conspicuous act of bravery.

The story, including this damn True Giles Test, continued to chase Pete around like an unwelcome guest, a fearsome unmet obligation. He hated it. Some Giles men had looked hard for wars to join so as to meet this test, even that one in Cuba at the beginning of the century. Pete's father had made a minor contribution, serving in the army during the Korean War, but engaged in no major heroics. If anything, that put more pressure on Pete, his only son, to perform. What a joke! The last thing Pete wanted to do was die bravely on some battlefield. Or be any kind of a hero. Going to college had kept him out of Vietnam. But for the life of him, he couldn't stop the dream, which on this occasion had included a pounding noise.

The pounding started up again. He looked at his bedside clock—11:30 p.m., late for any activity in sleepy little Glen Alpine. Maybe the screen door was broken. That chilly north wind from the Appalachians was blowing. He got out of bed and went downstairs. Turning on the dining room light, he heard the knocking again. It was the front door.

"Jesus Christ, Pete! I was about to throw a rock at your window. I heard you were home. Open up." It was Monk Tanner, Pete's oldest and closest friend.

"Get dressed, college boy, we're going to the movies. And bring some money. I'm tapped out."

"You've got to be kidding, it's almost—"

"Just do it, it's important," Monk interrupted. Pete could see that his friend was wired. With his long brown hair and mustache, Monk resembled a Southern rock 'n' roll musician, especially in his agitated state. His shirt didn't look warm enough for this strange weather. The temperature went from the thirties to the seventies in the space of the day when this wind blew, even in May.

"You won't be sorry." Monk looked unusually serious. "We'll be in time for the midnight show."

Pete sighed, went upstairs, threw on some clothes, including his Appalachian State letterman jacket, and joined his friend. Monk's silver Ford Mustang hit all the green lights on Highway 70, so it was a ten-minute straight shot to downtown Morganton. It felt longer to Pete on account of Monk's clenched silence. They hadn't spent much time together recently—not since last summer really—but Pete knew to leave Monk well enough alone during his episodes. He'd known him since first grade and liked him better than the college kids, including his football teammates, who he had spent the last three years with. Monk was pure "country," no two ways about it, but honest, funny, and loyal to Pete in all ways. A true friend.

They parked near Duggie's Bar and started to go downstairs. A tough looking guy stopped them. "That'll be ten bucks a piece," he said.

Surprised, Pete handed him a twenty-dollar bill, and he and Monk descended to the funky basement. About forty young men and several brave girls were crammed in, sitting in folding chairs in front of a beat-up old movie screen. Morganton was a Baptist town, and this was about as sinful as it got: Friday night porno movies. The Morganton cops turned a blind eye, as long as folks behaved themselves. Pete was thinking about the entrance fee. "That's a lot of money down the drain," he said.

"Just wait," was all Monk said. Then he went over to the makeshift bar to get beers while Pete settled in and relaxed, trying to make the best of it. He was on a short quarter break from App State, and his parents had asked him to watch the family house while they took a rare vacation. So why not a dirty movie?

Monk returned with the beer in plastic cups. The projector whirred to life. *Wild Valley Babes* was the title. "Jesus," Pete muttered to himself. It was like every sex movie, fun for a minute or two and then boring as hell. Why were they even here?

On the screen, for all the world to see, was Johnny Rolland, the finest baseball player to ever come out of the entire state of North Carolina, appearing in a stag film in a group sex sequence.

Pete was stunned, and then he sickened. This couldn't be true, but there he was. The memories flooded back. Rolland had been the star center fielder for a Morganton High School team that made it to the state tournament. He'd drawn comparisons to Willie Mays but mostly Mickey Mantle since he was white. In 1969, he'd signed with the Philadelphia Phillies right out of high school for bonus baby money, and Rolland quickly made it to Triple-A before he was badly hurt in a team bus accident. His right knee was shattered, along with his baseball career. *Now this*, Pete thought. It was really sad.

"That's why we came," Monk said, looking grim-faced. "Let's get the hell out of here. I can't watch this again. I saw the whole damn movie at nine o'clock. I heard Duggie and his buddies 'borrowed' the movie from a porno theater in Atlanta and are showing it six times over the weekend. But get this, in the credits he's listed as 'Glenn Alpine.'"

Pete recognized somebody he'd known in high school as they headed out. "You're gonna miss the best parts," the drunk guy said. Pete just nodded to him, still in shock, following Monk as he walked across the street and found a bench in the courthouse square. The rain had stopped, but the stately old courthouse building, illuminated at night, glistened from the moisture.

"Johnny was my hero. I was planning to go to Philadelphia one day and watch him play. I remember his stolen bases even more than his home runs. He could hit *and* run. Now I see this goddamned awful thing." Monk stuffed a wad of chewing tobacco in his mouth, maybe to keep his emotions under control.

Pete felt the same way. Two years behind him in school, he and Monk had gone to all of Rolland's high school games, keeping statistics and watching his awesome combination of power and speed. It looked as if nothing was going to stop him. The Phillies thought so too; the signing money got his family, such as it was, out of that crummy trailer park near the train tracks. The local newspaper showed a picture of Rolland, his mama, and whatever man was around then in front of their new little house in town.

Then on a foggy night in Pennsylvania, a flatbed truck ran a red light and slammed into the team bus. Most of the players were okay, sound asleep but Johnny was standing in front, shooting the shit with the driver. He was thrown clear out of the bus through the front window. Lots of blood, but his knee was the real problem. Multiple surgeries, followed by months of rehab in Arizona, couldn't put Johnny Rolland back together again. The Phillies tried hard, but he was finished as a baseball player. Pete lost track of him. Seemed like everybody else did too. The local paper stopped writing about him.

"Did you see his body in the movie, all contorted, bald head, huge chest, tiny legs?" Monk asked.

"Yeah, I saw it. That's weightlifter stuff, lots of bench pressing, plus steroids," Pete said, suddenly angry, not sure why. "What are we complaining about? He looked bad, Monk, maybe drugged up. Big deal. End of story. Nothing we can do about it." Pete wanted to break training and smoke a cigarette, but he didn't have any. And he was sick of this drippy, crap weather. It had been a wet spring. They were the only people in the town square. An animal, likely a possum, was snuffling in the hedge.

"He looked really sad to me," Monk said, "like he needed help."

"Come on, what are you, a psychologist? Did you see that Hollywood sign in the background? He's in California in a damn movie having the time of his life with those bleach blondes. Let's go home." Pete stood and started walking toward the car. Despite his words, he didn't really buy it either; he had sensed a troubled man behind the muscled and sexed-up physique. But it might be purely their shock and imagination. They didn't know Rolland anymore, maybe never had. He was a star to them, not a person.

Monk grabbed the back of Pete's jacket, trying and failing to stop him. Pete wondered if Monk was going to fight him. Monk threw down his ball cap in frustration. "Screw you, I'm not going home and just forgetting about this. I'm gonna take a vacation from the plant, drive to California, and save my friend. You can come or not."

Save his friend? It was the single craziest idea Pete had heard in his twenty-one years of life. He dismissed it out of hand, saying, "You've got to be kidding."

"I'm not," Monk responded.

They walked in silence back to the car. As Monk drove

back to Glen Alpine, Pete reflected on his automatic response. He'd always been so dependable—the good boy who got excellent grades, played high school and college football, dated nice girls, and generally made his parents proud. His father expected him to join the family lumber business after graduation. An uncomfortable thought entered Pete's brain. He realized at that moment that he was trapped in a pre-ordained life. What if, for once, he did something wild and crazy, like dropping everything and driving west?

Last Christmas, his father took him to the Giles Lumber Company. Pete knew it well, had done the hard, physical work at the mill during his summers, but this journey was different. William, a stern and often distant father, was excited. He took Pete to an office right next to his. It contained a beautiful old desk and was fully furnished, ready to use. "This is your office, son," William said. "When you finish college, you start here as vice president. I couldn't be prouder of you."

It had made Pete's stomach churn. Feeling trapped, he wanted to run for the door. Somehow, he managed to mumble his thanks and the two went home. Then Pete had to go through the whole charade again with his mother. He'd never been happier to return to school.

Nothing had felt right at home since. He'd even waited for his parents to leave before returning to Glen Alpine yesterday. Now, something wild and crazy was being presented to him. Could this idea work, the road trip of his life? Coach would be pissed. Spring practice was over, but the "voluntary" conditioning and weight-lifting sessions were starting soon. App State was no Clemson or North Carolina, but it took its football seriously. Could he be back in a week?

Pete's epiphany continued unabated. He began to realize that he was sick of football, not the games, which he still loved, but all the authoritarian BS that went with it. Coach could suck eggs as far as Pete was concerned. He was a starter. The team needed him next season. School was already set up to be an easy summer quarter. He was a double major, English for himself, Business to keep his family off his back. He could catch up fast. Maybe write about the trip for his American Literature professor and get credit for it. His mind was spinning.

As for his parents, they'd be gone for another eight days, in Belize of all places. His mother had finally gotten her husband a long way from the mill, where he couldn't call in every day. Pete figured the neighbor lady could watch the house, water the plants, and feed the cat. He would sweet-talk her, say it was about a girlfriend or something, so the neighbor lady wouldn't bust him later. She liked that romantic stuff. All the pieces might fit...

One big thing still didn't make sense. "Johnny Rolland wasn't our friend," Pete said to Monk. "We were two high school sophomores who idolized him, trailed him around like groupies. He barely knew who we were."

"Well, how about this, college boy, he's my kin," Monk blurted out. "Not real close, some sort of cousin on my asshole father's side. I only found out last year from a gossipy old aunt of mine when we were drinking cherry bounce moonshine up at the lake. It surprised the hell out of me. That makes it personal."

Pete didn't know what to say. They drove home in silence, each lost in their thoughts. "Let's talk in the morning," he said when Monk dropped him off at his big old Glen Alpine house. It was dead quiet after Monk drove away. Then Pete heard an owl making its hunting call, close by, maybe in the big poplar tree in the backyard that fronted the woods. It was after midnight, time for the creatures to hunt. He went inside and made sure the cat had food and water.

He felt like his life was tilting in an unusual direction. The image of that corner office at the mill, next to his father, was haunting him. It was exactly where he didn't want to be. Pete began to pack. But he knew there was a person he needed to talk to first.

***

"Brother" Jeremy was ladling out steaming bowls of grits and gravy to the unfortunates when Pete showed up at the Calvary Food Bank early the next morning. The food bank was located in an old warehouse on the east side of downtown Morganton where things began to get seedy. Without anybody ever saying anything about it, it was the one area in town, besides the factories, where whites, blacks, and even Mexicans (working at the chicken plant) could interact in the mostly segregated city without causing any trouble for each other. The fog in the air matched the haze in Pete's brain. He hadn't slept much.

He'd met Jeremy Simmons two years ago when volunteering at the food bank. Now they were friends of a sort. Pete had heard rumors that Jeremy, now in his forties, had some sort of complicated personal history that included time in LA. Pete had been careful to respect Jeremy's privacy in that regard and never asked. The consortium of churches that ran this food bank had hired Jeremy, and nobody quite knew why this Yankee had been brought to town. He was, however, good at his job. Pete's father, who tended toward orthodoxy, did not like Jeremy, simply because he was an outsider.

Jeremy handed off his breakfast duties to a volunteer and motioned for Pete to join him in his small office. "To what do I owe the pleasure of your company this morning? You look lousy, by the way."

Pete spit out the whole story in fast staccato sentences, the ideas sounding more outlandish as he went through it. He included the fact that Monk and Johnny Rolland were related. "Do you think I'm crazy?" he asked at the conclusion of his tale.

After a long pause, Jeremy said, "Yes and no," with a rueful smile. "You're asking advice from a man who's done more than his fair share of crazy ass things. I'm here in Morganton to atone for some of them. But here goes. First, you want a break from your overly organized 'good boy' life. I get that. A road trip to the West sounds perfect, and you seem to be lucky enough to have some time."

Jeremy hesitated again and sighed. "But, Jesus, Pete. I am duty-bound to shut up about Los Angeles and my doings there. But I can tell you that the pornography business in Southern California is run by some shady characters. It's more gangsters than Hollywood movie types. Hard drugs often are a part of it. I've been gone for five years, and I'm not allowed to return, ever. That's all I can say about that, and it's already too much." Jeremy stared at Pete, shook his head, and then pulled out his checkbook and wrote a check. He put it in an earthen jug on top of a filing cabinet and then pulled $200 in cash out of the same jug. "Heaven help me. Here's my contribution to your journey if you decide to go. If not, gimme the money back. But please be careful and split at the first sign of trouble. LA is huge. You likely won't find him."

"Thank you. Monk got the address of the company that made the movie from the credits," Pete said. "It's on Lankershim Boulevard in North Hollywood if that means anything." He handed Jeremy a scribbled note with the address.

"I know the area, not this particular place," Jeremy said. "So, you're just going to walk in there and ask for this Johnny Rolland character?"

"Yeah, I guess."

Jeremy wrote two names and phone numbers on the same piece of paper and handed it back to him. "You really are running blind. If you happen to run across these two, just say 'The Reverend' says hello. They'll know. And call me from the road if you get in trouble. You know my home number. Now get out of here before I talk myself into an even bigger heap of trouble."

***

Somewhere in Oklahoma, Pete mentioned this conversation to Monk, who watched every cop show on TV. Monk responded with, "Well, Pete, it sounds like your weirdo Yankee buddy is in Morganton courtesy of the feds. You ever hear of witness protection?"

CHAPTER THREE

May 9

I WENT OUT THROUGH THE front door of Mister Louie's and into chaos. The customers, the staff, and the musicians were milling around. To my surprise, JK was there trying to direct the human traffic and get witness statements. "How'd you get here so fast?" I asked, glad to see my partner.

"My cousin and I had just pulled into the Magic Lamp parking lot on our way to dinner when I heard the radio traffic and figured you needed help. My cousin's happy. I left him there in the bar. What's the status?"

"It's bad. Double homicide in a back room behind the stage. The shooter also fired at me from his car on his way out. Missed by a mile." The lie popped out. "I fired back, just to keep the guy off me."

"I heard. Dark blue Lincoln, driver and a passenger, the latter being the shooter," JK said. "What's your priority?"

"Do what you're doing. Get names and addresses, especially from the staff. There might be some kind of mob connection. I gotta find the bartender. The murder victims are likely wise guys, although that's just a hunch right now. There might have been a third occupant in the Lincoln, maybe the one who got shot, but I'm not sure of that."

I raised my voice and spoke to the crowd. "Folks, I'm Sergeant Jimmy Sommes of the San Bernardino County Sheriff's Department. This is my partner, Officer Kreuger." I gestured toward JK. "I'm afraid we've got a serious crime scene, with fatalities, behind the stage. We'll get you out of here as fast as we can, but we need to take statements. Officer Kreuger and these other officers will get to you as fast as they can. Please be patient. And there's no current danger. The suspects drove away."

I found Billy, the club's assistant manager. "This is just crazy," he muttered.

"The bartender, who is he, and where is he now?" I asked him.

"He's new, Benny somebody. Said he'd been promoted to general manager but wouldn't give me the time of day. He split after the shots were fired, literally ran out the door."

That figured. I needed to talk to my boss, Sam Fuller. He knew the LA and Vegas mobs better than anyone. Right on cue, I heard Sam's ancient Jaguar coupe before I saw it, its engine badly in need of a tune-up as always.

"Fill me in," he said when he got out of the car, no preliminaries needed. "Let's talk in back."

I told him what I knew, both facts and conjecture. Listening to me, Sam ran his fingers through his short slate-gray hair, always the Marine. The medical examiner had arrived. Two crime techs were fingerprinting the entire room and searching for bullets.

"Hey, Marvin, can I see their wallets?" Sam called out to the ME, who started to object but stopped at seeing Sam's glare. The medical examiner carefully extracted the wallets from the men's back pockets and handed them to Sam, saying, "I need those back right away." One was bloody. Sam examined both and found their driver's licenses. "We've got Vincent and Joseph Salerno, with the same Lankershim Boulevard address in North Hollywood. Very likely brothers. Both in their twenties."

Sam sighed, then looked at me. Could he smell the Wild Turkey on my breath? "Like you said, it's likely these now deceased gentlemen were armed and fired weapons, but the killer or killers scooped up the guns on their way out the door. Let's meet tomorrow at ten, my office. You and JK will be lead, but we'll need to put together a full team, including communications. The press will have a field day with this."

"Okay," I said. "We'll run the victims' sheets tonight, see if they have records. I'm betting they do. The shooter, that's another matter. He looked like a meth head to me, and he's got a driver named Monk. That's about it, except there might have been a third person in the Lincoln. I got a quick flash, plus I'm betting there's a blood trail out to the parking lot. The crime scene guys need to confirm that."

Sam nodded, thanked me, and started to walk away. Then he stopped. "Remember Joe Donatella, Joe Don we called him?" Sam asked me.

I nodded. He'd been a big shot in the Los Angeles mafia who'd lived a surprisingly quiet life in North Upland, not too far from where we were standing. He'd died a couple of years before.

"His guys ran a major gambling operation in Ontario out of Dave's Market. Still do. He stayed clear of that operation for the most part. Well, Joe Don was an old-fashioned gangster and a good Catholic in his own weird way," Sam said. "He'd made it to underboss for the entire Los Angeles mob before he died. He kept them out of drug dealing for one thing, at least around here. Joe didn't start pointless turf wars, and believed that gambling and loan sharking were the wise guys' most predictable and profitable businesses. He was no saint, plenty of rough stuff, but it usually stopped short of murder."

Sam hesitated for a moment and then continued. "What you don't know is that Joe Don and I used to get together from time to time for coffee, always unofficial and off the record, usually in places like West Covina. We sure as hell weren't friends but shared a common interest in wanting to avoid any crazy violent mix-ups."

Sam allowed himself a smile. "Sometimes I even bought some of his family's rotgut red wine."

"Now it's the wild west again," I said.

Sam nodded. "And everybody's dealing dope. See you in the morning." Sam shuffled off, walking like a man who'd seen too much violent death in his time.

CHAPTER FOUR

May 9 – Upland

JOHNNY ROLLAND KNEW WHERE HE was going. "Turn left at the next light, it's Euclid Avenue," he instructed Monk Tanner. He was double-checking a half-crumpled piece of paper, muttering to himself. "The address is 290 North Laurel. Take a right on Arrow Highway, below the train tracks, then a left on Laurel. It'll be the third house on the right. Pull into the driveway."

Monk did as he was told. He was a good driver, had even done some stock car racing in North Carolina. The garage to the right of the house was open. A middle-aged balding man in khakis and a blue windbreaker was in the front yard waiting. "Pull into the garage, close it after you, and then use the side door into the kitchen," he said. "You need a stretcher?"

"Not sure yet," Rolland replied. "You were ready for us."

"I heard all the noise on the scanner. Don't tell me anything more. Not my concern."

Monk, with his good southern manners, said, "Hi, I'm—"

"No names ever, pal," Windbreaker barked at him. "Call me the Medic. Now move."

Monk drove the car into the garage. It was spotless. Pete Giles lay in the back seat moaning, barely conscious. The Medic quickly maneuvered Giles into a carry position and moved him through the kitchen into a room with a hospital bed. "Looks worse than it is, probably just a shoulder wound, but he's in shock," the Medic said to Monk. "I'll stop the bleeding and get an IV started. Do you know his blood type? He'll need some." Monk didn't.

"You're a strong dude," Monk said to him, admiring the

carry position.

"It's all technique," the Medic replied with a smile that looked more like a grimace.

Johnny Rolland remained in the garage staring at his car, seemingly transfixed, unable to move. "Shit, this fucking hayseed got blood all over my car," he said to no one in particular. "I need a shot, Medic," he yelled, "but no smack, never."

The Medic walked out to Rolland. "You know the deal. Pay me ten grand to fix this guy up and I'll let you have whatever you want." He gave Johnny a long look. "I recommend Dilaudid since you're coming down off stimulants. You get a clean car and even a good breakfast if you and your crew are out of here by nine o'clock tomorrow morning. And one more thing, don't come back anytime soon. You're going to be on a kill list, along with your young friends." The Medic returned to the house to tend to his patient. He figured Rolland didn't know that Dilaudid was synthetic heroin.

Meanwhile, Rolland briefly considered harming the man, his customary solution to any problem, but realized he needed to agree to this plan so as to live to fight another day.

***

Pete Giles awoke early the next morning from swirling, deep purple psychedelic dreams. The searing pain in his right shoulder was made worse by having no idea where he was. He began to thrash around only to discover the handcuffs binding his left wrist to an iron bar that was part of his bed. He was about to scream when a firm hand further restrained him.

"Take it easy, son. You're my patient. You're going to be fine."

"Wh—who are you?" Pete managed to stammer, wondering for a moment if this apparition looming out of the darkness with the calming voice was some sort of an angel, except that he looked so ordinary, like that actor Robert Duvall.

"Call me the Medic. I take care of people. Johnny Rolland

brought you here."

Johnny Rolland, the crazy drug freak he and Monk had driven across the country to rescue. Monk's harebrained idea had now made the leap to full-blown disaster. Pete had gotten shot. Actually shot. It was almost beyond comprehension. He dimly recalled the hellish scene in that cramped room, the men slamming through the door and the gunshots that followed.

"It's a clean wound, right shoulder, and the bullet is out," the Medic said, apparently reading Pete's mind. "It missed the bone. I'm going to adjust the IV in your left arm, so hang on." He first removed the handcuffs. "But no basketball for a while," he added with a half-smile.

Giles watched him, again trying to come to grips with his circumstances and failing. Was it just yesterday? That crummy bar in Pasadena where they met up with Rolland, set up by the lady at the Palomino Club. Johnny was chain smoking Marlboros and pounding down beers and shots of bourbon when they encountered him at the bar, immediately making his nonsensical claims of innocence, saying that gangsters were dogging him for no particular reason. It failed any test of reason.

"Look, I ain't no saint," Johnny had said to them. "I do what I do to live my life, but these assholes are trying to kill me," grabbing Monk's arm as he spoke. Pete knew already that Monk was hopeless. He was drinking the proverbial Kool-Aid and buying the crazy stuff that Johnny was peddling, no critical thinking left in his brain. Monk seemed excited by this dark world. Pete feared he had lost his friend, and perhaps more importantly greatly endangered himself.

"Why do they want to kill you, Johnny?" Pete had asked, wanting him to incriminate himself for Monk to hear.

"Let's just call it a certain disagreement over who owns what, you know what I mean. He pulled a battered old valise over his shoulder. Enough talk, let's go. We're driving east on Colorado Boulevard out there, good ole Route 66," Rolland said, gesturing toward a busy road barely visible through a dirty window. Any vestige of the innocent young baseball player was gone. The man had become a thug.

"Pete, you stick with me. Monk, you follow in the Mustang, a nice set of wheels. Damn, it's good to see you boys." Rolland downed one last shot and threw a couple of twenties on the bar. "We've got a couple of stops to make, and I'm planning to score big tonight."

Getting into Johnny's Lincoln, Pete had asked him, "What exactly do you want with us?" Pete's eyes strayed to the door handle. Should he just bail out and run for it?

Rolland had flashed a feral smile at Pete. He'd noticed Pete's glance. "Leverage, kid. Pure leverage." He pulled an ugly-looking gun from underneath his seat. "And you fellas walked right into it. I suggest you enjoy the ride because you ain't going anywhere, son."

The Medic snapped the handcuffs back on Pete's wrist, abruptly bringing him back to the present. It was no better. "Sorry, those are my orders. Morphine will help with the pain," he said, then quickly and efficiently injected a needle into Pete Giles's left arm. It provided the young man with a temporary respite from a dilemma that offered not even the remotest possibility of a solution.

CHAPTER FIVE

May10

"***OKAY, WHAT DO WE KNOW?"*** Sam Fuller asked, starting the meeting. We were in Sam's small conference room at San Bernardino headquarters the morning after the shootings. Attending along with JK and me were two other deputies, Hank Phillips and a rookie named Laura Gutierrez. I'd heard they were partners. Perfect. Phillips was one step removed from George Wallace in his political and social views, and a Chicano partner was just what he deserved. And a woman to boot! I didn't look at Hank, afraid my smile would give the game away. Plus, the man still owed me on account of his misdirected tear gas canister shot that damn near got me killed up on Mt. Baldy two years before. He still apologized to me for that way too often. All I ever said in return was that we arrested the bad guys and I didn't get shot.

Beth Bolling walked in. She was press relations. We had history. "Nothing in the papers yet, boss," she announced to Sam, pouring herself a cup of coffee. I looked at JK, rolling my eyes. This was our case, and by my reckoning there were now three extra people in the room.

Sam saw my reaction. "We're not going to solve the case sitting around this table, so I'll keep it short. Sommes is lead. He'll direct the investigation and this small team, working it in the customary manner. My concern is that some sort of a mafia gang war might be happening on our turf. Hence, we need to tread lightly with the press and try to wrap this up PDQ before it becomes a bigger deal than it already is."

Sam looked at the rookie. "I'm sure you know this,

Deputy Gutierrez, but we work just as hard on homicide cases involving nefarious characters as we do on those involving upstanding citizens. And"—Sam allowed himself a wry smile—"you'll find out that the differences between those categories aren't always what they seem. So again, what do we know?"

I recited the basic facts about the two dead goons and their North Hollywood address, the getaway car with at least two, probably three occupants, and the blood trail indicating that at least one of them was wounded. I'd heard at least two weapons, maybe three, being fired.

"Nothing from the local hospitals, I assume," Sam said. "Any prints?"

"We're sending some partials to LA County for ID, the usual drill," JK said.

We all knew that was a slow process. Might help at trial later. Then I talked about the missing bartender and all the loose ends.

"I may have something on that," Phillips said. "There's this ki—Jewish guy—trying to make a move on the dope business out here. He's based in North Hollywood, just like the dead guys, but spending lots of time these days in Ontario. Izzy Weiss is his name. He's into everything, including porno, but coke and heroin are his major products."

JK looked up from his notes. "Jeez, I've got a Weiss too. The bass player at the club last night. First name Joey. All the other musicians have been around here for years and are older guys. Joey just showed up recently. They say he's got a good groove, but none of them really know him that well."

Just then, Sam's secretary came in. "Jimmy, you've got a call. He says it's urgent. It might have to do with last night."

Sam gestured for me to take it, so I left the room. Saved by the bell. How come Phillips knows about this Izzy Weiss character and I don't? Time for me to get my shit together and stop being distracted. Half-assed doesn't cut it in our line of work. For one thing, it can be dangerous.

I took the call. It was a patrolman who worked out of Rialto. "We've got something funky at the El Rey Motel on Foothill. You know the place, right?"

"Hell, son, everybody knows the El Rey. What've you got?"

"We've got a trashed motel room, a busted-up Ford Mustang, and a Mexican motel clerk who won't talk to us."

I was thinking business as usual at the El Rey, but then the patrolman got to the good stuff. "The Mustang has North Carolina plates, and the registration is in the name of a Monk Tanner with an address in Glen Alpine, North Carolina."

I flashed back to last night, the guy with the gun yelling, "Get us the hell out of here, Monk." Not exactly a common name.

"Hang tight, and don't let the motel clerk leave," I said. "I'll try to get there in ten minutes."

I rejoined the meeting. Sam had left. JK was running through the witness statements. Nobody had seen much.

"We're rolling," I said to JK. "The El Rey Motel in Rialto. We might have a lead on the driver from last night, a fellow named Monk Tanner."

Addressing the rest of the team, I told Phillips and Gutierrez to keep working the Izzy Weiss angle. "And find out who owns Mister Louie's. Probably some string of corporations, but it might lead to Weiss."

"What do you need from me?" Beth Bolling asked. Our fling from last year had ended on friendly terms—no harm, no foul, and very little emotion.

"Just try to keep the press off our backs if they get interested. We are in the midst of our investigation, blah, blah, blah. You know the drill."

***

San Bernardino took care of its roads, Rialto didn't. That's when I knew we were close to the El Rey Motel on old Route 66, now Foothill Blvd. The road got bumpy past the more famous Wigwam Motel, which was just that, concrete wigwams. Route 66 buffs stayed there with their charts and books. Someday I wanted to drive the entire length of Route 66, the "mother road," as they called it, from Santa Monica all the way to Chicago, with special attention to the Oklahoma part, since I'd been born there. Route 66 was long gone now, much of it replaced by interstate highways, but the bits and pieces I'd seen in California were fun. Carol Loomis and I had drag-raced once on a well-paved stretch of it just east of Barstow. Her Chevy Bel Air had beat my Charger, costing me a prime rib dinner at Lord Charley's.

"Hey, Jimmy, you missed the turn," JK said, pulling me from my memories. *Jesus!* I was still distracted. Pulling a quick U-turn, I parked in front of the motel's office, next to the patrol car. The door to Room 48 was wide open. The trashed Ford Mustang was parked in front. The driver's side window was smashed in, and the leather seats were slashed to hell. It looked like somebody had opened the trunk with a crowbar. Nothing subtle about it. Anger was involved. The trunk was empty.

"There's a small baggie of weed in the glove compartment," Larry, the patrol guy, told me. "Plus a cassette player and a bunch of tapes."

So, they'd been looking for something else.

"Clothes scattered on the floor, an empty duffel bag, shaving stuff in the bathroom, and some loose change. That's about it," JK said when I joined him in the motel room. The bed was turned over, a broken lamp next to it, and the pillows were slashed open. An ashtray full of cigarette butts had been dumped on the carpet. JK was looking at two shirts. "One's size medium, the other is extra-large."

"Two guys, one bed," I said. "Some kind of romantic rendezvous?"

"Sheets are clean. Bed doesn't look like it was used or slept in," JK replied. "Look at this." He pointed to one loose twenty-dollar bill on the closet floor. "We better dust it for prints."

"Agree," I said, "along with the room and the car. They might match up with last night's shooter."

I surveyed the room. "What do you think, two or three people hanging out in this room?" JK shrugged. This scene struck me as related to the Mister Louie's shooting, but I didn't have enough pieces yet to make any sense of it.

The female motel clerk had come on at 6 a.m. All the damage had been done by then. She hadn't called the Sheriff's Department. A motel guest had, but hadn't left her name. The night man had left, and Lupe, the frightened motel clerk, didn't know how to reach him. The room was registered in the name of "Yogi Berra," and paid for in cash.

Nobody at the El Rey Motel wanted anything to do with us. Cops were nothing but trouble to them. We'd find the night man, but he'd tell us he didn't see a thing, even though his small window, protected by metal bars, looked right at Room 48 and the trashed Mustang. Schemes, secrets, booze, drugs, hookers, and broken dreams fueled this motel, along with poor folks who simply needed a cheap night's sleep before resuming their restless journeys. I felt more in common with this motley crew than I liked to admit, maybe because we kept the same hours. I wasn't sleeping too well these days.

Allie, my sometime girlfriend—I'd met and fallen for her during the infamous Claremont bombing case, which all roads seemed to lead back to—was a full-fledged journalist now, working for a newspaper in San Jose. Our usual weekends, not that usual to begin with, were on hold. She was chasing the Patricia Hearst kidnapping story, obsessed by it. I had lots of time on my hands. I missed her, more than I wanted to.

"What next, boss?" JK asked, looking at me funny, probably seeing I was only partly there.

"Sorry, man. Not much sleep last night," I told him. "We gotta find out everything we can about Mr. Monk Tanner from Podunk, North Carolina. Some bad dudes are after him and his murderous friend. I'm going to get a county crew out here to impound the Mustang and secure Room 48."

I told the Rialto deputy to stay put until the crime scene

techs showed up. JK asked to stay too. "I'm going to sweet-talk the motel clerk over there into giving up the night man. It's probably her cousin, and we need to find him. I'll see you back at the station." He might succeed too. Everybody liked the guy and JK's Spanish was better than mine even though he'd been in SoCal for less than a year.

Instead of driving back to San Bernardino, I headed south and then west on the San Bernardino Freeway toward Pomona. I felt some welcome adrenaline kick in, my head clearing. This was a damn fine murder case; better than the chicken feed I'd been working on. I wondered if the premier private investigator in the entire Inland Empire, Carol Loomis, might be free for lunch. It was worth a try, and she probably needed a break from philandering spouses.

CHAPTER SIX

May 6 – New Mexico

MONK TANNER WAS BEHIND THE wheel about thirty miles east of Albuquerque, New Mexico, when a ton of rocks started falling on the Mustang. At least that's what it felt and sounded like. Hailstones the size of golf balls were flying down out of the sky through a dense white fog. "I'm pulling over, can't see a goddamn thing," he yelled.

He found a good spot with some elevation to it. Then the torrential rain started. Pete Giles was worried about a flash flood. "I hope we don't float away."

Monk stayed calm. "It rains harder than this in Glen Alpine. No big deal." Thirty minutes later, the storm passed, the sky cleared, and the young men were greeted with an amazing sight. A small herd of pronghorn antelope, lorded over by a big buck, were grazing in a field no more than fifty yards from them. "They look like half goat/half deer," Monk said. Neither had ever seen one before. The men got out of the Mustang quietly so as not to spook the animals.

The high mountains to the north looked close enough to touch. "It doesn't get any prettier than this," Pete said to Monk, enraptured by the sights, wanting to hold on to them. He got a strong urge to stop, call it a trip, and drive back home. They'd driven like fools, grabbing random hours of sleep here and there in truck stop parking lots, and living on burgers and diner breakfasts.

Pete knew for certain they weren't going to find Johnny Rolland, their fallen hero, now a creepy porno guy, among the millions of people in Los Angeles. As they got closer to the city, he realized he was scared. Hard drugs, porno? He was just a college kid. Maybe he could just keep standing where he was, watching the antelope.

"Let's go, Pete." Monk grabbed his arm as if sensing the indecision. After one more intoxicating view of this classic western scene and breathing in the clean, sweet air, Pete reluctantly walked toward the car.

"These dents are proof of this moment," Monk declared, surprising Pete with his philosophical approach to the damaged hood and roof. Normally, he'd be really pissed off. Monk had been smoking lots of marijuana in addition to popping Benzedrine pills during the day, which could account for his tranquil mood. Pete was avoiding the pot—he still wanted to play football in the fall—but had popped a Bennie from time to time to stay awake while driving.

The absolute majesty and size of the West amazed him. The hailstorm had cleared the sky, and Pete could see for what must be 100 miles to the north. A long freight train snaked along the base of the mountains, probably the Santa Fe line. His father liked trains and kept some old timetables next to a tin of pipe tobacco in his study at home.

Pete knew he was in for the lecture of his life from his parents when he returned home but did not regret the trip, at least not so far. It had something to do with reclaiming his life and not just constantly seeking to please others. Along those lines, Pete was considering flying home from Los Angeles upon their arrival, ditching Monk in the process.

Monk abruptly took the next I-40 off-ramp. "We need gas." The sign at the light read "Welcome to Edgewood."

Monk pulled a five-dollar bill out of his jacket pocket at the Shell station and gave it to the attendant. It was his turn to pay.

After the fill-up, Monk didn't move. He just sat there. "Okay, fuck it," he finally said. "I've been holding out on you, Pete, the whole trip. Johnny Rolland is no distant cousin of mine. He's my half-brother. We got the same good-for-nothin' father. Can you believe it? All through high school and I never knew. Sorry I didn't tell you."

Pete hadn't seen this coming, but it helped to explain Monk's unusual intensity, starting at the porno movie and never letting up. "Why wait to tell me?" he asked.

"I don't know. Nothing is making any sense to me. What are we doing? Driving toward this giant city where I don't know a soul, thinking I can convince Johnny Rolland, if I can find him, who doesn't know me from shit, to come home."

"He doesn't know he's your half-brother?"

Monk lit a cigarette. "I don't know. What I said about learning all this last year up at Lake James was true. I haven't seen Johnny in two years."

"Gimme one of those," Pete said. Monk handed him a smoke and he lit it. Training be damned. "We've been on the road for, what, three days and two nights. You've been stoned most of the time in case you haven't noticed. It's been a nice little vacation for me. Should we just turn around?"

Monk shook his head. "I gotta try to find him, man. But if you need to leave, that's cool, no hard feelings."

"I need a minute," Pete said and got out of the car.

He walked around the gas pumps toward a flower bed separating the station from the road. Monk had given him a clean way out. He could fly home from Albuquerque and return to his life. Nobody but Monk and Brother Jeremy would know any different. Hell, he had that corner office waiting for him in Morganton, his life set out before him on a platter, no thinking required. Or... He looked west to a stretch of highway he figured was another old piece of Route 66—they'd been chasing that road since Oklahoma. Or, he could blow everything to hell and continue this quest to find Johnny Rolland. He recalled the high school boy who used to run like the wind at center field, catch every single ball hit anywhere near him, and then win the game in the next inning with a home run. But now what was he? Most likely a damaged, drugged-out man who almost certainly didn't want to be found. It was an easy choice. Pete ground out his cigarette on the still wet pavement, slippery from the hail, and walked to the driver's seat. "Let's keep going," he said to

Monk. "I'll drive. We can be in Arizona by nightfall. Maybe grab some sleep in Flagstaff."

Monk nodded and moved to the passenger seat, knowing when to keep his mouth shut.

CHAPTER SEVEN

May 10

I *PARKED MY CHARGER RIGHT* in front of Carol's office. It didn't look like much from the outside. The painted sign in the window, starting to crack at the edges, read "GIDEON PITTS, PRIVATE INVESTIGATOR: Fast and Discreet." The office was located two doors down from the Wherehouse Record Store, a favorite of mine, in a small strip mall on South Indian Hill Blvd in Pomona. Pitts was old and mostly retired. Carol Loomis, still earning all her required hours for a full PI license, ran the show. She already had more clients than she could handle.

She smiled when I walked in. "Hi, stranger, got a hot new case for me?" There was no secretary, no Gideon Pitts. He likely was home napping.

"Maybe I do, but not sure there's any money in it. It's quiet in here. Don't you ever get bored?"

"Nah, I've got all these cases to keep me company," Carol said, pointing at the stacks on her desk. Carol loved working the files, putting the pieces together. I'd seen that when she was a Claremont police detective and it was the same in her new job.

"Got time for an early lunch?" I asked.

"No can do. I need to be in court in thirty minutes. But I figured I might see you today. Does this ring a bell?" Carol held up a plain white sheet of paper. "TWO DEAD IN FOOTHILL BLVD BAR MURDER" was printed at the top. "It's going to be the Pomona *Progress-Bulletin* headline this afternoon."

"Jeez, how do you get that stuff?" I asked.

"I've got my sources. But that's all I know, so give me some fast particulars."

"It looks like two mob hitters based in North Hollywood were after some guy or guys in the back room of Mister Louie's bar and got whacked by the intended victim. I just happened to be there checking the place out and heard the whole thing."

"Drinking at a dive bar on a school night?"

"No, *Mom*, the assistant manager was worried about changes to the place and asked me to take a look. I ran out the back door in time to see the getaway car, a Lincoln, drive away on Foothill. Nobody has seen the car since." Carol worried about me sometimes so I left out the part about getting shot at. "Sometime later, a room at the good old El Rey Motel in Rialto got trashed along with a Ford Mustang registered to a guy in North Carolina named Monk Tanner."

"Connected?" Carol asked.

"The last thing I heard last night was the shooter yelling at 'Monk' to drive them away, so yeah, I figure connected."

Carol gathered up her purse and took two files from the top of the stack. "Gotta run, but Jimmy, you've needed a big juicy murder case. Anything to keep you out of the dive bars. Call me later at home."

I didn't bother to correct her on the dive bar thing. Next stop was the nearby record store where I bought Taj Mahal's second album, a great country blues record. After a quick lunch at Taco Lita on Holt, I drove to the Fontana Sheriff's Department station on Arrow Blvd. Larger than my Alta Loma home base, it had an easy-to-use, toll-free telephone system. I supposed I should report to Bert Jenkins, the assistant undersheriff for San Bernardino County, while I was here. This was his station. But he and I didn't get along, and it was common knowledge that I reported directly to Sam Fuller, regardless of what any organization chart said. Jenkins and I avoided each other. Easy because he rarely was around. I grabbed an empty office equipped with a desk and a telephone.

It was time to find out about Mr. Monk Tanner, which turned out to be easier said than done. First the North Carolina Motor Vehicle Department put me on hold for half an hour while they considered my request. Then some clerk said I needed a warrant to get Monk Tanner's phone number. After pleading a life-and-death situation and threatening to call the North Carolina State Police—who I should have called in the first place—a supervisor gave me the phone number. There was no answer when I called.

Then I called the Glen Alpine Police Department. No answer there either. *Jeez, what if I lived there and was getting robbed or something?* My options dwindling, I next called the Glen Alpine City Hall and got Margaret, the Town Clerk. And struck pay dirt.

"Monk Tanner lives with his mother about a five-minute walk from here. Dorothy, his mother, works at Drexel Furniture. So does Monk, I believe. Did you say California? My Lord. Is Monk in trouble? I believe Dorothy works the day shift. She should be home soon."

"Is there a father, a Mr. Tanner, I could reach?"

"In name only. He's somewhere in South Carolina. Doesn't consort with his family. Do you want me to watch for Dorothy's car? Rocky, our policeman, is out on a call, and our other officer quit last week."

I thanked Margaret for all her help, gave her this Fontana phone number and my home number, and asked that Rocky give me a call. My mother enjoyed watching reruns of *The Andy Griffith Show*. I knew she'd be thrilled that I had gotten a little taste of small-town North Carolina. I did caution Margaret to keep my call confidential. Otherwise, I figured everybody in Glen Alpine would soon know of it. She agreed.

Rocky the cop called me back, all business, ex-military, I could tell by his voice and cadence. Before I even asked, he offered to pay a visit to Mrs. Tanner. "Monk works hard and plays hard," he said. "Drinks and for sure smokes weed. Maybe a little of that damn cocaine on payday. It's found its way here. He's gotten speeding tickets and was in one fight at work that the Drexel police handled with no charges filed. Let's see." Rocky was thinking about it. I appreciated his thoroughness.

"He's also real good buddies with Pete Giles, who's likely up at App State right now," Rocky continued. "Giles plays football, kind of a hometown hero. When Pete's home, those two hang out together. Something of an odd couple, but they're old friends."

Deciding I could trust Rocky, I filled him in on the trashed Ford Mustang, and the possibility that Monk might be involved in some trouble. I left it at that.

"I know the car. Monk wouldn't leave it without a very good reason. And California? That makes no sense to me," Rocky said. "I'll go real easy with Mrs. Tanner. I don't like the sound of any of this." Rocky signed off, promising to call me after talking to Monk's mother.

It was 3 p.m. I called Beth Bolling. "Is the paper out yet?"

"Yep. Just got it. Big headline, but the reporter doesn't know much yet. I fed him a few things that he'd find out anyway. Kinda playing it like some trashy low-lives going after each other. No mob connection in the story. It's only the *Progress-Bulletin* for now, no *San Bernardino Sun*. The story might die quickly, especially if there's some big car crash or something."

"Thanks, Beth. You're a pro." I recalled a flash of her red panties last Christmas, pulling them off, a tiny strip of pale skin almost lost in all the California tan. We'd had some harmless fun, at least it had seemed like that to me. I hoped she felt the same way. Did somebody always feel pain? Was it ever truly 50/50?

Which took my mind back to Allie, as it did far too often these days. Allie caused me no end of pain, but so far the pleasure made it worth it. As if I had a choice. No fifty-fifty deal in our affair. That was certain. I'd met her, Allessandra D'Amico, Pomona College radical, while investigating and then solving, with Carol, the famed Claremont bombing case.

Allie had even lived with the bomber for a time back in 1970 before Kent State.

She and I both knew that "Allie the radical" and "Jimmy the cop" was an impossible match, no matter all those sparks that lit up our unforgettable nights. She left town, and that was it. But Allie had reinvented herself as a serious journalist—she'd turned on a dime after graduating from Pomona—and that made some version of us possible. She'd come back to me, sometimes, and very much on her own terms. I never called it love, not once, and we never were "exclusive," to use that ugly modern word. Still a radical in many ways, Allie struggled with her feelings for me, a symbol of authority, but she liked my libertarian tendencies. I also knew her secret: she was a rich girl who'd grown up in Pasadena with maids in the house.

Allie didn't need me, at least not in any traditional way. And I wasn't about to chase this newly created, hard-nosed reporter around California or elsewhere. But my God it was good when we were together, in all possible ways. She elevated my spirit and my brain, in addition to making me randy as a goddamned goat. Allie had even charmed my hard-to-please mother. I settled for what I got, the periodic joy overriding the more or less constant loneliness. Carol, of course, and maybe even Sam Fuller knew it was taking a toll on me. Jimmy Sommes, the cocky bachelor, had met his match, and was reaching for the bottle a little too much. I still chased the ladies from time to time, but I always was thinking about Allie. The others meant nothing to me, which was an act of cruelty to them.

The phone rang, rescuing me from dark thoughts. It was my new pal Rocky from Glen Alpine. "Okay, Mrs. Tanner knew that Monk had taken vacation time from work about a week ago, saying that he was going on a trip. She doesn't know where. She actually charges him rent, saying he's an adult at twenty-one and can come and go as he pleases as long as he pays. She also said that she thinks Pete Giles might be with him. Monk was on the phone to him constantly before he left.

"I just drove by the Giles place, a big house on the hill," Rocky continued. "No lights on, nobody home, just a cat meowing at me through the door. So I called the Giles Lumber Company and found out that William Giles, the owner, is on vacation and not to be disturbed. That directive came from Giles's wife apparently, since it's their first vacation in years. Anyway, William Giles is due back on Sunday."

"Thanks, Rocky, for all the fine work," I said, meaning it but not sure where it led.

"There is one more thing, Sergeant Sommes," Rocky added. "I called Appalachian State, not sure of their calendar. It turns out the school is on a quarter break. School starts again next week."

"Hey, you ever come out here to sunny California, I'll give you a job." We ended the call.

This case was coming into focus. I pulled a Scenes of California calendar off the wall. The month of May 1974 showed a picture of a cable car clanking down a hill toward crystal-blue San Francisco Bay with Alcatraz in the distance. I started circling dates with a pencil. The Mister Louie's homicides took place on Thursday, May 9. Today was May 10, the El Rey Motel incident. Monk Tanner alone, or with Pete Giles, left North Carolina on, let's say May 4. That left plenty of time for them to get here by May 9. I knew that Monk was here on account of the now trashed Mustang, and maybe this other guy too. I should be able to reach William Giles, the father, on Sunday if I was lucky, or Monday for sure. That left the killer a complete mystery, or was Monk Tanner also a shooter? Or Pete Giles? For some reason, my gut said no. I had a soft spot for college athletes, which was dumb.

It was time to call it a day. Then the phone at my desk rang.

"Meet me at the Sycamore Inn bar ASAP," Sam Fuller said.

CHAPTER EIGHT

May 10

I ***KNEW PEDRO, THE BARTENDER*** at the Sycamore Inn. It occurred to me that I knew too many bartenders. Sam was sitting at a corner table, the only quiet spot. The restaurant was Friday night packed. I took my bourbon and water over and sat down. "You're working too hard, boss. I assume this is not a social drink."

"I've got a mess on my hands and need your help," Sam said. He had a beer in front of him that he wasn't drinking. "Let's get to it. Hank Phillips is dirty, a crooked cop, happening on my watch right in front of my eyes. I don't feel good about it. But that's why he's on your murder detail, to keep him close to us."

"Jeez, I knew he was a racist and a creep, but a crook?"

"Bought and sold to the LA mob. It's gambling debts, betting on the ponies at Santa Anita, and his choice was to help them or die. Today a crew was going to rob the Bank of America on Euclid Avenue. Phillips had it all arranged to be the first cop to respond, get his head banged in for his trouble, and then let the perps get away. It's this new gangster, Izzy Weiss—at least new to our region—putting the robbery plan together, trying to flex his muscles."

"Thanks for letting me know about the bank job." Sarcasm crept into my voice. I couldn't help it.

"Jenkins was running the show for us out of Fontana. And it's still closely held, but I'm taking over the operation now."

"Christ, I was just over there working the phones. He wasn't around." That explained it. Bert Jenkins was second in command to Sam, but due to retire next December. I thought he was incompetent. He thought I was a showboat. He wouldn't give me the time of day on any operation of his, especially if it was on my turf. "So why did Phillips finger Izzy Weiss today at our meeting?" I asked, pretty sure I knew the answer.

"To cover his ass and try to play both sides against the middle," Sam said. "Phillips isn't smart enough to pull that off. Anyway, the two murders last night spooked Weiss, too many cops prowling around, so he canceled the bank job at the last minute. He's furious with his crew for being anywhere near Mister Louie's last night, calling it 'nickel and dime crap.' We've got an undercover contact inside the operation—six months of work—and the person knows that the Bank of America job will happen in eleven days, May twenty-first."

"Sounds like you've got it wired," I said. "What do you need me for?"

Sam gave me a pained smile. "We don't know which Bank of America branch, except it won't be the one on Euclid. This Weiss character is superstitious, not your typical mob guy. He's into astrology, and supposedly the stars don't align again for that bank, or some such nonsense. Weiss is moving to the next bank on his list."

"Which is a mystery," I said. "Is Jenkins in on it with Phillips?"

"No, he's just stupid. Seven months from retirement and it can't happen soon enough. I should never have let him near this case, too complex, but had some pressure from above." Sam as undersheriff ran the department, but there was this politician, the actual "sheriff" in name only, who mostly went on junkets and pressed the flesh. The public liked his handsome face, and Sam was good at keeping him away from us working stiffs. But the sheriff liked Jenkins, because the latter kissed his ass. That was well-known.

"This political stuff is worse than murders," I said. "Makes me nervous about the new job you want me to take."

"We'll deal with that another day, or maybe this is a trial run. Political stuff *is* lousy. Hell, I voted for Nixon, and look what he's done, the biggest cover-up in history. Anyway, Phillips is scared of you because you're ruthless and tough, if sometimes a little, shall we say, unorthodox. Tomorrow, I'm planning to accuse you of consorting with hookers and cheating on your expense account and then chew you out very publicly in order to tarnish your reputation."

"Why?"

"Because I want you and Phillips to become buddies. We believe he knows, or will know soon, which branch is the next target. Our person—who I don't know, by the way—on the inside is getting frozen out, because Weiss is tightening the flow of information. We've lost our source, at least temporarily. Since Phillips is deeply flawed, he'll like you better if you're in trouble. Here's the file. You can study up."

"Who can know about this? I want JK and Carol in on it."

Sam paused for what seemed like forever, then took a sip of his beer. I waited him out. He knew I wasn't going to back down,

"JK sure, but goddamn it, Carol is a PI now, not answerable to me at all." I was silent. "Okay, then, but zip her up good. Jesus, you two are like one person sometimes." Sam smiled as he said this. "She keeps you on the ball, unlike that lady newspaper reporter who makes you so goddamn miserable."

I started to object, but Sam cut me off. "I've got some good news for you too. We have a strong lead from this same informant about who your killer might be. A low-rent leg breaker named Johnny Rolland who works for Weiss. But his location is up in the air. He ripped them off, the mob, for both money and an unknown amount of heroin. They want him dead and buried in the desert. This won't come out to the group tomorrow for obvious reasons. We don't want to burn our source."

"So to summarize, I'm to catch this Rolland character, if he's the shooter, before the mob gets to him, find out who the hell Monk Tanner from North Carolina is, and make friends with a dirty cop in order to stop a future bank robbery. Does that cover it?"

"And do it all really fast," Sam said.

That's when it hit me. Sam sounded ten years younger. "You're having the goddamned time of your life on this operation, aren't you? All this undercover stuff."

Sam knew he was busted. "I'll admit it's been challenging," was all he said.

We both burst out laughing, then finished our drinks and called it a night. Sam left before me. As I paid the bill, Pedro the bartender nodded to me. "You want another one for the road?" I considered it, then shook my head.

I called Carol as soon as I got home and asked her to meet me at 7:30 the next morning at Memorial Park in Claremont, near the little merry-go-round, and to bring Max if she wanted. She knew instantly that it was important and didn't ask any questions. I hung up.

Max was her cute little pug. I knew he could keep a secret.

***

"I love Sam, you know that, but this little scheme of his seems kinda far-fetched to me," Carol said when we met the next morning. It was cloudy. A marine layer had blown in from the coast. I'd filled her in on Hank Phillips, Izzy Weiss, and the supposed Bank of America robbery at an unknown location on May 21.

She remained skeptical. "You've been called lots of things, Jimmy, but all the cops, especially creeps like Phillips, know you're straight on the big stuff. And hookers? Not really your style. Last I heard, you didn't have to pay for it."

I was walking Max while Carol talked. We had the park to ourselves. No school today at Sycamore since it was Saturday, and it was too early in the day for the neighborhood kids to be here. Now it was my turn to talk. It felt like a confession of failure. "Yeah, well maybe I should come clean. While you've been real busy lately with your work, and happy with Annie, I've, well"—telling her the truth suddenly scared me—"been kinda off my game." How lame was that?

"What do you mean?"

"I've been slacking off, letting JK carry me on the job, drinking too much, thinking about Allie, the band busted up. Lots of stuff getting to me." The dog did his business in the ivy, oblivious to such revelations.

"Does Sam know this?"

"Sam knows I've been distracted, not giving the job my best. I think he's trying to use this bank job assignment, and the new promotion idea, to get me motivated again."

"Is it working?"

I considered her question. "Maybe. I stayed off the booze last night, thinking about my next moves instead."

"Good. What about Phillips?" she asked. "Like you, I knew he was a creep—he grabbed my ass once, probably doesn't even remember it—but not crooked. You been hanging around with him?"

"More than I like to admit. We frequent the same cop bar down on Mission. I usually drink alone, but sometimes I join him as he loudly complains to his buddies about just about everything. I never say much."

Carol sighed. "First, I know you hate this touchy-feely stuff, Jimmy, but pick up the phone once in a while for God's sake. You, me, even Annie, we're cemented for life. So, on second thought, good old Sam, I've got to give it to him. Maybe the drunk Jimmy with hookers thing might work as a cover." Carol punched my arm. "But I don't like it, the Phillips thing. Cops versus cops is always messy. That's why we all hate Internal Affairs types."

"You're still a cop at heart," I said.

"Goddamn right. And call me if you get in trouble. I don't consider you expendable."

CHAPTER NINE

May 7 – Los Angeles

PETE GILES AND MONK TANNER splurged on a motel room in Santa Monica after a long driving day from Flagstaff. The men slept late, ate breakfast, and then started their sleuthing. First stop was Westwood Village. Consulting a map, they saw it was adjacent to the sprawling UCLA campus. One of the names that Brother Jeremy had given them was Manuel. "Bartender at the Westwood Hamburger Hamlet" was scribbled after his name.

Driving east on Wilshire Boulevard and then turning left into Westwood, they got their first look at wealthy Los Angeles. The area was filled with clothing stores, restaurants, movie theaters, and banks. The sidewalks were bustling with a mix of college students and rich-looking shoppers, mostly women. Parking was hard to find. They squeezed the Mustang, which badly needed a wash, into a spot between a Mercedes and a Porsche. "Jeez Louise," Monk muttered under his breath.

It was lunchtime at Hamburger Hamlet and there was a wait. Not hungry, Pete cut in front to explain to the hostess that they were looking for Manuel. Was he working? She ignored him, busily seating paying customers, who gave him dirty looks as they passed. Pete thought he looked okay, wearing khakis and a golf shirt, but he realized the clothes were fine for western North Carolina, but not Westwood, California. He and Monk, who had his denim jean jacket on, looked like what they were: country boys in the big city. Even the college kids had a different air about them, and the girls' elegant jeans were so tight that Pete had no idea how they got them either on or off. During a short lull, he repeated his request to the hostess. The busy young woman, who sported a perfect Afro and was drop dead gorgeous, fixed her brown eyes on Pete and said, "Manuel's in jail, that's all I know, now please move along, I'm seating people for lunch."

Pete knew he should follow up, ask to speak to the manager, and invent some brilliant story as to why he needed to find Manuel. Instead, he scurried away, feeling intimidated and defeated. "This is just too weird, man," he said to Monk when they got outside. "Let's get out of here."

"Hang in there, buddy," Monk said with a smile. "I'll take the next turn at this detecting business." They drove to North Hollywood, over a high, dry mountain ridge full of mysterious foliage, not at all like a North Carolina forest, and suddenly viewed a vast sea of buildings, houses, busy roads, and shopping centers. The San Fernando Valley stretched for miles.

"How come North Hollywood ain't in real Hollywood?" groused Monk. During the entire trip, he expected Pete to know things about the West, about California. Pete had taken one trip to California as a kid with his parents, to visit Disneyland and some distant cousins, and they'd flown in from Charlotte. He didn't know anything about Los Angeles.

"Beats the hell of me," he said. "Keep checking the map. I don't want to get lost."

They found Lankershim Blvd, a long, ugly, busy street, and finally located the building listed as the address for "First Rate Productions," the company that had produced the *Wild Babes* movie. They parked, went into the small office building, consulted the directory, and climbed the stairs to the second floor. The sign on the door read "FIRST RATE PRODUCTIONS, dba Beaver Inc." There was a painted logo with a sexy, stacked redhead in a bikini holding what looked like a champagne glass. There also was a scribbled note taped on the door reading "Out to Lunch, Back Soon, Luv Tammy," complete with a smiley face. Pete was encouraged. Then he noticed all the mail piled up on the dirty hallway rug. It had overflowed the mail slot. They went downstairs to the rental office.

"Out to lunch, my ass. The bums owe me two months back rent," a bony lady in the office told them. "Haven't seen her in a month, the redhead with the fake boobs who runs the place," she said, firing up a Camel cigarette, which produced a phlegmy cough. The office stunk, and the woman had bad breath. Pete stepped back. Oblivious, the woman consulted an open calendar next to a half-eaten peanut butter sandwich. "In fact, we're going to clear their stuff out next week, spray it down for sex diseases, repaint it, and then rent it out again. End of story."

"That's Tammy, right, the redhead?" Monk asked. "Do you have a phone number or forwarding address for her or the company?"

"They make dirty movies. What do you think? When they paid it was in cash."

The young men trooped out and had just about reached their car when Monk got a gleam in his eye. "You go over to that hot dog joint across the street," he said, pointing to it. "I'll meet you in five or ten minutes. Order me a chili dog with everything on it, and some kind of drink."

Pete was glad to see Monk acting spunky for a change. He crossed the street and almost got hit by a truck making a fast right turn. The truck honked at him as he scuttled to the sidewalk. Pete put in their order, and a waitress brought their food and icy cold lemonade to an outdoor picnic table as Monk appeared with a big grin on his face.

"I think I just committed a federal offense, but who cares," he said after the waitress left. "Let's eat first. Damn, this is a goddamned good-looking chili dog and onion rings." They ate for a while, then Monk took off his knapsack and spilled the contents out on the table, careful not to get mustard or chili on the papers.

"I just stole all this mail from the porno company," he said. "But maybe, since it was outside the door, and the business is gone, and it was on the rug, maybe that's not 'stealing' under the law. Whaddaya think?"

Pete couldn't help but laugh. "Let's see what you got."

They did some organizing first, separating out the bills, then all the ad coupons, and finally the few personal items. They used a napkin holder and their wallets to keep stuff from blowing into the street. Luckily, it wasn't too windy.

"Let's start with these," Monk said. This was his operation. There were several manila envelopes. He opened one, turned bright red, looked to the sky, and said, "Lord, you have punished me for my sins."

Pete took a look. It was a glossy photograph of a young man with long blond hair holding his erect penis in his hand. It was his resume, so to speak. That was it, plus a phone number. Pete wasn't sure how his advisor at App State, a female English professor, would react if he wrote about this. She might think it was funny. He wouldn't show her the photo.

There were three more "resumes," two of naked women, and a last one of a limber couple in a variety of poses. "Man, I never even knew one of those positions was humanly possible," Monk said. "Could be dangerous to your body."

"Okay, what else we got?" Pete said. He was embarrassed by the pictures. After sorting through some boring stuff, they got lucky. There was a postcard of the Los Angeles Union Pacific train station. It read:

> Tammy, tell Izzy not to look for me. I'm gone and diserve what I took. D at the Club knows where to find me, but only in emergancy. You still owe me $200 for that last movie job but you can give that to Izzy.
>
> HA HA. Johnny

Pete felt a little thrill at finding their guy. Johnny had

never done well in school. A star baseball player who couldn't spell.

Monk snapped his fingers. "Get that paper you have with the names on it. The one the guy at the food bank gave you." Pete did, and Monk looked at it. The second name was Dolores, bartender at the Palomino Club.

"Might fit, she might be the 'D,'" Monk said. "Johnny always loved his country music, and I've heard of this club, a big county-western place. Kinda like Nashville West." He went up to the hot dog counter and asked if anybody knew where the Palomino Club was. The manager did. It was close by. Monk came back with the address written on a napkin and two more chili dogs. He handed one of them to Pete. "Eat up, college boy," he said. "We may need to do some afternoon drinking."

Monk snuck up the stairs and returned all the mail to the rug next to the First Rate Productions door—making sure that bony lady didn't see him—and then the men headed off to the Palomino Club. Pete drove. Monk was having a blast. He popped a Benzedrine.

The famous club was nearly empty at 3:30 in the afternoon. They sat at the bar and ordered beers. An attractive, older Latino woman with her long black hair tied back in a ponytail, wearing jeans and a maroon polo shirt, asked for ID. They each forked over their North Carolina driver's license for her inspection. "Doc Watson and James Taylor," she said with a smile. "That's about all I know about North Carolina. Never been there."

Pete looked over her head. There were pictures of musicians on the wall behind the bar, some he recognized: Linda Ronstadt, Kris Kristofferson, Willie Nelson, Dolly Parton. "What brings you boys out here to the big city?" the woman asked when she brought their beers.

"Well, it depends," Monk said. "Are you by any chance named Dolores?"

"Last I checked, yes." She stared at Monk. "You're too young to be a process server. My ex wants me to support him. No chance," she said with a smile, putting a bowl of pretzels out for them. She left to close out a bill for another customer. The place was starting to fill up, mostly men.

They each ordered another beer and watched Dolores go about her business. She was good at it and knew most of the folks by name. During a lull, she came back over to them. Not wanting to miss his chance, Monk went to work. "There's another North Carolina guy, Dolores, that we know, an old friend of ours. His name is Johnny Rolland. We're looking for him. Can you help us?"

Her face froze. She walked to the other end of the bar and began washing glasses. Pete watched her, trying to decide when to play the "Reverend" card. Not yet, he decided. An up-tempo song was playing on the jukebox.

"That's Buck Owens, Pete, the guy from *Hee Haw*," Monk said. "He's been a star out here forever."

Pete was more concerned with Dolores's shift in mood. She hadn't liked the Johnny Rolland question, meaning she knew him. She served a couple mixed drinks at a nearby table. There was no cocktail waitress. Finally, she came back and said with a blank expression, "No. I don't know anybody with that name. That will be eight bucks for the beers."

Monk started to answer, but Pete interrupted him. "Dolores, the Reverend said to say hello."

Dolores nearly dropped the glass she was holding. Linda Ronstadt was singing now, a sad country song. Dolores fixed her gaze on Pete. "What the hell. I'll need a phone number for him."

Pete wrote it on a napkin and gave it to her.

"Boys, I was having a nice boring afternoon thinking about having dinner tonight after work with my cousin, who's a good cook. Her chile rellenos are better than mine. Maybe a little tequila, watch a movie on the tube, and you come in and hit me with this shit." She was quiet for a moment.

"Get out of here now. Come back at 11 a.m. tomorrow, before we open. I'll let you in."

"Thank y—" Monk started.

"Don't thank me for anything yet. Now go."

Pete knew they had upset her and wondered if she and Brother Jeremy, or whatever he called himself out here, had been lovers. His mood upon leaving the club was an odd mix, but mostly a feeling of triumph. "She knows Johnny."

"Damn straight," Monk said. "Now can a country boy make a request? I want to see the Pacific Ocean, maybe even stick my toes in it."

CHAPTER TEN

May 11

OUR SMALL TASK FORCE RECONVENED at 9:30 a.m. Except for Sam, although I knew he would appear soon. We were working this Saturday morning. Every murder investigation had a ticking clock. The longer it went unsolved, the harder it got to close the case. I'd quickly briefed JK beforehand on the bank robbery thing, saying it was hush-hush and that we would talk more later. At the meeting I reported to the group on the entire North Carolina angle. Beth discussed the newspaper article. Lots of murders these days, she observed. No big deal so far. JK had no luck finding the night manager at the El Rey Motel. He'd vanished, at least for now. Too many cops hanging around.

"What about ownership of Mister Louie's?" I asked.

Laura Gutierrez was starting to answer when Sam burst in, his face flushed. "Sommes, in my office, now," he barked.

"Boss, I wonder could we—"

"Exactly what part of 'now' didn't you understand, *Sergeant*?" Sam spit the words out, then muttered, "But maybe not for long."

I got up to leave and shook my head, feeling embarrassed in spite of myself. Sam was putting on a good show. "Beats me," I muttered to the perplexed-looking group on my way out.

Sam's office was maybe thirty feet from the conference room. He slammed the door when I came in and started yelling at me. His voice easily penetrated the thin government-issue walls. I was pretty sure the entire floor could hear him. "Are you trying to throw your entire career away, for Christ sakes, over some hooker named Suzie Diamond?"

I started to answer, but he interrupted. "Zip it, Sergeant. You talk when I say you can talk." Sam was holding up a stapled report, even though nobody could see him. "And then you try to expense it! Five separate nights at that motel in Claremont. Griswold's is LA County. Was that on purpose? Claremont, for Christ's sake. Plus the fancy dinners, the bottles of champagne. Have you lost your mind? Internal Affairs is going to bust you to patrol duty, Sommes, with my blessing."

It was my turn to yell at him. "This is a pending case, sir. I don't run to you for permission for all the work I do. We've got a chance to break up this prostitution ring working the Ontario Airport motels, run by a goddamn dangerous pimp. Suzie's his manager with the girls." I was making this story up as I went along.

"Bullshit. No case file. Your supposed supervisor at the Fontana station knows nothing about it. I bet JK doesn't know either. How stupid do you think I am?" Sam paused, then softened his tone. "Look, that Portland thing, killing the hitman, Carol getting torn apart by that guy. I told you to see somebody, talk it out. But no, you're Mister Tough Guy. Trying to drink it all away. You think I don't know about that?"

I was mute. He was hitting too close to home. This game of Sam's could turn dangerous. He gave me a thumbs-up, trying to soften the blows.

"Here's the deal, Sergeant," Sam continued, his voice raised again. "I've got these damn murders to solve, so I'm giving you two weeks to solve them. I'll keep IA off your back for now. But you lied to me. That I will not abide. Period. Now get your ass out of here and close this case. And don't you dare even think about seeing this Suzie Diamond again, or whatever the hell her real name is." Sam rarely raised his voice, but it always had immediate impact. And he was a pretty good actor.

Margaret, Sam's longtime secretary, had her head down when I walked by her. Christ, people were going to believe this shit, no matter what happened later, and the gossip was going to fly around the office like a raging wildfire. Just what Sam wanted. I wasn't thrilled about this whole business.

The conference room was quiet when I entered. "Just a misunderstanding," I said. "Don't worry about it. Officer Gutierrez, you were about to tell me who owns Mister Louie's." She didn't know yet, but they were working on it; a bunch of shell corporations were involved. "No surprise, that's how they do it in Las Vegas too," I told her.

I could tell everybody wanted to get out of the room, so I said, "Let's reconvene at 3 p.m. Every hour counts right now."

Then Hank Phillips, true to form, said with a smirk, "They do say diamonds are a girl's best friend, Sommes," as he walked toward the door. I wanted to smash his face in but couldn't do that. Not until I befriended him and then busted him and got him sent to prison.

I hated dirty cops.

***

"Jesus, I can't keep any of this straight," JK said to me. And he wasn't a complainer by nature. We were drinking coffee at the Donut Queen near the steel mill.

"You don't have to," I said, "in fact, better if you don't. Your job is to find this leg breaker, Johnny Rolland, and arrest him, along with Monk Tanner. My job is to find out the next bank robbery location."

"How?"

"Well, I'm going to bust up the teams, for one thing, supposedly on Sam's direct orders. I'll partner with Phillips, you ride with Gutierrez. You're getting the better of the deal, believe me. I have to endure Phillips's filthy Oldsmobile. Sam's going to flatter Phillips on the side, tell him he's got to babysit me, keep me under control."

JK was quiet. "C'mon, man," I cajoled my partner. "Gutierrez is smart, a USC grad, her dad's a cop in Inglewood, and even in those clunky clothes she wears, very attractive."

Jesus, what was I now? A matchmaker? "The team meets at 3 p.m. at the Alta Loma station. I'll announce all this then."

JK finally laughed. "Okay, what the hell. See you then."

***

I did what I do sometimes: headed up the mountain, got north of Foothill, where I could think and breathe. I didn't need coffee and wasn't going to drink beer at lunch. I chose a pull-out on Mt. Baldy Road that had a view of the dam and Pomona Valley stretched below it. I was in luck. The smog was light, a brown smudge in the direction of the Chino Hills but light blue sky otherwise. I could see the jets landing and taking off from Ontario Airport. Behind me, Mt. Baldy and the San Gabriel Mountains stood watch over everything, unchanging except for the fires, and indifferent to all our personal struggles. I liked being here. It helped me to keep things in perspective. Most of my work these days was done south of Foothill, in the ugly flatlands near the speedway and the freeways, where there was too much violence and too many drugs—at worst, this led to murder. I loved my work, chasing the villains, but often needed to decompress up here or at my cabin, seeking the old Southern California of my youth—found well north of Foothill.

Sam was giving me the big test, trying to figure out if my lazy, distracted ass was up to the challenge of complex police work. I could chase crooks and murderers. We both knew that. But could I navigate people, lead a group, make others better at their jobs? Did I even want to? Right now, Sam saw me as a slowly sinking ship, a man who could do his job until retirement but who was losing a step every year, and losing interest. I wasn't sure he was right but couldn't rule it out either.

Just two years ago, in 1972, I held a pretty simple view of myself. I apprehended bad guys for a living, played my fiddle in a pretty good band, and met some ladies along the way who kept me interested, but not involved. For some reason, probably related to my father's death the year before, I just didn't want to feel too much.

The bomber case messed everything up. My biggest triumph at work had also changed me. I was practically holding that hitman in my arms as he died from my gunshots, looking right through me, not at me. That son-of-a-bitch even looked a little like me. Had I killed a really bad version of myself? Maybe I did need to see a shrink, but I hated the thought of all that bullshit, baring my soul to some smirking asshole who smoked a pipe and nodded his head like he knew everything. I might punch him in the face instead. The thought made me smile.

And then there was Allie. Time to quit fooling myself. I loved her, and she didn't love me. She liked me better than any other man, maybe always would. My old self would have thought it was perfect: a sexy girlfriend with no strings attached. But it was those very strings that I now wanted, more than anything I'd ever known, to bind us, to connect us. Maybe it was time to roll the dice, risk everything and tell her that I loved her. And then watch her run away.

For now, I needed to descend off the mountain and get back to work, something I usually understood. Sam had cooked up this complicated double case for me. He had other good men who could handle the bank robbery investigation, leaving JK and me to find and arrest the murder suspects. It was my kind of case, and a really good one. But no, Sam was determined to push me way past my comfort zone. To see if I could get better at what I did, not worse. I realized as I looked down at my valley, and his valley, that it meant the world to me what he was doing—and I wanted to make him proud of me again.

CHAPTER ELEVEN

May 9 – Los Angeles

Pete and Monk showed up at the Palomino Club at 11 a.m. as Dolores had instructed. They accepted her offer of coffee. "You checked out with the Reverend," she said, "although he told me to never call him again, for 'everybody's sake,' he said. Quite mysterious."

"He runs a food bank for poor people in our town," Pete said. "We don't know anything about what his life was like out here."

"Best that you don't know. The Reverend created more than his fair share of chaos in our world, and in my world, before he disappeared." Dolores lit a cigarette and took a big drag. Sadness pulled at her features. Pete assumed they'd been lovers.

"As for a much less complicated man, Johnny Rolland, I wish you'd turn around, go back to North Carolina, and forget all about him."

"We can't do that, ma'am," Monk answered.

"Ma'am? Christ, am I getting that old?" Pete thought she was attractive, and even sexy, in a real-world way. Dolores caught him looking at her. Her eyes thanked him. "Anyway, Johnny Rolland, when he's off drugs and booze, can be a polite young man who loves country music and baseball. And for some reason, he likes me. But Johnny's always loaded these days, one way or another, and he's a mean son-of-a-bitch. My men have had to throw him out of this club on occasion. He's down to two friends in the world, me and Tammy, a lady with big boobs who runs a porn studio. Everybody else wants to either kill him, or at the very least beat the living hell out of him."

"Is there a particular reason?" Pete asked.

Dolores was slicing limes and lemons as they talked, getting ready to open for the day. The front door opened and a man entered. "Hey, we're not open yet," Dolores told him. "Come back at noon." The man gave us an odd smile, then departed.

"Okay, you did not hear this from me, but Johnny mostly works for Izzy Weiss, a local gangster here in North Hollywood, as a collection agent and sometime drug courier. Guys don't pay their debts, Johnny helps them change their minds. He does some protection racket stuff too. For all I know the owner here pays off Weiss. It's his neighborhood."

Right out of Al Capone, Pete thought, *and a long way from playing baseball.*

"Okay, boys, I'm going to say two more things that you never heard from me, and then you're leaving. And this is only because of the Reverend. I'll add it to his other debts to me." She lit another cigarette.

"Word on the street is that Johnny ripped off Weiss on a delivery of heroin out in Ontario, kept both the money and the dope—about the only drug Johnny doesn't use. It wasn't much, in the scheme of things, but ripping off Izzy Weiss means he's a walking dead man."

"Jesus," Monk muttered.

"There's something else," Dolores said. "He called me last night, or rather this morning, about 2 a.m. I told him about you two being here. First, he hung up. Then called me back. He wants you to meet him at Sol's Hideaway Tavern in Pasadena today at 3 p.m." She handed Monk a piece of paper. "Here's the address."

"Why?" Pete asked, wondering what in the world he and Monk would encounter.

"I have no idea," Dolores said. "And I repeat, get in your car and drive back to where you came from. Don't meet him in Pasadena. I should have never told him about you. Don't even know why I passed on his message." She walked off toward the kitchen without another word.

"Let's go," Monk said to me. "Where's Pasadena?"

***

"Did you hear what she said, Monk?" Pete was way too pissed off to enjoy his chili dog. The men had gravitated back to the same hot dog joint on Lankershim. Monk was chomping away on his lunch, acting like he didn't have a care in the world.

"Your gangster half-brother is likely going to get himself killed," Pete continued. "And you want to get us right in the middle of it. Are you nuts?"

"Look, I just want to hear Johnny's side of it. Dolores might be exaggerating things."

"She's about the straightest shooter I've ever met. None of that Southern women bullshit we've been listening to all our lives. Come on! You watch all the cop shows. Crooks loan money to losers at high interest, then send thugs like Johnny to collect. Or Johnny sells drugs to the losers, then collects the money or breaks their legs. Only this time, according to Dolores, he went rogue, kept the money and the drugs. What don't you get?" Pete threw his drink into the trash can so hard it tipped over. The other customers were getting nervous. It was Pete who looked like the crazy one.

"Settle down," Monk said. "Like I said, I want to talk to my half-brother about all this. Then we'll make a plan."

Nonsense, thought Pete. Monk's absent father was a gambler and small-time crook. Pete had seen it more than once back home: rednecks trying their best to escape their upbringing and limitations but crashing back to their old ways. He and Monk had drifted apart in the last year or two. That was clear to Pete. Had his friend gotten lost? He didn't know. What he did know was that Monk was dragging him into a god-awful mess. He considered taking Dolores's advice and getting the hell out of LA.

An unwanted image tore into Pete's head. It was Josiah Giles lying dead at the Battle of Shiloh, his body blown apart by Union artillery. The dream, that stupid dream. Was Pete allowing himself to walk into his own twisted version of it, embracing the type of danger the Giles men seemed to revere beyond reason? But for what conceivable purpose? It had nothing to do with Johnny Rolland. Pete didn't care about him. Was he trying to save Monk, his best friend? Or was he testing himself? He was feeling a rush of adrenaline, something like what he experienced before playing a game against a team that was better than Appalachian State. When he was hoping to upset South Carolina or some other bigger school. Except he was about to play the most important game of his life in which the stakes were higher than he'd ever known, namely, his life.

"Okay, let's go," Pete muttered to Monk. It was a short easy drive to Pasadena. With some time to kill, Pete drove up into the hills above the city. The entire Los Angeles basin stretched out below them. Pete thought it looked clean, innocent. They could see the Rose Bowl, gleaming in the sun. Then they descended to their rendezvous with Johnny Rolland, and whatever danger it portended.

They found plenty. There was Johnny Rolland, in the back room of the bar, wearing black jeans and a large Hawaiian shirt. As in the porno movie, he was bald and possessed a mismatched body, skinny legs and a massive weightlifter's chest. Pete never would have recognized him as the brilliant fleet-footed center fielder who had almost made it to the bigtime. Through a constant mix of cigarettes and alcohol, Rolland outlined his grand plans. Monk made the immediate jump to follower. He'd found his long-lost brother, and he was heedless of the risk that he and Pete now faced.

CHAPTER TWELVE

May 11

I'D TAKEN TWO GULPS OF beer before our team's three o'clock meeting, enough to get it on my breath. "Gutierrez, you ride with JK until we solve this murder case. And Phillips, it's your lucky day, you get me. Have you cleaned your car lately? These are orders from above, by the way, so don't blame me." I quickly moved on before the grumbling could begin.

"Nobody has claimed the dead bodies of our murder victims, and I doubt that anyone will," I said. "The San Bernardino morgue will keep them refrigerated for the time being. The autopsies were unremarkable. Booze, meth, and burritos."

"That'd make a good title for a country song," Beth remarked. There had been no further press about the murders, so she was in a good mood. And it hadn't yet made it to the television news. Just a couple of murders, ho hum.

"Actually, Lowell George of Little Feat did that already." I couldn't resist showing off. "I believe it was 'give me weed, whites and wine,' which is pretty close."

"What's our next move, boss?" JK asked, wanting to move things along.

"How about you and Officer Gutierrez pay a visit this evening to Dave's Market in Ontario? Just to shake the tree. Let the mob know we're thinking about them. If Izzy Weiss is muscling in on the action out here, that market will be one of his hangouts."

Gutierrez looked confused, but before she could speak, Hank Phillips chimed in. "The back room of that crummy market is where the mob runs its gambling business in this valley, and beyond. How come not us, Sommes? That sounds like fun."

"First, it's either Jimmy or Detective Sommes," I said to him. "And I've got other ideas for us, Hank. Stay on afterwards for a minute."

We talked strategy for the Dave's Market visit. JK and Gutierrez were to be polite but persistent, wanting to know where every person at the market—usually five or six hoods would be milling around—was on the night of the Mister Louie's murders. JK would also flash morgue photos of the Salerno brothers, asking the crowd if anybody knew these murder victims. Even real grocery customers were going to be interviewed.

"What's the purpose of all this?" Phillips asked, still irritated about being excluded.

"Like I said, Hank, we're delivering a little love note to Mr. Weiss, letting him know we're on to the mob connection in all this."

"If there is one," Laura Gutierrez said.

"Very good, Officer Gut—"

"Call me Laura, for Christ's sake. So far we have hunches and ideas, no real evidence."

I was noticing a certain lack of respect for me at this meeting. Good. It was part of my new persona for this gig.

"That's why JK and you are shaking the tree," I said and ended the meeting.

Phillips lingered as requested. He didn't waste any time. "You've always been a cocky asshole, *Sommes*, and I know you think I'm a low-life loser, so what's the deal? Why am I part of this detail?"

"Because Sam made me include you, so let's make the best of it. I need a drink. You coming?"

There was a corner bar near our San Bernardino headquarters that seemed like it belonged in some small town in Wisconsin, but the drinks were ample and cheap. *Just no polka music, please.* Phillips and I ordered beer and shots of bourbon. The barmaid was wearing a frilly, low-cut blouse. She leaned over to serve our drinks and we both enjoyed the view.

"Okay, Hank, here's the deal. I'm sending goody-goody-two-shoes JK and young Officer Gutierrez to plant our flag at Dave's Grocery, to get the mob's attention. When it gets rough, and it will, that'll be you and me, and lots of backup. Bring both your guns."

"What about the killer?"

It was time to send Phillips in the wrong direction. "I think it's somebody from Vegas. My sources there don't have a name, but let's just say that Izzy Weiss is not a popular guy in that town. The Vegas bosses liked Joe Don because he was smart enough to stay in his lane. Weiss is different, more like Bugsy Siegel, not just because he's a kike, but because he wants whatever he can grab."

Phillips was quiet, trying hard to think. I ordered another round. I could hear Carol's voice in my head, saying, *Take it easy, boy*.

"What now?" Phillips finally asked—the same question as JK.

"Take Sunday off, Hank. No press on the murders means Sam will be off my ass for a change. That guy's getting a little old for all this."

"Was he right about you, this hookers thing?"

I paused so he would think I was wondering how much to tell him. "Yes and no. There is a gang of crooks robbing businessmen at the airport motels, using hookers as lures, but I may have gotten in a little deep. Let's just leave it at that. But I won't be seeing that Suzie Diamond again, because I can't afford to lose my job over any woman, no matter how goddamn gorgeous she is." The waitress showed up with the drinks. I powered down the bourbon and thought about putting a five-dollar bill between her fresh, young breasts as a tip, but managed not to. This was fun, this drinking thing, even with a nitwit like Hank Phillips.

One thing led to another. Hank and I ended up at the cop

bar on Mission Boulevard in Pomona. I shifted to tequila. We called each other "assholes." We ate burritos from someplace. At one point, we were peeing in an alley behind the bar. Why not? Hank got morose somewhere along the line, saying that he used to be a really good cop, but his supervisors never gave him any credit. His pay raises weren't worth shit. Hotshot cops like Sam and me thought he was worthless. Blah, blah, blah. I managed to dump about every fourth drink when Hank wasn't looking but was still out of my head.

I took every opportunity to complain bitterly about Sam too. Saying things like he was going to bust me to patrol duty in two weeks after we solved the murders, even though I was a really good cop, because he didn't give a shit about any of us anymore. So what if I screwed a hooker. That was my business, not his, but he was going to cut my pay anyway and mess up my life because I no longer worshipped his ass. "I gotta pee again," I told anyone who was listening and headed out toward the alley.

"They've got toilets in here, Sommes, you Okie redneck," Hank said.

"Yeah, well fuck you, Hank. You're going down the tubes with me. Get used to it. We're both screwed so we might as well enjoy the ride." I stumbled out the door and started to look for a dark place to do my business. Phillips was on me before I knew it.

"Fuck you too, Sommes." Then he took a swing at me and connected. Right hook to my jaw, not much power, but it hurt. To hell with this. I hit him in the gut. He doubled over in pain. I considered kicking him in the balls but instead grabbed him and threw him against a trash can, but he managed to hook my left leg with his right leg as he went down, taking me along with him. It was a nice move. We both lay sprawled on the dirty gravel as the metal trash can tipped over and spilled garbage all over us.

That was too much. We started to laugh, howling like monkeys at the zoo. The whole neighborhood must have heard us. One of Hank's buddies came out, saw us, looked disgusted, and returned to the bar.

"You can't punch worth a shit," I told Hank when I could talk again. My clothes stunk. I might have to throw away the denim shirt I was wearing. I got up and tried to brush the garbage off. The strongest smell was old tacos. It could have been much worse.

"Yeah, well, you're an asshole," Hank said, also getting up. His vocabulary was limited, especially when he was drunk. I tasted bile in my mouth but didn't want to puke in front of Hank. *Live your cover, man, hang tight, stay in the groove*, I advised myself, barely able to avoid another burst of laughter.

"I'll see your miserable ass on Monday, Phillips, and that's an order," I said, leaving him in the filthy alley.

I made it halfway home, stopping at a diner to order coffee. I sat at the far end of the counter and slurped it down, hoping that people wouldn't come too close. I then drove north to my cabin without crashing my car or falling asleep at the wheel. I stripped naked on the deck, leaving the smelly clothes outside. The raccoons might want them. Then I went inside, showered, and slept for nine hours.

What was I doing with this crazy case?

CHAPTER THIRTEEN

May 10 – Barstow, California

JOHNNY ROLLAND TOLD MONK AND Pete that robbing the liquor store in Helendale, a small Route 66 town west of Barstow, had been a spontaneous decision. "There I was in the store, just me and this old broad behind the counter, about to buy a bottle of Jim Beam—not my brand but the best they had—and some cigarettes for Monk. Then it came to me, why not just rob this lady instead? Man, you should have seen her face when I drew down on her. Thought she might have a heart attack."

He threw the pack of Marlboros to Monk. "Got two hundred fifty bucks and the booze and smokes for my trouble," he said with a cackling laugh.

Rolland had been in a terrible mood since they'd cruised past the El Rey Motel earlier that day and seen the cop cars. He'd parked their miserable gray Ford Fairlane station wagon the Medic had provided them in a strip mall parking lot next door. All the store signs were in Spanish. Wearing shades and a cowboy hat, he did a quick walk by the motel and saw the trashed Mustang in front of their motel room, its door wide open. Pete recalled that Rolland had left some of his cash in the room yesterday. They'd spend a short time in the motel room yesterday before going to the music club.

He came back to the car shaking his head. "That cost me some real money, boys, which really pisses me off. I figure it was your fault. You likely got tailed to that bar in Pasadena. Sorry about your car, but this is the big leagues, Monk, and if you want to play you gotta get better at it quick. I lost some dough, but I still got my stash. It never leaves my side." He patted the leather valise Pete had first seen at the Pasadena bar. He patted the leather valise Pete had first seen at the Pasadena bar.

Pete remembered the man Dolores had sent away at the Palomino. He'd had a strange, icy smile. Maybe they had been followed to Pasadena. It was not his job, or his world, to know stuff like that. He shifted in his seat, and his shoulder barked at him. The Medic had provided Rolland and the young men with clean clothes and the nondescript station wagon for this trip to where, Pete had no idea. "You might want to change the license plates soon," the Medic had said to Rolland, handing him a spare set.

The Medic had rigged up a bed of sorts for Pete in the back seat. He took the shoulder pain as a good sign. Now it felt like a football injury. He would heal and wasn't going to die. Monk kept giving him pain pills, which helped. Other than that, the two of them were not talking much. Pete knew he was a prisoner in this crazy business. Monk, however, had veered over the edge. He was an accomplice. He'd driven the getaway car twice now. Pete was having trouble even looking at Monk.

"Let me explain our next move, gentlemen," Rolland said. "There's a motel down the road a ways, about five miles. My buddy manages the joint during the day. He's gonna give us their biggest room, a suite tucked in back. We'll park behind it and get this invalid here set up in a bed." He pointed back at Pete. "That'll give me some time to figure things out."

"Come to think of it, Giles," Rolland continued, "I never liked you much, even in high school. You were the rich kid, looking down your nose at us trailer people. Not like my buddy here, Mr. Monk." Rolland pulled his ball cap down. "I'm gonna close my eyes for a short catnap. Wake me up when we get to the Sunset Inn. It'll be on the right side of the road after the Route 66 Motel, if my recollection is right. We'll hole up there for a day or two."

***

Dinner was Kentucky Fried Chicken, including all the usual sides. At least there were three beds. Pete thought Rolland was acting a little less crazy. Maybe all the drugs were wearing off, although Rolland and Monk were sharing that stolen bottle of Jim Beam. A baseball game was on television, the Dodgers at home against the Cubs. Rolland seemed to know what pitch was coming next, based on the batter and the circumstances. "The ball doesn't carry worth a shit at Dodger Stadium, so the pitcher can get away with fastballs down the middle and they'll end up as long flyball outs. Those same pitches at Wrigley Field end up in the bleachers as home runs," he said. "The pitcher needs to throw more sliders at Wrigley. I hated hitting against sliders, except when the pitcher hung them. Then you could knock the hell out of them, as long as you stayed back and kept your weight off your front foot. Nothin' worse than pulling a home run ball foul off a hanging slider. Nothin' in the whole world."

Pete's mind kept going back to the shootings while Rolland did his baseball talk. Had it only been last night? They'd used the drive-through at a burger joint and then parked Rolland's Lincoln behind a building. Pete could hear music coming from the building. Some guy waved them in and then directed them to a storeroom. Johnny handed him a wad of bills. The man gave Johnny a baggy of white powder, saying something like "we'll do the smack deal at intermission." Pete was flat out terrified by all this depravity, wanting to run away no matter what the consequences. For the second time that day, Johnny seemed to read his mind. "You ever fired a .44 Magnum, college boy?" he'd asked Pete, taking his pistol out of his coat and spinning the cylinder, making sure it was loaded. "Maybe I'll give you a lesson sometime soon. Hey, Monk, why don't you spread us some lines of coke. It better be good for what I just paid."

Pulling out his gun had saved Rolland's life, and likely Pete and Monk's, because that's when things went crazy. The storeroom door burst open, and two men entered, weapons drawn. One of them made the stupid mistake of starting to say something. Johnny Rolland shot him two times in the gut. That's when the other man started firing, but it was too late for him. Rolland shot him just as Pete felt a massive punch to his shoulder. Things got hazy after that. He knew he'd been shot but had no clear memory of getting to the car or driving to the Medic's house.

Things now seemed pathetically ordinary in this motel room, as the ballgame droned on. Pete tried to relax. But one reason he was reliving, and rethinking, the shooting was to determine if Monk Tanner, his best friend until now, was a criminal. Pete had been considering law school for a while. He knew he wasn't good enough to play pro football, and he dreaded the thought of working for his father. If nothing else, law school would buy him some time.

He'd taken a pre-law course last fall, and they'd briefly covered the topic of "felony murder." For example, if three people robbed a bank, and one of them shot and killed a guard, all three plus the getaway driver, if there was one, could be charged with murder because all of them were bank robbers, a felony. Rolland had killed two people right before Pete's eyes. Monk had served as the getaway driver. Was the shooting in self-defense? Possibly, but everything Rolland did was criminal in nature, including holding Pete hostage against his will. Monk was cooperating. In Pete's mind, Monk had crossed all the lines. He was a criminal.

Pete wasn't handcuffed but figured he might be tonight. It filled him with rage, at both Monk and especially at himself. He vowed that every single thought and action from now on would focus on escape. That included choosing pain over the pills that made him groggy.

He looked up and saw Monk looking at him, his expression hard to read. "How ya doin', Pete? Havin' fun yet?" Monk took a swig of bourbon.

Pete was silent at first, then said, "Yeah, feeling better. Thanks for cleaning my wound, and gimme that bottle." He swallowed a gulp and felt the burn. From now on, he planned to lie to Monk about everything. Rolland would be harder to fool. That asshole was watching Pete too, with that feral grin on his face. It as much as said, *Don't even think about it, motherfucker. You belong to me.*

Pete realized he was playing linebacker again—in a more deadly game—and he was really good at it. Rolland might be elusive, like the best running back he'd ever faced. Like that guy playing for The Citadel last season. But Pete, using muscle and brains, was going to chase Johnny Rolland down, from end zone to end zone, and destroy him.

If Monk got in the way, he was going down too.

CHAPTER FOURTEEN

May 12

SUNDAY DAWNED HOT AND SMOGGY. I slept late. My hangover was moderate, better than I'd thought it would be. Looking back on my evening, it felt dispiriting and weird, me selling Sam out the way I had. But I was doing what he wanted me to do, and there were no half measures. I'd learned that in Yucaipa years before, spending two weeks with a biker gang whose members would have cut my throat if they'd known I was a cop. Hank Phillips hadn't dropped his guard last night, even as drunk as he was, but he had begun to complain about money troubles. That was going to be my way in, even if it took a big bite out of me.

Today, thankfully, there would be no Hank Phillips. JK and I were meeting soon at the Fontana station with a goal of reaching William Giles of Glen Alpine, North Carolina. I had his home number courtesy of Rocky, the Glen Alpine cop. I found myself hoping that his son, Pete, the football star, was not mixed up in the murderous business out here along with his buddy, Monk Tanner, who most surely was.

After a breakfast of four aspirin, coffee, a banana, and the last Hostess donut in the box, I considered picking up my fiddle for some practice. Then rejected the idea. Music was as stale as that donut. No need to force it since our band was on hiatus. I called my mother, and we had a cheerful conversation. She asked about the possible job promotion. I told her, true enough, that Sam was giving me some extra work that fit right in with that plan. She was glad to hear it.

Two minutes after we hung up, the phone rang. I figured it was my mother remembering some piece of family gossip she'd forgotten to convey. Instead, it was a smoky female voice that I knew well. "I'll be sitting at a corner table in the lobby bar of the Biltmore Hotel tonight at 7 p.m., trying my level best to fight off horny journalists seeking my company. I'd much rather it be you." Then she hung up.

Allie. She loved these sexy games. So did I, if it was all I could get. My hangover vanished. Now it became a matter of occupying myself for the rest of the day without thinking too much about her. She likely had a room at the Biltmore. I'd pack a small bag... wouldn't need much. My mood went from zero to sixty. She did that to me.

I was looking forward to the North Carolina phone call. Maybe we'd get a lead on the elusive Monk Tanner. The Fontana station was quiet when I arrived, which meant no unusual Saturday night violence had befallen the town. JK, as usual, had arrived first. It was a genuine pleasure to work with such a dedicated partner. We calculated that it was 3:30 p.m. in North Carolina. I called, and a woman, presumably Mrs. Giles, answered after three rings. I identified myself and asked to speak to her husband. Perhaps I should have been more diplomatic. I heard the receiver hit the counter. I'd upset her. I heard her say "a deputy sheriff from California" in a fast whisper to her husband.

"Hello, this is Bill Giles. What's this about?" he stated in an authoritative tone. It was the voice of a boss.

I explained that we were looking for a Mr. Monk Tanner, whose car had been badly damaged in San Bernardino County where I worked. We believed that Mr. Tanner was in the area.

"Have you talked to Dorothy Tanner?" he asked.

I realized that I should have talked to Monk's mother rather than just taking Rocky's word that she didn't know where her son was. In any case, I told him that we'd heard that Mrs. Tanner was unaware of her son's whereabouts but knew he'd taken vacation time and gone on a trip.

"Look, uh, Deputy, we just got back from a vacation and haven't even unpacked. I know our son, Pete, and Monk are close friends, but I believe that Pete's gone back up to school. He'd been watching the house, but I think he has classes tomorrow. I'll give him a call. That's concerning about Monk. What's your phone number? I'll get back to you if I find out anything."

I gave him the number, and he hung up. I then immediately called Mrs. Tanner, giving her less information, merely saying that Monk's car had been found and that we were looking for him. She was friendly enough but oddly unconcerned, repeating what she'd told Rocky, namely that Monk was a grown man and could go where he wanted. She did repeat that he'd taken vacation time from the Drexel Furniture Company, where both of them worked. He'd been gone a week, and had taken two weeks off.

"I don't know about you," I said to JK, "but if my mother had gotten a call about me from a cop three thousand miles away when I was twenty-one, she'd have really freaked out. Safe to say that Mrs. Tanner doesn't worry too much about her son."

"My mother would freak out even now if she got a call," JK said with a grin. "I guess we've got good moms."

The phone rang. It was Bill Giles calling back. "Okay, some things back here aren't making sense. What's your name again, Deputy?" He sounded angry, like it was my fault.

"My name is Jimmy Sommes, sir."

"I've discovered that my son is not at his dorm at App State, and according to our next-door neighbor, he apparently left our home a week or so ago. He was supposed to be watching our house while we were away, so at a minimum he's in big trouble with us. I am now convinced that he's with Monk Tanner. What the hell is going on out there, and let's cut through any BS. A law enforcement officer from California calling my home strikes me as serious, so let's have it."

I heard a female voice in the background whispering, "Bill, settle down," or something like that.

"Mr. Giles, there was a double homicide in San Bernardino County last Thursday night. The victims were not your son or his friend Monk Tanner. At this point we have no direct evidence indicating that your son was involved, but it is an ongoing investigation. The situation is less clear regarding Mr. Tanner. The likely shooter that night called out 'let's get out of here, Monk' to the driver of his vehicle, a Lincoln Continental. I remember that first name because it's unusual. Finally, the next morning we found Mr. Tanner's vehicle vandalized at a nearby motel."

"My lord," Bill Giles said. "Does Dorothy Tanner know all this?"

"Not all of it. I rarely discuss the details of an ongoing investigation, but given the circumstances, I likely will talk to her again soon. She knows we found her son's vehicle, but I left it at that, not wanting to unduly alarm her."

"She doesn't alarm easily. Could you please hold on a minute, Officer Sommes?"

I could hear murmuring again, both of them this time. Putting myself in their shoes, this call must be terribly upsetting and frightening. JK passed me a note. It read "Johnny Rolland?" I nodded. It was a good idea.

Giles came back on the line. He was quieter, subdued. "First, Officer Sommes, thank you for answering my questions. I realize you are doing your job. My wife and I need to talk to some folks here, think on this, pray on this, as we are very confused. We are going to visit Dorothy Tanner, among other things. Is this the best number to reach you?"

I gave him the number of the Alta Loma substation, my home number, and JK's. I respected this man and his wife. Before he hung up, I stopped him. "Mr. Giles, I'm sorry. Could I ask you one more question? Does the name Johnny Rolland mean anything to you?"

Another pause. "Hmm, Johnny Rolland. He was a baseball player around here, a really good one as I remember. He went to Morganton High School, just like Pete and Monk, but he was a little older than them. Later on, Rolland got hurt, I believe, couldn't play pro ball. I haven't heard his name in years. Is he mixed up in this too?"

"We honestly don't know at this moment, but his name has surfaced."

"Okay, I need to go now, Officer. My son Pete is a good boy, a good man. We love him. That's all I know." William Giles hung up the phone. There was emotion in his voice. His life, and that of his wife's, had just changed, perhaps irrevocably.

I gave JK the number for the Biltmore Hotel in LA; the hotel guest was Allie D'Amico. "Don't call unless a total catastrophe that you can't handle is unfolding," I told him. "Call Sam and tell him the team will meet in his office at noon tomorrow if that's okay with him."

"Okay," JK said. "I've been trying to piece together some information about Johnny Rolland. We need to know more about him."

"Good idea. See you tomorrow."

CHAPTER FIFTEEN

May 12

THE SUN WAS STILL HIGH in the sky when I headed west on the San Bernardino Freeway toward LA and Allie, my anticipation at a fever pitch. It never felt perfect, because I'd lost control—Allie was calling the tune. But the smile on my face told a different story. I couldn't wait to see her.

The Biltmore lobby bar was open and brightly lit. Good. I'd been in too many dark, smoky joints lately and didn't really need any more booze. I stopped near the front desk and saw Allie, maybe fifty feet away, sitting in the cocktail lounge at a small glass table to the right of the elegant old cherrywood bar—where movie stars used to hang out, drink whiskey, and tell lies.

Allie was wearing a short black cocktail dress that fit snugly over her magnificent breasts, showing just the right amount of cleavage. The dress matched her raven hair, cut medium length now, not that long, straight hippie girl hair she'd featured two years before. A single strand of pearls hung from her neck. I knew she was wearing matching stud pearl earrings. She didn't like the dangly kind. I could see the gleaming black D'Amico high-heeled shoes on her feet. Her daddy had made his fortune making and selling those shoes. But the heels were moderate, not stiletto, since she was a working journalist who needed to move fast when chasing a story, which for her could happen anytime day or night. I guess she was like a cop in that sense. The unexpected dictated our days and nights.

She saw me and smiled. My heart jumped. Feelings of

loneliness disappeared. Only the present mattered. Her look thrilled me. I floated the rest of the way to her table, now starring in my own movie.

"Hi, cowboy," she said, moving her purse and sweater off the other seat. "I hoped you were going to show up. I saved a place for you."

I sat down, gave her a quick kiss, said some stupid thing like "better than wine." The words didn't matter. I was with her. "What're you drinking?"

"A Black Dahlia," she said. "It's their signature cocktail. In honor of you know who."

The liquor in Allie's martini glass was jet black. Even the olives were black. I signaled the barman, pointing at Allie's glass. He nodded his approval and started mixing the drink. "Miss Elizabeth Short, the Black Dahlia," I said. "LA's most famous unsolved murder. She was last seen here."

"Are you going to solve it?" Allie asked, looking at me, playful.

"Nope. I've got my own set of murders to solve."

"Me too," Allie said. "I've got mine to cover, plus a certain kidnapping that's gone completely haywire."

Allie's chocolate eyes flashed as she talked about chasing her big story. I knew the Patricia Hearst stuff, at least the basics. A spoiled young newspaper heiress was kidnapped by a ragtag gang of radicals in Berkeley. Then held for a ransom the demands of which kept shifting depending on the murky mindset of the SLA, the Symbionese Liberation Army. Even Allie, still an ardent socialist of sorts, thought this smallish group was flat-out crazy, and violent. Even before kidnapping Hearst, the SLA had murdered a popular black public official in Oakland and proudly told the world about it. Then the news that made this wild tale even more of a worldwide story. Patty Hearst joined the gang! And robbed a bank in San Francisco.

The drink came. I'd had one once before. Gin and a touch of vermouth, mixed with blackberry liqueur. An odd combination but perfect for this bar.

"I'm chasing a rumor that the SLA might be relocating to Los Angeles," Allie said. "Their leader is an LA guy, and the FBI is finally getting closer to busting them in San Francisco. But thus far I've got no frickin' leads, nothing down here." She paused. "Except for you, Deputy Sheriff Sommes. I've got you." She grinned, and it transformed her face from tough to mischievous, as if she possessed a delicious secret that she may or may not be willing to share. That's all it took.

I signaled the barman for the check and threw down a ten-dollar bill. "Let's go to your room. I'd arrest you, but I didn't bring my handcuffs."

We kissed in the elevator. I couldn't wait a moment longer. Her room had a view of City Hall, blocked when I closed the curtain. With one quick move, she had the little black dress over her head and off, followed by a trail of royal purple lingerie drifting to the rug. I threw my clothes all over, not caring. We didn't even make it all the way to the bed, not the first time. She may have kept her shoes on. The sex was fast and urgent, as if we'd just met. In some ways it was true. Three weeks away from her felt like an eternity.

Later, after long showers and forgettable room service food, we explored her massive hotel bed, and each other, for what seemed like hours. Allie altered my sense of time. We settled in as lovers, not frantic strangers. "Penny for your thoughts, cowboy," she said in her throaty voice.

"No thoughts, just feelings. You're a very sexy lady."

"Thank you, sir. Would I wreck it if I smoked?"

"Hell no. I even miss your stinky Camels when we're apart." Then I almost broke the rules. To tell her that I loved her. That I wanted more, that I wanted everything with her. But she'd likely stiffen, pull away. Our magic, and it was magic, needed to be in the moment. The future, like the past, didn't exist. I knew the rules. I held my tongue and relaxed, luxuriating in her husky laugh and rich body. Perhaps that crazy thing about dying in your lover's arms held elements of truth. I was deeply happy. For now, that was more than enough.

We parted after an early breakfast the next day, each a little shy, aware that we continued to live in different worlds. Each saying we would see each other soon, unsure if it was true, but both hoping. Then, to hell with it, I broke the rules as we embraced, saying, "I love you, Allie." She hesitated for an instant, then her arms held me closer.

"Back at you, cowboy," she whispered, giving me an extra squeeze. With that she was gone, but her fragrance and touch lingered, elevating my mood. My world felt like a better and less lonely place. Was I reading too much into it, that last embrace and her words to me? I doubted it. From the day we met, she'd always been honest, sometimes to a fault, but I always knew where I stood.

Later on, while heading east down the freeway, my thoughts centered on Allie and our fine time together, the radio tuned to a soft rock station that was playing a corny love song, my Charger almost got smashed by a big semi-truck in El Monte as it merged heedlessly into traffic. Its booming airhorn brought me back to my senses. *Okay, Jimmy, settle down.*

It was time to get back to work, and this cowboy needed to be in San Bernardino by high noon.

CHAPTER SIXTEEN

May 13

IT WAS A SHORT MEETING with our investigative team on Monday morning. Sam wasn't around. I told them about my call with William Giles, and that he obviously was trying to find out if his son, Pete, was involved in all this. Hell, maybe Pete had gone to Florida or wherever Southern college students went for springtime fun. Again, since there was no new newspaper coverage regarding the Mister Louie's murders, we felt no outside pressure. Normally, my internal murder clock would be racing, but the inside information regarding Johnny Rolland helped to slow it down. JK and Gutierrez's trip to Dave's Market hadn't yielded much. The folks there were used to cops and without a search warrant wouldn't talk. Still, it planted the flag with Mr. Izzy Weiss.

I told everybody to keep working and later confessed (falsely) to Hank Phillips that I'd drunk my ass off last night and needed a nap. The last part was true. JK managed to grab me long enough to stuff some Johnny Rolland research notes into my pocket before I left. Was I living my cover to fool Phillips, or slacking off, or both? My back was pleasantly sore from something that either Allie, or I, or both of us did last night in that giant bed. I wanted to be back there. I went home and crashed.

***

The phone woke me from a deep sleep. It was Carol. "I've got a new client that might interest you," she said. "His name is William Giles from Glen Alpine, North Carolina. Ring a bell?"

It took a moment for my mind to focus. "What time is it?"

"Six p.m., on Monday, May 13. Are you hungover?"

"No, I was with Allie last night in LA. We didn't sleep much. How's *your* love life?"

"Just swell. Let's get dinner someplace really good. On me. Mr. Giles arrives tomorrow and is offering a large retainer."

I realized that I was very hungry. "Lord Charley's in an hour. Meet you in the bar."

"Done," Carol said and hung up.

That gave me just time enough to shower, shave, and drive to the best prime rib restaurant in our area. I was puzzling over the abrupt upcoming visit by Mr. Giles when Carol arrived. I noticed she was dressing better, more corporate, now that she was a big-shot private investigator. My friend Rick, the maître d', got us a secluded table under an alcove.

"This is some kettle of fish, isn't it," Carol said, getting right to it. "I want you to tell me everything you can about this goofy murder case, now that I've got a dog in the fight, so to speak."

"You first, how did William Giles find you?"

"One of our superior court judges went to the University of North Carolina undergrad and he and Giles were friends. Giles called him last night and asked who the best private investigator in San Bernardino County was. The judge was kind enough to recommend me, even though I'm technically LA County. Anyway, I'm gonna owe that judge something big down the line." Carol paused to eat a bite of salad. Lord Charley's menu was simple: salad followed by a generous slab of prime rib, cooked to order, accompanied by a baked potato and a puffy Yorkshire pudding pastry. The latter was very English. I'd never even heard of it before I'd started coming to this restaurant.

"You can order a drink, Jimmy. I promise not to get on your case. Especially if you depleted all of your bodily fluids during your tryst with Allie. Was it fun?"

"Yeah, but I'm not going to jinx it by talking about it." I signaled the waiter and asked for a Budweiser. Carol ordered a glass of red wine. "I'm trying to remember what I told you about the case."

"Lemme try," Carol said. "Two hoods show up at Mister Louie's to kill some guy in the back room, and the guy kills them instead and shoots at you—you failed to mention that to me—while escaping in a dark blue Lincoln. Somebody named Monk is driving the Lincoln. Blood spatter on the wall in the back room indicates that a third, unidentified person, very possibly Peter Giles, was shot. Do you have blood types?"

"O positive, and neither murder victim was O positive," I said. The prime rib arrived. "Let's eat first, then talk." We made relatively quick work of the delicious food.

Carol resumed her summary with the coffee. "Early the next morning, a San Bernardino Sheriff's Department patrolman is alerted to an incident at the El Rey Motel in Rialto that includes a damaged Ford Mustang owned by one Monk Tanner, a resident of Glen Alpine, North Carolina. Correct?"

"Yes, you have the basics, except I've got some significant new information." *Should I be telling Carol this?* She was a PI now, not a cop. But I'd asked her new client about the guy, so she'd soon find out anyway.

"There's a new person of interest. His name is Johnny Rolland. He's a loan shark enforcer for the LA mob and is also from North Carolina. An informant mentioned him as possibly involved in the Mister Louie's murders." I was using cop talk to Carol. We never did that. She gave me a funny look.

"You holding out on me, buddy? What's this person of interest business?"

"Yeah, sorry. This is a first for us. Me, the cop, you the PI working the same case. Sam's giving me some trouble about you. Let's go to the bar and each order a margarita and figure this out." Rick the maître d' showed up at the perfect time and took our order.

"Sam's not always right, you know," Carol said, chewing on her lower lip, a sign she was in deep concentration. "Yeah, this situation is new for us, but I'll respect your confidences. Anyway, Mr. Giles is convinced that his son is with Monk Tanner and, thus, is in big trouble. That's why he's flying out here tomorrow. He asked me if five grand was an adequate retainer. I said sure. Money clearly is no object."

"Good for you on the money. Does he know that somebody else got shot, likely Monk or Pete? It's almost certain that Johnny Rolland killed those mob guys." Our margaritas arrived. I slurped some down, licking the salt off the rim of the glass.

"I didn't tell Giles that somebody else got shot because we don't know any details yet," Carol said. "Mr. Giles has a generally low opinion of law enforcement. It wasn't personal as to you, but he isn't confident that the Sheriff's Department can help him."

"Sometimes I agree with him," I said. "Also, he's kind of right. JK and I are tasked with finding and arresting this Johnny Rolland character and apparently his driver, Monk Tanner. Pete Giles is stuck in the middle, unless I'm reading it wrong and he's a bad guy too. Maybe I'm cutting him too much slack."

"I don't know either," Carol said, "but everything about him checks out fine so far. Obviously, I'm being hired by Giles to find and save his son." Carol crumpled up her cocktail napkin. "This is a weird case. I'm trying to put myself in your shoes. Does Rolland have an arrest sheet?"

I pulled out the sheet of paper that JK had given me summarizing his research. I was too embarrassed to tell Carol that I'd barely looked at it. She could tell anyway. "Lemme see it, Jimmy," she said, a touch impatient. "Hmm. Two arrests, felony possession of a small amount of cocaine nine months ago. Case was thrown out, some sort of illegal search. Then in January of this year," Carol continued, always happy to get the data, "a misdemeanor indecent exposure arrest. An entire porno crew filming in the backyard of a rental house in Reseda was rousted by LA County Sheriff's Department personnel, after a neighbor complained. Rolland was one of the actors and got caught with his pants down, so to speak. Must have been quite a show. But everybody involved with the movie got off with a fine."

It was my turn to take the research notes back, while Carol ordered another margarita for each of us. "A company called First Rate Productions based in North Hollywood, also a defendant in the case, covered the legal fines," I said. "JK called the LA Sheriff's Vice Squad. They confirmed that Izzy Weiss, one way or another, owns the company, but apparently First Rate Productions has closed its doors."

"Those arrests answer a key question," Carol said. "It shows that Rolland has been here for at least the past year, presumably working for this gangster named Weiss. How did you know that?"

I smiled. "Can't really say, but the information is solid," I said. "That's also how we know Rolland is the likely shooter. Let's see, Rolland was born on June 20, 1951, at Morganton Hospital in North Carolina. He'll turn twenty-three next month. Tanner and Giles are both twenty-one, so a little younger. Mr. Giles confirmed that they all went to the same high school."

"Rolland is the key to this," Carol said. "Two young men, Monk Tanner and most likely Pete Giles, left North Carolina a week or so ago and drove all the way across the county to Mister Louie's club in Upland to hook up with him. Why do that?"

"Just in time for Rolland to kill a couple of hoods," I said. "Mr. William Giles is not going to be a happy man tomorrow."

"Agreed. Also, how long are you and Sam going to sit on this Johnny Rolland information? You've got a killer on the loose, even if his victims were two-bit hoods. In my humble opinion, maybe JK can tell your investigative group that he got Rolland's name from an LA Sheriff's Department source."

"That might work, Ms. Hot Shot PI of the month. Crack

this case and it might get you the centerfold in the *Private Eye* monthly magazine."

"Which doesn't exist, but maybe I'd look good with a Colt .45 in my hand, a Humphrey Bogart fedora on my head, and a white tuxedo jacket discreetly covering what needs to be covered." We split the bill and left.

CHAPTER SEVENTEEN

May 13 – Barstow

THE ROOM SMELLED GOD-AWFUL, EVEN with the door open. Body odor, remnants of fast food in the trash, and a toilet that barely worked were contributing to the odor. Barstow was hot and dry as a bone. There was no breeze to speak of. Pete wasn't sure if Johnny Rolland had taken a shower during their three days at the Sunset Inn. He had, however, brought in a barbell holding several heavy cylindrical metal weights. Monk spotted him during the training sessions with Rolland using motel chairs pushed together as his bench.

"Too bad you're wounded, Giles," Rolland said, "or you'd see that I can out lift you any day of the week. Three sets of ten lifts each with the bar holding two hundred fifty pounds. That's my maintenance routine."

Pete knew he could match that without much difficulty due to his football weight training, although not that many reps, but he said nothing in response. The less he said to Johnny Rolland, the better. His shoulder was improving. The Medic had done a good job, and Monk was diligent about changing the dressings. That was about the only vestige left of his old friend. The rest of Monk had gone dark. The group had only left the motel room to get food and liquor (Monk always drove while Rolland kept his eye on Pete, their prisoner) with one frightening exception.

It was hard for Pete to keep the days and nights straight in this motel sameness, but he knew that crazy, terrifying journey had happened their first night there. It had been close to midnight. Rolland had rousted Pete from his uneasy sleep, uncuffed him, and marched him to the car. "Come on, college boy, we got a drug deal to make." Monk was driving as usual. Rolland had an arsenal of weapons. Pete saw two pistols and a sawed-off shotgun. Monk got on the I-15 in Barstow and headed east toward Las Vegas.

"The key to a good drug deal, my young friends, is finding a location where the other guys can't kill you. Because they may want to, depending on the circumstances. I like gas station parking lots, people always there but not too many. Monk, you stay on I-15 until we get to the East Yermo Road off-ramp. Then turn right and drive until you see this Mobil gas station on the left. It'll be all lit up, about the last gas before the desert takes over."

He handed Monk one of the pistols. "This deal will be easier than most," Rolland said, clearly enjoying showing off his expertise, but also nervous. "No cash is involved. They get the heroin. We get the cocaine. I've worked with them before."

"Do they know you're on the run?" Monk asked.

"I'm betting my life they don't," Rolland said, jacking two rounds into the shotgun, "because me and their head guy need to sample the products before we do the final hand-off. No reason they would since they're not part of Izzy's crew. My deals with them are always side deals."

Pete saw the gas station on the left. A motel called the El Rancho something or other was across the street, its small sign reading "Vacancy, Last Stop before Oblivion." Its lobby was bright, with customers milling around inside, even late at night.

"Monk, I want you to turn left into the gas station, but stop at the edge," Rolland said in a low voice. "Keep the engine running. They'll have two cars, both Pontiacs."

Pete saw only one other car, a late-model sedan parked at the gas pump. No attendant was in sight. "Okay, flash your headlights on bright three times," Rolland said. Monk did as he was instructed. From the other side of the station, hidden in darkness, a different sedan flashed its lights back.

"Okay, boys, it's showtime," Rolland said. "Drive halfway to that car that flashed us and stop near the gas pumps. Then cover me." Monk eased the car along. Rolland, still quick as a cat despite his bulky frame, jumped from the car, shotgun in one hand and a bag in the other. A man from the other car did likewise, holding a bag but no gun. But twenty feet away, a man from the first sedan got out. He was aiming what looked like an army M-16 at Rolland. Monk trained the .44 Magnum on that man. Pete watched Monk become a criminal. He was a natural.

Standing five feet apart, Rolland and the other man with the bag conversed in Spanish. Each pulled one package from their respective bags. Somebody nearby gunned a car engine. It startled Rolland and the other man. Then they relaxed, a false alarm. The other man was grinning at Johnny Rolland. Pete didn't know why. Each man put a small plastic package, the sample, on the patchy asphalt. Then they backed away. A different vehicle, a small pickup truck coming from the west, started to pull in for gas. It was a woman driving alone. The man with the rifle from the first sedan waved her off with a threatening motion, his gun held high. The pickup truck reversed and disappeared into the night with a screech of its tires.

Rolland and the other man each picked up the other's package. Still cradling his shotgun, Rolland made a tiny slit in his with a switchblade, scooped some powder out with his finger, and snorted it. The other man did the same. Each seemed satisfied. Rolland returned to the station wagon. "Here's the final deal," he said, giving Monk his satchel of heroin. "Drive very slowly up to the car that flashed its lights at us. When I say 'go,' throw it to the driver. He'll do the same to you. Now move."

Several men in the other sedan were outside their car now, all covering Rolland's car with their weapons. Monk crept along. Pete thought it was a 50/50 chance they would get killed. Rolland was badly outnumbered. It might all depend on whether his "customers" believed he was still protected by the LA mafia. Apparently, they did. News must travel slowly to Barstow. The drugs were exchanged without a hitch.

Rolland was a happy man. "Those fellas got a good deal on the smack, but I don't care, because I got enough blow to keep us happy for a while. Make sure neither of those Pontiacs is tailing us, Monk. You're a born wheelman, my brother. I just love the town of Yermo. My kind of place. Turn left here, then right on old Route 66."

There was no tail. They were clear. Everybody breathed a little easier as they drove in darkness of the desert night. A battered old Route 66 Barstow sign loomed in their headlights.

"Slow down," Rolland ordered Monk. Then quick as a cat, he drew his .44 Magnum and fired a shot at the sign, already riddled with bullet holes. They heard it clang off metal as they sped off.

"It's a tradition," was all he said. Then the three of them hauled ass back to the Sunset Inn, Monk and Rolland chattering away, telling baseball stories.

Even Pete felt good. It beat getting killed.

***

Rolland and Monk spent the next two days bingeing on cocaine, listening to country music on a portable cassette player, and watching movies on television. Monk contributed his considerable marijuana stash. At one point, they forced Pete to snort some coke. He didn't feel much of anything, maybe a mild buzz, but did notice it made him want more. Rolland said, "Don't waste it on the college boy."

Pete knew some of the music they were listening to, the popular songs by Johnny Cash and Loretta Lynn, but much of it was new to him. They played one song over and over again, a cowboy song about "Pancho and Lefty." It was haunting and sad. At one of their quieter moments, Rolland said, "That's us, Monk. I'm Pancho and you're Lefty. But I don't want to die, man. Those Federales ain't gonna get me, not yet. You neither, brother." Their party continued. Pete wondered if Rolland even listened to the words. Apparently, he missed the part of the song where Lefty sells Pancho out. Pete doubted if Monk had noticed either. They were too high to care.

Later, not knowing if it was day or night since all the curtains were closed tight while the air conditioning blasted, Pete awoke from a restless, troubled sleep. Was there any other kind? The morning TV newsman said it was Monday, May 13. Monk was crashed out and snoring on his bed. Rolland emerged bleary-eyed from the bathroom. He stunk to high heaven. Approaching Pete, he flashed his switchblade knife and snapped it open. "Sitting on the toilet in there, I just got a grand idea on our next move. I figure you are worth some real money, Giles. Why risk robbing a bank, my other idea, when I can hold your rich ass, no offense, for ransom." Rolland broke out into his evil cackling laugh. Pete thought he sounded more like a hyena than a human being.

CHAPTER EIGHTEEN

May 14

EVERYTHING CHANGED ON TUESDAY. FIRST, Sam and I agreed to go public with the Johnny Rolland tip. A BOLO was issued using his mug shot from the cocaine possession arrest. It merely said that he was a person of interest in the Thursday, May 9, slaying of Joseph and Vincent Salerno, formerly residents of North Hollywood, California. Anyone with any information was asked to contact the San Bernardino Sheriff's Department. Rolland was considered to be armed and dangerous.

At our morning staff meeting, JK announced that he'd gotten the Rolland tip from LA County Sheriff's Vice Squad, and had no further information about "the person of interest." We knew Hank Phillips would immediately pass this on to Izzy Weiss, but the LA angle should serve to protect our confidential informant from getting blown. We hoped so, but the life of any confidential informant consists of living on the edge.

Then Carol called me. Late last night, William Giles had received a ransom demand by telephone. His son, Pete Giles, had been kidnapped. The kidnapper asked for $150,000 in unmarked bills in exchange for the safe return of Pete Giles. No other details were discussed. The caller had then hung up. Carol volunteered to report the crime to the San Bernardino Sheriff's Department on behalf of Mr. Giles.

Sam Fuller and I met in his office to discuss the new development. Our likely killer of two North Hollywood hoods now was also a likely kidnapper. I told Sam that Mr. Giles, a take-charge kind of man, already had retained Carol Loomis to find her son and "assist law enforcement" prior to even getting the ransom demand. His plane was scheduled to land this afternoon at Ontario Airport. "Apparently Giles doesn't think much of cops as instruments of justice," I told Sam.

"He'll be a handful for us to handle," Sam said. "Boss types usually are, but in his shoes I'd want immediate results too."

"According to Carol, prior to leaving for the airport this morning, Mr. Giles instructed his lawyer back in Morganton, North Carolina, to begin the paperwork on a new second mortgage of the Giles Lumber Company in the amount of a hundred fifty grand."

"He'll want to pay," Sam said. "I imagine Carol Loomis can likely slow him down in that regard. How did she land Giles as a client?"

"A local judge that Giles knows recommended her. She's already the best around here."

"Just remember, Jimmy, she's still a PI, not a cop anymore."

"Roger that. I have one further request, Sam, and you're not going to like it. I want to meet with the confidential informant you have inside the Izzy Weiss operation."

"Why?"

"To get some understanding of both Weiss and this Johnny Rolland character. Is he just a hophead psycho? I've got one image of him in my head: a skinhead with a gun shooting at me, a crazy smile on his face, and a loud cackling laugh. It just screamed drug addict to me. He's not some sort of criminal mastermind. If I'm right, he'll need more dope. They always do. That's how we catch him."

"The informant talks to only one person. It's not me, but he's a good officer. You know how weird these things are. But I don't disagree with you. Let me see what I can do."

Sam looked at his watch. "One more thing," he said. "We've got about twenty-two hours from right now before I'm going to let the FBI know about the kidnapping."

"No state line issue. No minors involved," I said.

"Correct. But it's departmental protocol and I follow it. Let's find this son-of-a-bitch fast, and clear both the murders and the kidnapping. And this takes priority over Hank Phillips and his tawdry operation. Both the press and the FBI will be all over us soon enough, whether we like it or not."

"Got it." I left to find Beth Bolling. Luckily, she was in her office and already busy on account of the Johnny Rolland BOLO.

"Jesus, now he's a kidnapper," she exclaimed when I told her. "Do we have to go public with that too?"

"No. It might not be him, for one thing, and it might be counterproductive. I want to meet with William Giles first."

I commandeered one of Sam's conference rooms as my temporary office and called Carol. "Can I go to the airport with you this afternoon? I would like to meet Mr. Giles."

She hesitated. "Actually, no. I've got to meet him first, find out how the client wants to play it. I may end up negotiating with you and Sam on Giles's behalf. Plus, he'll be exhausted. His plane from Charlotte left at 6 a.m."

I couldn't help but smile. "I knew we'd end up on one of these cases together sooner or later. But a kidnapping of a North Carolina college football player with a rich daddy, by a drug-crazed thug. Jeez."

"Not that rich apparently. He didn't have a hundred fifty thousand sitting around in a bank account."

"Who does? I'll let you figure out the ethical PI/client stuff. I just want to catch this Rolland bum ASAP."

"Me too, as long as Pete Giles doesn't get killed in the process." She hung up.

It left me feeling odd. Today, she was all business. Working with Carol to solve cases and apprehend criminals had always been exhilarating. Everybody thought we made a great pair, her the brains, me the brawn, but both of us knew that was a simplistic description. We'd made each other better at our work. When she was a Claremont detective, we were always on the same side, save for petty jurisdictional nonsense that neither of us cared about. Now, it was going to be different. She was going to bring her formidable A-game to work for a private client who most likely didn't give a rat's ass about catching Johnny Rolland. William Giles would want his son back unharmed, period. My job, I realized, was to effectively make those two objectives work together. Where the other man, Monk Tanner, fit into the puzzle was anyone's guess.

CHAPTER NINETEEN

May 14 – Barstow

R*OLLAND AND MONK THOUGHT PETE* was asleep. The raucous binge had concluded. The cassette player was turned off. It was daylight. Rolland was speaking quietly but urgently to Monk. Pete kept his eyes closed but listened. The subject was Mexico.

"I want us to go to Guadalajara in the very near future. There's a doctor there. I want him to get me off the meth and the coke. I can kick meth on my own but not coke. I live for the damn stuff. But we need more cash to pull it off, to get us to Mexico, and I've got a plan, a good plan. In fact, I made some calls last night, first to a buddy of mine who knows how to get things done, and then to somebody else."

Pete heard the hiss of a match being fired up, then the smell of marijuana. "Who else did you call?" Monk asked after exhaling.

"Okay, and don't get all excited, it was to Pete's old man," Rolland said. "We need to ransom Pete. Trade him to his folks for some real money, maybe a hundred fifty grand."

Pete almost cried out. *My God*, he thought. They're bringing my dad and mom into this. It was unthinkable. He restrained himself as best he could.

Even the newly corrupted Monk was upset. "What the fuck, Johnny, you're talking about my best friend. I can't do that."

"You already have. Pete's my prisoner, and you've been helping me keep him that way. He sleeps cuffed to the bed for god's sake."

"But that partly because he got shot, and I'm taking real

good care of him."

"Keep your voice down, Monk. I know you're taking care of him. But we've gotta talk this through. I'm not going to hurt him, even though he's a rich punk. You've got my word on that. That big house on the hill—I remember the Giles house—they have plenty of money. He gets to go home, have his shoulder looked at by a bunch of doctors, and we get to go to Mexico. Everybody wins."

"What about me?" Monk said. "Glen Alpine's my home too. I've got a job back there. I don't know anything about Mexico."

"Hate to break it to you, pardner, but you're already knee deep in all this shit. You're a damn fine wheelman as a matter of fact, but if I go down, you're going down too and looking at doing some hard time in prison."

There was silence. Then Johnny Rolland played his last card. "After all, Mr. Monk Tanner, what are brothers for? You think I don't know that miserable son-of-a-bitch down in South Carolina is a father to us both, at least did right by the two of us, brother?"

"How long have you known?"

"Last year sometime, he wrote to me asking for money and spilled the beans. I was downright touched, Monk. You're a good man, better than me. That's one reason I was glad to meet you boys in Pasadena. Did you know? I figure that's why you came to beautiful Southern California to see me."

"Yeah, I knew, from maybe a year back too. I didn't know where you were, and thought I'd probably never see you again." Monk paused. "Look. I've got to take a walk, think about stuff. Put that joint out, will ya."

Pete heard the screen door open and slam. Then a heavy hand landed on Pete's good shoulder.

"You get an earful, college boy? It's all gonna work out perfect, you'll see." Rolland's breath smelled like an open grave. "Open your eyes."

Pete did so and saw Rolland holding his knife blade out

again, this time about one inch from Pete's neck. Blood was trickling from Rolland's nose, and his eyes looked dead. "You've got maybe a fifty/fifty shot of living through this, boy, so you'd better fucking help me make this ransom thing work to perfection."

CHAPTER TWENTY

May 14

CAROL CALLED ME AT 10 P.M. "Can you meet me at the Los Amigos Bar in half an hour? William Giles is driving me crazy. I need to talk and tequila might help."

"Let me check my calendar... Looks like I'm free. See ya soon." Carol almost never called me at night, rarely needed alcohol to solve a problem, and had never before complained to me about a client. From my brief phone calls with William Giles, I sensed his "take charge" executive type manner was getting to her. Sam and I figured he was going to be a handful, and from Carol's tone, we'd been right.

Carol was already drinking a margarita when I arrived. "My limit is two," she said. I ordered a Budweiser. No hard stuff for me tonight.

"I've never been judged so aggressively as I was today by Mr. William Giles, and constantly found wanting," she said. "My clothes, my car, and especially my crummy strip mall office were not at all to his liking." Carol paused and drank half her margarita. "This is getting to be a habit," she said with a rueful smile.

"Did Giles say anything to you about any of that?"

"Not really, but I could see the disappointment in his eyes, especially regarding the office. He clearly expected a suite in an office building and maybe a secretary. Jeez. He really got to me, made me doubt myself. Also, I feel very guilty because what he and his wife are going through is just terrible, and here I am worried about myself."

"First, you're the best. Did he hire you? That's the main thing."

"Yeah, I've already deposited his five-thousand-dollar check. I'm expected to work full-time on this case, and my expenses come out of the retainer. He'll get refunded what I don't earn at my hourly rate. I expect to earn it all pretty fast."

"Is this barroom meeting billable?'

Carol smiled. "Sure, since I'm liaising with the leader of the San Bernardino Sheriff's team that is going to solve the kidnapping, namely you. But he doesn't want to meet with you, only with Sam. Bosses are his thing, and you're a flunky. He's also this close to contacting the FBI, saying he's going to pray on it tonight. This praying stuff. I'm never going to visit the South, ever."

This was the reverse of our usual pattern. Tonight, I needed to help Carol settle down. "Okay, let me buy the drinks. Mr. Giles clearly is distraught over the kidnapping of his son. I would be too. How does he want you to help him?"

"First get the money to a local bank. I suggested Sumitomo Bank of California. But he said no to a 'Jap' bank. Accordingly, we will visit the Claremont branch of the Bank of America tomorrow morning and arrange for the money to be wired from his bank."

"Has there been any further contact from the kidnapper? It's got to be this Johnny Rolland character, which is good news."

"No further contact. Why good news?"

"Because he strikes me as a rank amateur at the kidnapping business, and something of a dumb shit. We're smarter than he is."

"Yeah, but he's also a dangerous drug addict who has just killed two men."

I nodded. "There is that. I do need to talk to Mr. Giles tomorrow whether he wants to or not. Monk Tanner has not been kidnapped to our knowledge. What the hell is going on with him? Is he a kidnapper too? Giles must know something about their interaction."

"Okay, but maybe Sam has to be in the meeting too as a

gesture of respect to Mr. Giles. Plus, I think bringing the FBI into this might be a good idea. How many kidnappings have you worked?"

"Well, there was this pissed off ex-husband who stole his two kids from an Alta Loma elementary school during recess in a custody dispute with his ex-wife. We caught him at Bodene's bar that night bragging about it and threw him in jail. He'd left the kids with his new girlfriend. They were returned immediately to the ex-wife unharmed. Does that count?"

Carol laughed. "I wouldn't mention that stellar crime-fighting episode to William Giles if I were you. Come to think of it, I'm going to stop at one drink. Sorry for dragging you out. I just needed to vent."

"Come on. I've done way more venting than you have over the years. You deserve one once in a while." I paid the bill and we left for our respective homes.

William Giles should have liked Carol's cherry red Chevy Bel Air. It was practically a classic, and I thought Southerners liked fast wheels.

***

I had just gone to bed when the phone rang. It was Sam Fuller. "Our contact inside Izzy Weiss's crime operation is willing to meet with you."

"When?"

"Now. You're to drive to my garage and wait. I told her you drive a Dodge Charger. She'll get in your car and talk."

I was tired, but the trusty Benzedrine tablet I always kept in my wallet was designed for this. I popped it. "You said 'she,' so it's a woman. Have you seen her?"

"No, only a phone call tonight, when she agreed to meet with you. The woman is scared of Weiss, and she knows Johnny Rolland."

"Sounds promising. I'm on my way."

There are advantages to living alone. I never had to explain to anybody where I was going and why. There wasn't even a dog to feed and walk. I was a free agent. I guess loneliness had its virtues. That, of course, was self-serving bullshit, but who cared? I had work to do.

I followed Sam's instructions when I got to his sprawling north Etiwanda property. The garage was located to the left of the old wood-shingled house. I turned off my engine and waited. A woman wearing a loose-fitting coat walked quickly to the car. She looked to be in her thirties, about my age, and had long red hair tied in a loose ponytail. "Just drive," she said. "I don't care where, except no restaurants or bars. Izzy has spies everywhere."

"My cabin is safe and private."

She hesitated. "Fine, but no funny business. I'm Tammy Lee Bottomly." She laughed. "My stage name, so to speak. It's as good as any."

That began to define her world. It was full of dangerous men. She used a "stage" name. That was okay with me. She was an information source and had asked for this meeting.

"Well, I'm Sergeant Jimmy Sommes of the San Bernardino Sheriff's Department, and that's the only name I've ever had. And no funny business."

She was quiet. I drove home on Baseline. It was after midnight but still warm. There was no wind. I decided that talking on my deck might help her relax. Jumpy, she looked around while we climbed my steps.

"I'm going to have a beer. Do you want anything?" As I was talking, she took off her coat. Her figure was spectacular.

"Sure, I'd like a beer." She saw me looking at her and gave me a wry smile. "That's another reason for not going to a bar. Men tend to notice me."

You can say that again. I brought the beers. "Okay, thanks for meeting with me. I know this is risky for you. Why don't you start talking. Do you mind if I take some notes?"

She nodded okay and took a pull on her bottle of beer. "I started off in the pornography business in LA after getting kicked out of high school in Phoenix. They're real, by the way," she said, following my eyes and cupping her large breasts, covered by a flimsy sweater and a bra. "I made some movies, the usual awful crap, just to survive, and lo and behold, it turned out that I was really good at the business side of things, becoming an efficient producer. It's lots of work, by the way," she said, throwing a smile my way, "putting together a good dirty movie. Anyway, Izzy Weiss noticed me and decided I should run his company, First Rate Productions, in North Hollywood, on the condition that I become his mistress. It was a cold-blooded arrangement, but I didn't mind. I've tried to run a good, honest shop, not exploit the young women more than necessary, and avoid using directors who are junkies. As for the men in the porno movies, what a bunch of creeps. Most of them drift off into who knows what."

"You knew Izzy Weiss was a mob guy, correct?"

"Sure. When that movie came out, the one with Marlon Brando, he began to think of himself as the 'Godfather' of the San Fernando Valley, a good gangster, whatever that means."

I decided to try and shake her up. "Then why are you selling him out? A lovers' quarrel?"

She laughed out loud. "Hardly. We don't sleep together much anymore. He's found a younger version of me. No, that's not the reason. The son-of-a-bitch made me give up my business, just walk away from it, stiffing the creditors, giving me a bad name. Said the company was too conspicuous. I have no idea what he meant by that. I think it was pure spite. He didn't want me to have any success, thought I should just be happy giving him weekly blow jobs and shopping at the mall with his money. What an asshole. That's a good reason to sell him out, plus there's just too much dope and too many murders in his 'work,' as he calls it. The 'good gangster' thing is impossible, especially for him, a Jewish man working with a bunch of Italian mafia hoods who'd just as soon stick a knife in his back because he's not in their made men brotherhood.

"Is it that dangerous?" I asked. *She really should be talking to the Feds,* I thought. *They can offer witness protection.*

"He's safe as long as he makes the bosses a shitload of money, which he's been doing. Anyway, he gets off on it, the danger. Izzy's an attractive, intelligent hood, but still a dangerous, violent man, and I want out."

"What about Johnny Rolland?" I asked.

Tammy sighed. "Poor Johnny. He's a mess. Too bad. A nice enough kid before the cocaine and meth got him. I hired him in a couple of movies, just for the hell of it. He had the, uh, equipment for it, but it was just a joke to him. His real job was doing whatever Izzy wanted him to do, usually strong-arm stuff."

"Stealing heroin and money from his boss. Is he that dumb?" I asked.

"I think he's self-destructive. Every once in a while, he talked about his baseball career. What could have been. I don't think he cares much what happens to him anymore. It's a downhill run. Can I get another beer? All this talking is thirsty work."

I came back with two beers and two blankets, one for each of us. It was getting a little chilly, but I didn't want to break the mood. "Did you know the whole deal at Mister Louie's was going down, the planned hit on Rolland?"

"Not a clue. Izzy and his son, a wannabe musician, rent a fancy apartment over in North Cucamonga. I stay there sometimes, and I heard Izzy screaming bloody murder, no pun intended, at some of his soldiers about the fuck-up there and how it blew the timing of the bank robbery job. He yelled at them to move the bank robbery operation to May twenty-first at 'the next bank' on the list. Then he saw me listening and told me to pack a bag and get my ass back to North Hollywood and stay away from him. I haven't talked to him since, and he thinks I'm there. I told my regular cop contact all this." She was getting tired.

"Yeah, I know, but there's been a new development. Your friend Johnny Rolland has decided to go into the kidnapping business. He's got a hostage, a young man from his hometown in North Carolina, and Rolland is pledging the hostage's safe return in exchange for a hundred fifty grand from the father."

Tammy opened her purse and took out a pack of Salem cigarettes and drew one out. "Jesus, Johnny's operating way out of his league now," she said. "Do you mind if I smoke?"

I told her okay and handed her an empty plastic cup to use as an ashtray. It made me flash on Allie and her stinky Camels. Would she be jealous of this particular house guest? She'd say no. I say maybe.

"I agree he's out of his league, and we've got to catch him before more people get hurt. Speaking for my good friends at the FBI, I'm pretty sure you can get yourself a brand-new life if you help us catch Johnny Rolland. We don't know where the hell he is. Any ideas?"

Tammy hesitated. Perhaps the crime lady in her was resisting ratting out Rolland. Then she sighed and relented. "Izzy wants him dead. You want him dead or alive, so Johnny's running out of options. He loves the desert, Palm Springs, 29 Palms, even Barstow for God's sake. What a pit, but that might be his favorite."

"Best guess is he's got one accomplice and the one hostage."

Tammy snapped her fingers. "He sells dope to a gang of crooks that operate out of Barstow, Mexican guys. Izzy and I thought about filming a flick out there, but it was too damn hot. Hey, I'm really tired, and I've told you what I know. Can I sleep here tonight?"

It was almost two in the morning. "Sure. Take the bed inside. I'll sleep on the couch." I was supposed to meet with Sam at 9 a.m., and it was going to be a long day with William Giles. I needed some sleep. Tammy's information was really good, and I hoped it would pan out. We went in and crashed in our respective places.

Sometime later a hand on my shoulder woke me up. Tammy was standing next to me, wearing just her bra and panties. "I can't sleep. Can you come to the bed? We don't need to do anything. I just need you to hold me."

I followed her into my bedroom. In bed she moved her lush body against me. Notions of "not doing anything" began to fade. My body wanted her. Then an image of Allie came blasting into my head. She was smiling her crooked smile, like she was in on the joke. She wasn't angry. She was simply there, a permanent resident in my heart.

I turned over but not away from Tammy. I liked how she felt against me. Her body seemed to understand. We drifted off to sleep that way. It was deep and dreamless.

CHAPTER TWENTY-ONE

May 15

W*HEN I WOKE UP, I* heard Tammy running water in the kitchen, a cozy domestic noise. I put on shorts and a T-shirt and walked in, already preparing to give my speech. She was wearing one of my shirts which barely covered her ass. That was going to make the speech even harder to pull off.

She beat me to it. "Look, even though we were just pals in bed together last night, it might be hard for you to explain. Don't worry about it. You're a cop, and I'm all mixed up in this Izzy Weiss mess. It was a one-shot deal, such as it was. But… thank you all the same, Jimmy. I needed some comforting."

"You stole every single word of my speech," I said. "Thank you. It turns out I needed some comforting too."

"You want coffee?"

"Sure. I have an idea about stashing you in a safe house today, so we can talk more later about finding Mr. Johnny Rolland. Where's your car?"

"A block from your boss' house. I hope I didn't get a ticket."

"If you did, I'll fix it for you. Hell, I'm a big man in these parts."

She looked up and down my body. "Yeah, I figure you may be a big man in certain parts. I'll never know."

"Don't flirt with me, lady. I've got work to do."

I took my coffee on the deck, a smile on my face, and started to map out the day. It was 7:30 a.m. I was due in San Bernardino at nine, but JK could cover for me. I'd call him.

First, I decided to call Carol at home to see how she was doing. I was glad I did. She answered, all excited. "The kidnapper called Mrs. Giles last night. He's going to call my office at 10 a.m. I called the FBI at Mr. Giles's instruction. They're setting up recording and tracing equipment in my office as we speak."

"Does Sam know?"

"I didn't call him. That's your job."

That strange feeling that Carol and I were playing for different teams and maybe working at cross purposes began to intensify. But I still needed her help. "Is Annie's apartment empty? I need a safe place to stash a witness. It's connected to this case."

Annie Hoover and Carol lived together in Claremont. But Annie, who ran a legal clinic in Claremont, maintained her Upland apartment for business purposes. Even in liberal Claremont, there were times when the two career women needed to be discreet about their relationship. Carol had told me it also gave Annie a place to go when they had one of their rare fights or, more commonly, needed to work all night on a legal brief.

"Yes, it's empty. Hold on a minute, let me check with Annie." She put down the phone.

"Annie says yes, but tell him not to mess up the place."

"It's a her, and I'm sure she'll be very neat."

"Jimmy, Jimmy, Jimmy, what are you up to now?"

I was blushing like an idiot but kept my cool. Hell, I felt guilty and hadn't done much to warrant it. "Nothing at all. This is potentially an important witness in our case."

"Okay, fill me in later. I've got to get to my office and deal with the feds." She hung up.

I called Sam. "Carol called the FBI at the instruction of her client. The kidnapper's going to call her office at 10 a.m. The FBI is there and is going to try and set up a trace on the call. I plan to attend if Mr. Giles will allow it. It's LA County. I don't have jurisdiction."

"My friends at the FBI will likely be irritated with me for

not contacting them immediately," Sam said, "but I was within the twenty-four-hour protocol. I'll call my friend at the Westwood headquarters, so plan to be there for the call as my representative. It's not up to Mr. Giles. How was your meeting with the informant?"

"Significant. She knows a lot. Rolland might be hiding out in Barstow, or somewhere else in the Mojave. But my hunch is Barstow. I'm going to stash her in a safe apartment for the day. She might help us find him." We signed off.

Tammy and I drove to get her car in Etiwanda. Both of us were quiet. Her life was in shambles, and she knew it. "Your regular contact at the Sheriff's Department, did he offer to help you, bring you in?" I asked.

"Not really. Once I told him I didn't know the location of the next bank job, he kind of lost interest. I felt abandoned. Until Sam Fuller reached out to me, via my contact. And now you, a bonus," she said smiling.

We'd just about reached her car when she said, "Wait! I remember something. We were in Barstow, and I'd been smoking pot." She grinned. "Sorry, Officer, about that, but anyway Johnny said he had this buddy at this motel. We went there and partied some more."

"Do you know the name of the motel?"

"I'm trying to remember. It's something real obvious... maybe Sunrise... No, it was the Sunset Inn. That's it. Kind of a dump."

"Thanks. That's a big help."

Tammy followed as I drove to Annie's apartment on Arrow Highway as fast as I could without attracting the attention of any local cops. Hank Phillips was a dirty cop. Who knows if Izzy Weiss had other lawmen working for him. We got to Annie's place a little after 9. I promised to call Tammy by lunchtime. "If you smoke, go out on the balcony, but wear shades and keep that body of yours under wraps. Like you said, it attracts attention." She agreed and I left for Carol's office.

I pulled my car over near Pomona College on Sixth

Street, needing a moment to gather my thoughts. All this man/woman stuff remained a mystery to me. I really liked Tammy, and the way she felt in the night. It wasn't just pals. Did I just cheat on Allie? She'd say no, and that gave me permission to do whatever I wanted. My mother, not that I'd dream of telling her about it, would say of course you cheated on her. My verdict: I didn't cheat on Allie and felt good about it.

I put all that aside and asked dispatch to patch me through to a buddy of mine in Barstow, a deputy sheriff. I requested that he put an unmarked car near the Sunset Inn to keep an eye on the place, but not to get made under any circumstances, since I didn't know what we had. He said sure. He knew the place. Lots of cover nearby. Then I called JK in San Bernardino. I told him about the kidnapping and the upcoming call at Carol's office. "Hey, are you alone?"

"I am," JK said. "The team is cooling their heels in the conference room."

"Dismiss the team for the day. Invent any excuse you want. Then meet me at Carol Loomis's office on Indian Hill as close to 10 a.m. as you can make it. All manner of stuff is going down today. The FBI is involved. You and I likely are headed to Barstow later."

***

It was hard to find a parking place in Carol's strip mall lot. Four shiny black Crown Victoria sedans surrounded her office like a school of sharks. The feds were here in force. I didn't know any of them and had to show ID to get in the door. That got me a quick smile from Carol from across the room, who for years as a Claremont detective had to show ID to get through various doors. She was familiar with being underestimated. Finally, the fed who seemed to be running the show said, "You're Sommes, right? I'm Jensen." We shook hands.

It was getting close to the time for the kidnapper's call. The feds were milling around getting ready. I introduced myself to William Giles and got a quick handshake and no eye contact. He was preparing himself for the call as well.

It was 10:05 when the phone rang, and a nervous William Giles picked up. There was a teleprompter taping the call and showing the transcript simultaneously on a monitor, which was a nifty new piece of equipment. "This call will be fast to all you folks listening," the kidnapper said. "Say something, Pete Giles."

Another voice. "Hi, Dad, I'm here." William Giles turned white.

Then the first voice returned. "Cable Airport, main runway, tomorrow, May sixteenth, at 1 p.m. Ground any flights, no airplanes. Place the satchel with one hundred fifty thousand dollars in unmarked bills on the runway near the control tower. I'll pick it up, count it, then you get your son. No helicopters flying around either, or I kill him."

"Is there—" Bill Giles started to talk. The kidnapper hung up. "Holy mother of God," Giles exclaimed. He looked dizzy, stricken. Carol tried to comfort him. He shook her off.

"Anything?" Jensen barked at one of the telephone technicians.

"Seven-one-four area code. That's all we got," the tech guy replied.

"That narrows it down to about five hundred thousand square miles," I said, unable to resist the moment. It drew some dirty looks.

Giles looked at Carol. "Let's set up the money."

"Sir, I'd advise that you allow us to run through our databases and look for any similar operations," Jensen said. "There may be opportunities to apprehend this criminal. I'll touch base with the local authorities."

"That would be me," I said, mostly to remind the FBI who I was. "Jimmy Sommes, San Bernardino Sheriff's Department along with my partner, Officer Kreuger, who is just arriving from San Bernardino headquarters. We are checking out some leads on the kidnapper right now."

"Thanks," Jensen said. "I'll give Undersheriff Sam Fuller

a call to discuss the particulars. My boss in LA speaks highly of him."

"Cable Airport is in Upland, but the San Bernardino Sheriff's Department works closely with the Upland PD. Sam will want to know ASAP," I said. "I'm sure he'll provide whatever local assistance you need."

JK had taken one step inside the room. "Let's roll," I said.

Carol ran after us as we walked to our cars. "Are you holding out on me?" she asked. "What do you have?"

"I'll tell you more when I know more, but I don't want a stampede of FBI agents going where I'm going right now. Trust me."

"I'm trying to," she said, not very convincingly.

"Back at you," was all I said as she stalked off.

"Two cars?" JK asked.

"Yeah. I've got one stop to make. Let's meet at the Denny's restaurant in Barstow, in maybe two hours. I'll fill Sam in." I hoped Tammy hadn't done a runner. Confidential informants got spooked easily.

CHAPTER TWENTY-TWO

May 15 – Mojave Desert

JOHNNY ROLLAND ORDERED MONK TO put Pete in the back seat of the Ford wagon and cuff him to the makeshift bed that was still in there. Pete didn't need the bed anymore as his shoulder was beginning to heal, but Rolland didn't care. "Hang in there, buddy," Monk said as he snapped the handcuffs tight to the metal rod of the bed. *Talk about a mixed message*, Pete thought. He had no idea if Monk liked the Mexico idea and wasn't about to ask him. He didn't want to talk to his lost friend about anything. It was moving day, although Pete had no idea where they were going. All of their meager possessions had been packed up and thrown into the back of the station wagon. Pete noticed that Monk's stash bag for his marijuana never left his side. The Sunset Inn was history.

Rolland drove several miles west to a gas station on the outskirts of Barstow. It was hot, even at 10 a.m. "Stay here," Rolland said to Monk, who he was treating as both a subordinate and a fellow criminal. Rolland glanced around for onlookers and when he didn't see any, he cuffed Pete to his wrist and headed for a telephone booth.

"Don't say nothing except 'Hi, Dad. I'm here,' or I'll cut your throat," Rolland said, showing Pete the knife. Then he entered the phone booth and made his call while Pete waited outside the booth, his cuffed arm slammed by the phone booth door. Then Rolland grabbed him, pushed him into the booth, and told him to talk. Pete followed orders, but about broke down as he spoke his lines to his anguished father. *This is all my fault.* Rolland shoved him out of the booth, his cuffed hand still connected to the kidnapper.

Rolland headed back to the car, threw Pete in, directly on his hurt shoulder, and restrained him again. Pete was nothing but a commodity now, a piece on the chessboard. "This is great, boys," Rolland exclaimed. "We are in play, and one day away from a goddamn great payday. All those cops listening in on the call think I'm stupid, some kind of drugged-up country hick. Maybe so, but I'm wily as hell, just like that coyote." He threw Monk the car keys.

"You drive, pardner. Head east on Route 66, then get on I-40 towards Needles." Rolland had some sort of a wrinkled old map in his hands. "Like it or not, I'm gonna stay sober as a judge today for our next adventure." Monk nodded his head as if he knew about the plan.

Pete watched the town of Barstow as they drove past it this time. He believed it was important for him to stay focused on their surroundings, and to note the condition of both Rolland and Monk. He figured it might be important for him later, if he even had a later. He wasn't at all sure that Rolland would let him live, even if he got his money.

But Rolland's stupid half in/half out of the phone booth stunt hadn't worked. Pete had heard the rest of the call. He knew they were going to Cable Airport at 1 p.m. tomorrow, wherever that was. This news contained a ray of hope. Were they driving or flying? Pete didn't know. He hoped for the latter. Neither of his captors knew that Pete, at the urging of his father, had taken some flying lessons. He was no pilot yet, but he knew enough to take off and land a small plane. He hid this secret away as if it were a precious jewel.

***

Rolland suddenly turned around toward Pete and stared at him. "Monk, take the next off-ramp and then pull over when you can." They were in the desert now, so Monk easily got off I-40. There was little traffic except for the trucks that seemed to inhabit the interstate highways 24/7. Rolland got out of the car and moved into the back seat.

Then he quickly placed a pillowcase over Pete's head and cinched it with rope. It was loose but effective.

"You were looking a little too alert, college boy. From now on this operation runs on a strict 'need to know' basis. And you don't need to know nothing." Rolland laughed at his own joke.

"I'll keep you company back here for a spell." He handed Monk a piece of paper and the wrinkled map. "That tells you where to go, wheelman. No loose talk now."

Pete felt a fresh surge of anger run through him. He wanted to kill Johnny Rolland with his bare hands. He knew that Rolland thought he was a wimp, a football player but not a fighter. That was effective cover for now.

Pete assumed they were headed for an airport. They were still going east, and it was hot and windy. That's all Pete knew for sure.

CHAPTER TWENTY-THREE

May 15

I RETURNED TO ANNIE'S APARTMENT to check on Tammy. She was nervous, purse in hand, ready to leave. "Look, I've got to get back to North Hollywood, to my apartment. Izzy has people watching me. A night away, that's okay, but any longer, and it goes into a report. And I might get disciplined."

I agreed she needed to get back. Things needed to stay as normal as possible in view of the scheduled May 21 bank job. "What does 'disciplined' mean?"

"He never really hurts me. Let's just say he has some kinky ideas that don't make it into my movies."

I wanted to meet this Izzy creep and have a little chat. Maybe after we arrested him next week. Maybe he'd resist arrest. Maybe I'd discipline him.

Tammy followed my train of thought and smiled. "My hero," was all she said. She really was something. She'd retained a degree of freshness, of ironic good humor in the midst of living a life that I figured normally would kill those qualities.

"The kidnapper called. He wants his money tomorrow. My partner and I are driving to Barstow today. We found out about the Sunset Inn, thanks to you. You've had some more time to think. Is there any place, or any person, out there that you recall that might help us find Johnny Rolland if he's not at that motel?"

Tammy thought for several moments. "Maybe. Johnny's got a thing for authentic old diners. He says they remind him of home in North Carolina. Anyway, there's this place called

The Country Kitchen or something like that, way out in the sticks east of Barstow. He loves the place. He dragged our entire film crew out there for dinner one night. We practically took over the place. We made the management nervous, our weird crew, not to mention the several truckers that were eating at the counter. They couldn't keep their eyes off our women. God knows what kind of chaos might have ensued. The food was no great shakes either, but it made Johnny easier to deal with."

"One more question. Do you know if Johnny Rolland knows how to fly a small plane?"

"Sorry, I don't. But Izzy uses small planes for his business needs. All the drug smugglers do, that's for sure. Flying in and out of Mexico is a breeze."

"Okay, thanks." Suddenly, I felt tongue-tied.

Tammy got up and prepared to leave. We looked at each other, both feeling it, something sweet, but also elusive and definitely ending. "Okay, I gotta go," she said. With that, she started to walk out, no kiss no hug, but sadness in her eyes. It was as if we'd never really met. Last night's intimacy was just an illusion. She paused at the door as she was leaving my life and said, "Take care of your woman, Jimmy." Had I talked in my sleep? Or perhaps it was obvious.

I called Sam, desperately needing to get back to work, back to the chase. "Cable Airport tomorrow at 1 p.m.," I said.

"I know. Jensen called me. We're to assist in any way possible, but it's their show, the airport angle seals it, the FAA and whatnot. I listened to a tape of the call. It's pretty obvious that Rolland is planning to fly in, pick up the money, and dump the hostage." There was a touch of strain in Sam's voice. He'd been through these FBI full court presses before.

"I agree with you, and I'm of no use there," I told him. "The feds will have Cable Airport blanketed. JK and I are headed out to Barstow. The informant gave me some tips. It's mostly a hunch, but I think it's a good play."

"Do the feds need to know? Does William Giles need to know?"

"I think it's too sketchy right now. I'll call you tonight if I find out more. A fleet of federal Crown Victoria sedans descending on the town of Barstow will accomplish nothing except maybe alert the kidnappers, if they're even there." I noticed that I was now including Monk Tanner as a participant.

"Okay. But I want reports. The sooner, the better." Sam did not sound entirely convinced. Dealing with the FBI on his turf was always difficult.

***

I got tired on the hot, shiny drive to the desert. Way down on sleep and not wanting to take any more Bennies. I stopped for coffee in Victorville instead. Afterward I found a Bakersfield country music station that helped get me to Barstow, a serious desert town. I was singing along to Dave Dudley's "Six Days on the Road" as I closed in on Barstow. Then Janis Joplin broke my heart with Kristofferson's "Me and Bobby McGee." That got me all the way to the Denny's parking lot. I'd barely sat down inside when JK arrived and hit me with some bad news. Rolland and the other two men had indeed stayed at the Sunset Inn, but they left this morning prior to Rolland making the ransom call to Bill Giles.

"How do we know this? I hope nobody talked to the motel clerk. He might have tipped Rolland off."

"No worries," JK said. "One of the Barstow cops knows a maid that works there. She filled him in and knows not to say anything about it. She also said the room was beyond filthy."

"Christ, Rolland could be anywhere now," I said. Perhaps I'd been underestimating Johnny Rolland. His team was operational now, and in the wind.

"It's not all bad news," JK said. "We've got the make of their car and the license plate number, courtesy of the motel maid. It's a 1970 light gray Ford Fairlane station wagon with California license number 693 FVA. Registration is up to date, but it was stolen two weeks ago from a San Diego chiropractor who was attending a Padres baseball game."

"Okay, let's go over to the sheriff's patrol station here in Barstow. It's close by. We need to set up a team and get the Barstow police on board too. I'll call Sam."

"I've got that in process, Jimmy. Lieutenant Ortega of the sheriff's office is setting up a room for us."

***

Two hours later, a team of six, including two Barstow city police detectives, was in place. The information we had to share was quite limited: Rolland's mug shot from the porno bust and the BOLO on the Ford Fairlane wagon.

I started the briefing. "Okay, we're working the front end, or the ass end, depending on your point of view, of an active kidnapping case. A young man named Peter Giles, age twenty-one, from North Carolina is being held, we believe, by a Mr. Johnny Rolland, a muscle guy who works for a gangster named Izzy Weiss as an enforcer. The ransom demand is in the amount of a hundred fifty thousand dollars. The money is to be left on a runway at Cable Airport in Upland at 1 p.m. tomorrow afternoon."

"Is this a mob operation?" one of the Barstow cops asked. "We're hearing that Weiss is getting into the dope business out here too."

"We believe Rolland has gone rogue and stolen both money and a quantity of heroin from Izzy Weiss. Rolland is also the chief suspect in two homicides that were committed in western San Bernardino County last week. The victims likely were mob hitters seeking to kill Rolland. There may be a self-defense aspect to it, but that's for the San Bernardino District Attorney's Office to figure out. We just want to catch the guy."

"Jesus," one of the Barstow sheriff's officers exclaimed. "If we find this Rolland character, we might have mob guys breathing down his neck. They want him dead."

"Yes and no," I said. "We've got an informant close to Weiss. According to the informant, Weiss is a businessman and has other jobs in progress that he likely considers more important than Rolland, who he views as a distraction that can be dealt with later. Weiss instructed his people accordingly." No dirty cops in this room as far as I knew so I didn't mind letting them know what I knew. Or thought I knew.

"The FBI is working this case from the Cable Airport side of things," JK said, changing the subject. "The San Bernardino Sheriff's Department is assisting them. Also, the father of the kidnapping victim is onsite. He wants to pay the ransom."

"What's our job here?" the Barstow cop asked, sounding a touch impatient.

"Fair question," I said. "The feds are placing their resources at Cable Airport. The working assumption is that Rolland is planning to fly in, grab the money, and then fly away. He's either flying the plane or hiring a pilot. I'm guessing there is no way in hell the kidnapper is going to get away with it. What I'm really worried about is what happens to the victim in this airplane scenario. My thinking is that if we find Johnny Rolland, Pete Giles, and a third person of interest named Monk Tanner out here and prevent them from flying to Cable Airport, it breaks up the kidnapping at this end. There's an airport out here, right?"

"If you can call it that," the Barstow sheriff's deputy answered. "It's out past Daggett to the east. The army built it during World War Two. But it's ours now, San Bernardino County."

That's when I heard the helicopters arriving. We had company.

CHAPTER TWENTY-FOUR

May 15

THE ENTOURAGE TROOPED IN. JENSEN, the FBI leader, was in front accompanied by several of his men. Then I saw Carol and her client, William Giles. *The gang's all here.* During my last call with Sam, he told me this might happen. Actually, it was fine with me. I wanted to catch Johnny Rolland and recover Pete Giles unharmed. If reinforcements improved our odds, so be it.

The Barstow Sheriff's patrol station had a cafeteria. On account of the new arrivals, we took it over. Folks went around and identified themselves, including a tense and tight-lipped William Giles. I went over the information again. The near miss at the Sunset Inn, followed by the 1970 Ford Fairlane information. A local deputy described the Barstow-Daggett Airport.

"When did you get the tip on Johnny Rolland and the Sunset Inn?" Jensen asked me, no accusation in his tone. The man was smooth.

"About 9 a.m. this morning from a confidential informant embedded in Izzy Weiss's outfit. I put someone on the inn immediately after I found out. That why my partner JK and I drove out here after the ransom call this morning. It wasn't exactly a tip, more like a possibility. We've been after Rolland since he killed the two hoods last week. I'm beginning to think he's sharper than I thought, or at least shiftier. Leaving the motel before making the ransom call was smart."

"But still a rank amateur as a kidnapper," Jensen said. "He's making it up as he goes along."

"Did the motel maid see Rolland, Tanner, and Giles leave this morning?" Carol asked.

"No," the Barstow sheriff's deputy answered. "She was cleaning another room. But we've preserved the room as is. Definitely three people sleeping there. We've got the motel clerk, Phil Jefferson, in custody. He had a wad of cash on him. Supposedly he and Rolland are buddies."

"It's imperative that Jefferson not be allowed to contact Rolland. Did he lawyer up?"

"Not yet, but a public defender is on the way," Lieutenant Ortega answered.

"We need to scare the shit out of the public defender, play the national security card," Jensen said, gesturing to one of his associates. "No leaks to Johnny Rolland."

There were lots of nodding heads in the room.

"I'm sorry, but what the heck is going on here?" William Giles said. "I've got the money ready and am willing but not happy to pay the ransom and secure the safe release of my son. My wife has family staying with her back in North Carolina while I get this done. She's beside herself with worry. I'm here in this room because Miss Loomis, my representative, asked me to be here. This operation you're mounting sounds like it's going to get my son killed."

"Perhaps this would be better discussed privately, Mr. Giles," Jensen said.

"I don't need mollycoddling," Giles said.

"Actually, Mr. Giles, we're trying to protect your son," I said. "Johnny Rolland, the likely kidnapper, is a violent drug addict. As Agent Jensen just pointed out, he's making this up as he goes along. We are assuming he knows how to fly a plane or has hired a pilot for this job. He's going to drive to the airport, which seems close to impossible because that leaves him no escape route. Thus our assumption. We're here in Barstow to try and apprehend him before this whole kidnapping scenario goes to the next level, if it can be accomplished safely."

I hoped Carol was going to back me up. She remained

silent and refused to make eye contact with me. Giles said nothing. My speech seemed to fall on deaf ears. We moved on.

"Is there a BOLO out on the Ford Fairlane?" Jensen asked.

"Yes, sir," Lieutenant Ortega responded, "but with a warning to approach no closer than fifty yards, no sirens, and to contact this office or the Barstow Police Department immediately."

"Good. We need some accurate maps and photos, particularly of the airfield." Jensen was rolling up his sleeves, taking command and getting to work.

After briefly conferring with JK, I walked over to William Giles. "I'm very sorry this is happening, sir. Is there any chance we could talk?"

He looked at Carol, who nodded. We walked outside and got hit with 100 degrees of desert heat. "How about Denny's? It's air conditioned."

JK stayed behind to work with the FBI team, and Carol, Bill Giles, and I drove to Denny's on old Route 66. There was no small talk. The rapport between Carol and her client seemed limited. Once there, we all ordered coffee, nothing else. I'd missed lunch and was hungry but didn't want to push it.

"What's on your mind?" Giles asked. He was stretched so tight I thought he might fracture.

"Monk Tanner is on my mind. He's the wild card in all this. Tell me what you know about him, even if it seems unimportant."

"I agree, Mr. Giles," Carol added. He ignored her.

Giles sighed and started in. "My family and several others founded the town of Glen Alpine. Our business is lumber and has been for close to a hundred years. The town is small, maybe fifteen hundred people. My father moved our company east to the bigger town of Morganton over fifty years ago, but Glen Alpine has remained our home. My son, Pete, met Monk Tanner in first grade at Glen Alpine Elementary

School. They've been close friends ever since."

"Even when your son left to attend college?" I asked.

"Maybe less so. My wife and I haven't seen Monk as much these last few years. But the boys, young men, still saw each other when Pete came home for summers and holidays. We've worried some, my wife and I, that Monk is not the greatest influence for Pete given his drinking and smoking and whatnot. But Pete's an adult now, just barely, so we don't raise too much of a fuss."

"Are you social friends with Monk's mother?" I asked.

Mr. Giles gave a brief smile, almost more of a grimace. "Not really. We socialize, and go to church, with different folks than Dorothy Tanner. People go where they're comfortable. It's as simple as that. Dorothy may be a Methodist. We're Baptists."

"What about Johnny Rolland?" Carol asked.

William Giles scratched his head. "From what I recall, he lived with his family in a trailer park in Morganton, near the freight yard. Dorothy Tanner is respectable. Not so the trailer park folks. Look, why do you want to know all this? Shouldn't we be getting back?"

"It's important because Monk and Pete made a very abrupt decision to take a road trip west, apparently to find Johnny Rolland. Why would they do that? We'll get back to the station soon. Don't worry."

"Of course I'm worried. Are you nuts?"

"Forgive me. I didn't mean it like that. Please, is there anybody back in Glen Alpine or Morganton that your son might have confided in about this trip? I get the feeling that it's not like him at all."

Giles stopped, ran his fingers through his hair, and after what felt like a full minute, he said, "Good Lord. There might be someone. There is a man, a Yankee, who was recommended to us, if that's the right word, to run a soup kitchen in Morganton. Some higher-ups in the State Baptist Church advocated for this Jeremy Simmons, saying something about redemption for sinners. He's a defrocked minister. I learned that later. Anyway, he and Pete became friends. I don't know why. And you're right. This escapade isn't like Pete at all. We don't understand it."

"We need phone numbers now for this Jeremy Simmons," Carol said. This was right up her alley. She looked at her watch. "It's 6 p.m. back in North Carolina, right? We need this man's home number."

"I really don't—"

"Mr. Giles, time is short," Carol said with welcome authority. "We're scheduled to take that helicopter back to Cable Airport in about two hours. Make some calls, please. That will be easier to do back at the sheriff's station. Let's go."

Giles for once followed orders. We used a small office back at the station. It took three calls and twenty minutes to obtain Jeremy Simmons's home number. "If he's involved in this, I'm going to get him prosecuted and put in jail," Giles said through clenched teeth. He was pissed off already and didn't even know if Simmons was involved.

"Let me talk," I suggested. "It's official police business."

Simmons picked up after three rings. I identified myself, gave the Barstow location, and said it pertained to Pete Giles and Monk Tanner. I had the speakerphone on.

"Excuse me," Simmons said. "How do I know you are who you say—"

Giles snatched the phone out of my hands, forgetting about the speaker. "This is William Giles. Pete's been kidnapped. Tell the deputy sheriff everything you know about any of this, you reprobate."

I took the phone back. Giles's directive to Simmons was crude but effective.

I heard Jeremy Simmons sigh loudly before he spoke. "Okay. Pete came to see me maybe ten days ago. They had seen Johnny Rolland, the former local baseball star, in a pornographic movie at Duggie's Bar the night before." Giles flinched at this; Carol patted his arm. We needed him quiet now.

"The young men, at Monk Tanner's urging, were considering a fast road trip to Los Angeles to see if their friend was okay. Pete asked my advice. I mostly said be careful if you go, that the pornography business in LA was dangerous. Then I gave him two possible contacts for finding Johnny Rolland. I, uh, also gave him two hundred dollars for the trip if he decided to go."

Bill Giles screamed at him, "This is your fault, you miserable spawn of Satan. You funded the trip. God forgive you."

I practically had to restrain Giles. "Wait a minute. There'll be plenty of time for those discussions later." I understood his rage. I was not a big fan of Jeremy Simmons either at this moment.

"We'll need those names, Mr. Simmons. What else can you tell us about your conversation?"

"The big piece of information that Pete relayed to me was that Monk Tanner, who I don't know very well, is related to Johnny Rolland, some sort of cousin. Pete said that's why Monk was acting so intense and crazy. He was going to Los Angeles to find his cousin whether Pete went or not. I got the impression that Pete partly wanted to go in order to protect his friend. He also wanted a break, Mr. Giles, from trying to be a perfect son to you. That's hard work."

It looked like a blood vessel was about to burst in Giles's temple. "You are so fired, Simmons."

I told Simmons to hang on for a moment, then asked Carol to escort Mr. Giles back to the main room, saying it was important that they check on the FBI's progress. I mentioned that I had some routine technical questions left for Jeremy Simmons, nothing else. Giles, for all his bravado, followed her meekly, close to tears.

"Mr. Simmons, several FBI agents are in the next room," I said, following a hunch. "Maybe you can save me some time and trouble. Because time is very short. How do you happen to have contacts in LA that would know how to find either a gangster or a pornographic actor?"

Simmons was silent for a long moment, then said, "No good deed goes unpunished. You'll find out anyway. I'm in witness protection, permanently barred from returning to Southern California. The FBI field office in Charlotte can provide the particulars. I'm likely done in Morganton now too. William Giles is a man to be reckoned with. How bad is it, the kidnapping situation?"

"Bad. Johnny Rolland killed two men last week. There was a possible self-defense element to it—the thugs were trying to kill him, but he may feel that there's not much to lose. Thus, the kidnapping. He's a drug user and needs money."

"Has Monk Tanner joined with him?"

"He drove the car away from the killings. He's been with Rolland for several days now. It's likely."

"According to Pete, Monk's a pretty classic Southern redneck with a heart of gold. It's difficult for me to see him selling out Pete though. They're very close. But stranger things have happened. I call it the apple never falls far from the tree syndrome, as our wise old granny might say. I see it every day where I work. A man or woman who has tried very hard to escape their upbringing and their prejudices, only to fall back to their old ways. Drugs and alcohol often play a role."

Jeremy then provided me with the names and phone numbers. "There's an outside chance that Dolores at the Palomino Club might know what Johnny Rolland is doing in Barstow, but please, please, keep the FBI off her. She's a fine lady. If you talk to her, say that 'the Reverend' says hello, but she's going to be furious."

I thanked him and hung up, still thinking he should have stopped Pete Giles from coming west and getting into all this trouble. With no time to spare, I called the Palomino Club in North Hollywood. It was famous. Hell, I'd always wanted to play there, to follow in the footsteps of my musical heroes like fiddler Byron Berline or the Nitty Gritty Dirt Band. No time to worry about that now.

Dolores came within a fraction of a second of hanging up on me when I mentioned the Reverend. Finally, she told me I had one minute.

"Okay, your friend Johnny Rolland has kidnapped a North Carolina man and is threatening to kill him."

"One or two men?" she asked. "Two of them came into the club last week." I hoped her questions didn't count against my minute.

"One for certain and Rolland wants a hundred and fifty grand tomorrow afternoon to free him. The FBI is all over this. Rolland may well die, and maybe the two young men also."

I heard Dolores whispering to somebody. She came back on the phone. I heard her strike a match, followed by a long exhalation. "Christ," she said. "Now you have five minutes. I've stepped outside."

"I'm in Barstow. Rolland and the young men left the Sunset Inn earlier today. We don't know where they are. Any ideas?"

She paused. "There's this one ex-army pilot, this crazy dude that Johnny parties with sometimes, and works with too as far as I know. The army kicked him out. Something happened in Vietnam. He came here to the club once with Johnny. He's dark, might be half American Indian or something. Johnny calls him 'Robin Hood' sometimes. I don't know why."

"We need a name, Dolores."

"I don't remember! Leave me alone."

I again thought I'd lost her.

"It might be Sherwood, like the forest," she said, then hung up.

I rushed back to the cafeteria. The group seemed mainly to be looking at maps. Others were on the phone. I didn't have much, but it was better than what these guys were doing. "I may have a name, boys," I said loudly enough for them all to look my way.

CHAPTER TWENTY-FIVE

May 15 – Mojave Desert

P*ETE'S FACE WAS SWEATING FROM* the damn pillowcase wrapped around his head. Monk and Rolland were whispering so Pete couldn't hear most of their words, but it sounded from their grunts like they might be lost. They kept saying Yermo, or something like that, and rustling their map. Finally, Rolland said, "Here it is, turn left."

It was a rough, unpaved road. "Go all the way to the top," Johnny instructed Monk. *Isn't Monk getting tired of this dictatorial crap directed his way?* Pete knew Monk wouldn't have taken it from anybody else.

After they parked in some sort of enclosure, Rolland uncuffed Pete and pushed him into some kind of building. Once inside Rolland yanked off the pillowcase. It was a trailer, and the blinds were drawn. There were two rooms at least. An air conditioner was cranking away, so it was cool inside.

"This is the cat?" A trim-looking man with a dark brown ponytail, his arms covered up and down with tattoos, inspected Pete like he was a piece of meat. "You worth a hundred and fifty grand? I hope so." The man was wearing sunglasses even in the dark trailer. "You can call me Willie, no last names," he told Pete, his breath smelling like garlic and onions. "I'm the best damn pilot in this here Mojave Desert. By the way, you men need a shower if you're gonna sleep here tonight, because you stink."

So this is the deal, Pete thought. Willie was no flunky. He was the pilot who would make the kidnapping work, or not. Johnny Rolland was quiet for once. Something was really bugging Pete about this encounter. Why was this man showing himself so clearly, possibly making it easy for Pete to later identify him? He looked like he'd been in prison, with all those tattoos. Did Pete even have a chance in hell of surviving? Willie was every bit as scary as Johnny Rolland. They seemed to be partners. Rolland had briefly left their room at the Sunset Inn yesterday after instructing Monk to keep Pete handcuffed. It must have been to set up the details of this kidnapping operation with Willie.

"Come on, Johnny, some of this won't hurt you none," Willie said, carefully pouring perfect lines of cocaine onto a small mirror and then cutting it with a razor. "You too, pal," he said to Monk. The three of them snorted the product, several lines following the first.

"That's enough," Rolland said. "We're operational, man, gotta keep our shit together."

"Yeah, whatever," Willie replied. Nothing seemed to bother him.

Rolland pulled two twenty-dollar bills out of his wallet. "Hey, Monk, we need some damn food. There's this place near here up on Yermo Road called the Burger Hut, good burgers, good tacos. Cheap too. Why don't you get about eight of each, plus a bunch a fries and some Coca-Colas to drink. That'll feed us, plus the college boy over there," he said, gesturing toward me. "Think of it as a condemned man's last meal."

Willie flashed Rolland an evil look. "Just kidding there, college boy," Rolland added. "Soon you'll be reunited with your mommy and daddy, you pussy."

Rolland threw the car keys to Monk. "He's a good wheelman," he said to Willie. "I'm training him good."

Willie wasn't so sure. "You know, I think I'll go with Monk here to the Burger Hut. He might need help finding the place or carrying all that food. There's cold beer in the fridge." The two men departed. Rolland cuffed Pete to the bed, then lay down on the beat-up old couch and closed his eyes.

Well, that idiot let the cat out of the bag, Pete thought. *I'm a dead man, unless I figure out a way out of this.* Rolland was treating Monk like dirt now that his new friend, partner, was on the scene. Maybe Pete could get to Monk now. He knew he had to try.

***

Several hours later the trailer was quiet. They'd eaten all the food and washed it down with Cokes and Miller High Life. Rolland was snoring on the couch. Willie was outside smoking a joint. Pete motioned Monk to come over. He was still cuffed to the bed. "I think they're going to kill me, Monk. After they collect the money. You better watch yourself, too, *wheelman*."

Monk looked at him through empty, sandblasted eyes. *Is he even there anymore?* Pete wondered. "Nah, everything's cool, Pete. These guys are pros. They know what they're doing. Keeping you alive is the key to the whole deal." With that, Monk got up and went outside to help Willie finish off that big, fat joint. Pete felt nothing but despair.

CHAPTER TWENTY-SIX

May 15

AGENT JENSEN LOOKED UP FROM his airport map. "What name?" he asked me.

"Johnny Rolland has a running boy out here, possible last name of 'Sherwood,' ex-army pilot, got kicked out. I don't have a first name."

"How solid is the info?"

"Moderate at best, but it beats nothing, and it fits with the kidnapping plan."

"Source?"

"Lemme hang on to that for now. I sweated the witness pretty good. We won't get any more out of the witness." I could feel Carol's eyes on me again. It made me uncomfortable.

Jensen grabbed one of his men. "Go over to the jail where we're holding the motel clerk, what's his name, Jefferson, find out if he knows Sherwood. But keep the public defender away. This is need-to-know. I don't care if Jefferson gets out of this later, on account of this. He's not important."

"We've got to fire up all the databases," JK said. "Federal, Military, State of California."

"Agreed," Jensen said.

Jensen addressed Lieutenant Ortega. "Do you think we could get some sandwiches, chips, and sodas or coffee for everybody? We may be here longer than I thought."

I went back to the smaller room, called Sam, and gave him a detailed update. He was sometimes able to work miracles with the data folks in Sacramento. He agreed to help. "How are William Giles and Carol holding up?"

"As well as could be expected," I said. "Normally Carol and I would be working hand in glove, but I can't do it on any of this, partly because I know her client just wants to pay the money and be done with it."

"How about the feds?"

"Very professional. Doing their jobs, but not producing much."

"Okay, find this Sherwood guy. I'll work my sources too. One other thing. Hank Phillips asked for permission to work Cable Airport tomorrow. I said yes, but will keep him out of the line of fire, so to speak. Maybe you can shut this thing down at your end before we get to Cable." Sam hung up.

I'd forgotten about my other pending assignment to stop a bank robbery at an unknown location. First things first.

A hit on the BOLO caused commotion in the cafeteria. A sheriff's deputy had spotted a gray Ford Fairlane station wagon traveling west and then turning left just past the Country Kitchen diner in Yermo. But he couldn't get the license plate because his car got stuck behind a US Marine tank convoy. The BOLO said no sirens, and the deputy knew better than to mess with the Marines. By the time he was able to make the turn toward Daggett, the Ford was gone. He was pretty sure it was a 1970 model. The deputy knew cars.

"Only in fuckin' Yermo," one of the locals muttered. "Lucky the Marines didn't blow up his vehicle with a bazooka."

"Hey, people," Jensen said, "how many ugly gray 1970 Ford Fairlane station wagons are going to be driving around or near that airport? Let's call it a probable." The crew took a fast meal break.

Carol approached me. "Can we talk?" she asked.

"Sure. Where's your client?"

"He's in Lieutenant Ortega's office talking to his wife, trying to console her. I needed to give him some room. What a mess."

"Yeah, but I'm hoping we can nail these guys here. Cable

Airport will be really dangerous for everybody. I don't see the FBI letting Rolland and whoever else fly away clean."

"Maybe, but they've given Mr. Giles their word that no aggressive action will take place until his son is freed."

"Right now, I'm more worried about the kidnappers harming Pete Giles. I keep flashing back to that dope fiend Rolland and his cackling laugh as they drove away from Mister Louie's last week. He's a very unstable dude."

"Look, I know you're being careful about your sources, even with the FBI. Is there anything I can know that might help you and me solve this thing?"

I hesitated, but Carol's brain could often find solutions that escaped me. "Okay, I don't think anything in Barstow matters. The car, if it was the car, was spotted in Yermo. The airport is near Yermo, ten miles east of here. Here's something that only Sam and JK know—Johnny Rolland apparently is partial to some diner in Yermo called the Country Kitchen. JK and I need to get out to Yermo ASAP, but a fleet of FBI agents, even just local law enforcement, may attract too much attention. I'll know more when we see it. The Ford was spotted west of the diner, but still in the vicinity."

"When do you plan to head there?"

"I'm ready now. I'm not accomplishing anything sitting around here. JK and I are going to check out the airport too." I gestured toward two young FBI men studying topo maps and aerial photographs. "Not my thing. I need to see things with my own two eyes. Will you do me a favor?"

"Sure. What do you need?"

If anything breaks on this Sherwood tip, call my office and they'll patch you in to me.

"Not a problem. We were scheduled to leave soon by chopper to Cable Airport," Carol said. "Now Jensen is saying it likely will be 9 p.m. by plane rather than helicopter. It's about six now."

That helped me make up my mind. "I'm going to grab JK and split. Yermo's less than ten minutes away, taking I-15. My Charger is perfect for these desert towns. Fits in better than the FBI Crown Vics. I'll tell Jensen we'll be back soon and easy to reach."

"Call me, Jimmy, if you find anything," Carol said. I nodded and went to find JK.

***

The Yermo Country Kitchen was quiet during the late afternoon. The waitress was friendly and enjoyed talking about her little desert town. I ordered pie and coffee to keep her talking. There was a tourist attraction nearby, she told us, a real ghost town that Mr. Knott of Knott's Berry Farm fame had been busy restoring. I saw JK's blank look. He'd wolfed down a burger as she talked.

"Every little kid in Southern California went to this fake western town in Orange County called Knott's Berry Farm," I told JK. "It has stagecoach robberies, old trains, damsels in distress, dusty saloons, the whole deal. Not nearly as good as Disneyland, but worth a kid visit every few years. I didn't know he'd been involved in a real ghost town up here."

"Does it help us solve our case?" JK asked.

I laughed. My partner could be single-minded. "Not one bit," I said, starting in on the cherry pie a la mode. "Just giving you some local color. Let's go cruise the Barstow-Daggett Airport once I finish this. San Bernardino County owns it."

On the way out, I showed the waitress a copy of the BOLO with Rolland's picture on it. She hadn't seen him, at least not lately. She said he looked familiar, maybe from last year, but wasn't even sure of that. Another dead end. I left the copy with her. We then drove south toward the airport, turning left where the gray Ford had turned earlier in the day. The Marine base was to our left, and some school buildings were on the right. We passed a beat-up old trailer park. I got a mild shot of cop radar as we drove by. Johnny Rolland grew up in a Southern trailer park. Then we got stuck behind a long freight train heading east out of Barstow. It was a busy area in that sense. Both I-15 heading toward Las Vegas or Los Angeles, and I-40 heading toward Arizona were visible from the train tracks. Not a bad place to move all manner of contraband, including drugs.

We turned left on old Route 66 after crossing the tracks. The "mother road" took us right to the airport. The first thing we saw was about fifty ramshackle bungalows, some deserted, located to the west of the actual airport. The army had built this entire operation during World War II, and the age showed. It brought back my Germany military police memories. All military bases had a certain sameness. A neglected old water tower stood nearby, and then something truly unusual came into view. It was a long wooden aircraft hangar, probably two football fields long. It was the biggest hangar I'd ever seen, definitely from World War II days. The paint was peeling away. As we drove around to its right, I saw the two Crown Victoria sedans, the FBI's calling card, parked near the hangar. Good. Jensen must have dispatched them. Two agents in each car, wearing sunglasses and blank expressions. JK waved to them. No response.

I could see that a number of planes were parked in the hangar, some of them old military. Small modern structures were tucked away further to our right, including the aviation manager's office and a fueling station. There was activity at the north end of the hangar. We did a drive-by. There was a guard gate and lots of barbed wire. Some sort of military facility.

Reading my mind, JK said, "Looks like classified spy stuff to me." I turned around before any guards got too curious. Instead, we drove south to higher ground near I-40 where we could observe the entire airport. I saw three small planes parked adjacent to one of the two runways. The general aviation component of the airport struck me as limited. The planes we saw there likely belonged to the FBI group leaving tonight. I saw no sign of the Ford Fairlane.

I wasn't sure we learned much, but now we'd seen it. And something about the airport bothered me in relation to the kidnappers. It was quiet, but not quiet enough, for their operation, particularly in view of the mysterious military activity. They'd need another takeoff location from the Barstow area to Cable Airport. I planned to relay this thought to the FBI when we returned.

"There's a motel near the Country Kitchen back in Yermo," I said to JK. "Let's double back and check it out."

Just then my radio crackled to life. "We've got a lead on a William Sherwood," the FBI dispatch officer said. "He goes by Willie and was released from Vacaville State Prison in 1973 after doing three years for assault and home invasion. We got a Barstow address from his parole officer. The team is heading out now." He provided the address. It looked like what I'd told Carol was wrong. There was action.

Carol called two minutes later. I said we were on our way and drove straight to the address. It turned out to be a small empty house in west Barstow, not too far from the Sunset Inn motel. The FBI team had arrived and entered. No Willie Sherwood. The crime scene techs were dusting for prints. They'd called the landlord. It was indeed rented to a William Sherwood. The place wasn't much, what I'd expect from a single ex-military man. A neatly made bed, a refrigerator with two bottles of Rainier Ale in it, a small TV, a portable fan, and an old couch. Everything reeked of cigarettes, but the ashtrays had been emptied. A Barstow newspaper from yesterday, turned to the sports page, was on the couch. The bathroom was empty, but he'd made one mistake. The crime techs found and bagged two used syringes. They'd been left in the trash can by the toilet. That was it, the life and times of Mr. Sherwood, ex-military, ex-convict, and current druggie. I was guessing meth. It was our second near miss today. As Sam Fuller always reminded me, that's why they call it police work. It's only easy on television shows.

"Well, shit," Jensen said, summarizing how all of us felt. "Let's regroup at the station."

Upon our return, I saw Jensen, Lieutenant Ortega, William Giles, and Carol duck into Ortega's office. I wasn't invited. Their meeting didn't take long. Afterward Jensen made an announcement to the entire group with William

Giles standing next to him, looking both impatient and angry. "In view of our tight time frame, the FBI focus now will shift back to Cable Airport. We believe Rolland and Sherwood are the kidnappers, and that Monk Tanner is involved in a more ambiguous capacity. In consultation with San Bernardino Undersheriff Sam Fuller, we believe that any interdiction of the kidnappers at Barstow-Daggett Airport or elsewhere poses too great a risk to Pete Giles. A team is currently placed at the airport to monitor the activity, but not to intervene. Thanks. We've got planes to catch."

Jensen came over and thanked me for the leads that I'd provided. It was gentlemanly of him, so I refrained from saying that, so far, the FBI hadn't accomplished much of anything. Jensen ran a good meeting. That was it.

"Are you staying?" Carol came up to me.

"Yup," I said. "I'm tired of these law enforcement circle jerks. But I want you to call me tonight here, no matter how late, after you get Giles settled. This must be awful for him. I'll have cots brought in for JK and me. We're missing something big, Carol, not getting this case at all, me included. Just chasing our tails. Call me."

She nodded and the FBI entourage departed, and not in a blaze of glory.

CHAPTER TWENTY-SEVEN

May 15

"*WHAT ARE WE MISSING, JK?*" The two of us had gone back to Denny's. The waitresses were getting to know us. I ordered a tuna sandwich instead of a burger, remembering it was Carol Loomis's go-to food. I wondered if Carol was enjoying all the whooshing all over hell with the FBI and her stressed-out client in chartered helicopters and planes. Probably not.

"Sherwood," JK answered. "I talked to his parole officer. He's an ex-military pilot who received a dishonorable discharge. Spent time in Nam doing classified work. Lives in Barstow now after his prison stint." JK was having his second burger of the day. After all, he was ten years younger. "The one in Yermo was better," he said, providing a rare restaurant review.

"I figure Sherwood's a drug smuggling pilot for hire," he continued. "Mostly broke because his money goes for hard drugs and," JK's face broke into a grin, "fast women. Just like you, Jimmy."

"Yeah right, except for the hard drugs and fast women parts. I'm just an unemployed fiddle player moonlighting as a deputy sheriff." We ate silently for a while. I'd ordered coffee. It was going to be a long night.

"I agree with you but figure he's small-time because he's undependable," I said. "My guess is that he runs bricks of marijuana up from Mexico for local dealers and guys like Johnny Rolland. Likely, he has his own small plane stashed somewhere and gets work because he's a good pilot."

"A hundred fifty grand is quite a score," JK said. He was

drinking Pepsi instead of coffee. "Rolland is cutting him in for good money since the kidnapping plan requires Sherwood to get them in and out of Cable Airport tomorrow, fast and in one piece."

But how, I wondered. The FBI would have the airfield blanketed. They would tag the plane in the air with radar. "I think Rolland might collect the ransom money and hang on to Pete Giles, giving them new instructions on where they'll release him, hoping that William Giles will agree to the new plan on the spot, while the FBI guys have another meeting."

"He might," JK said. "Rolland could say that Pete Giles will be found tied to a tree in some city park in San Bernardino at midnight, as long as nobody follows their plane."

"I still think the feds follow the plane, or maybe they'll put some kind of tracking device in with the money that Rolland wouldn't know to find. The FBI has lots of good toys. In any case, I need to talk to Sam about our status. Does he just want us to stop working the case at this end? I doubt that."

***

There was activity at the Barstow Sheriff's patrol station when we returned. A junior FBI man had stayed behind and was organizing an additional team to augment the agents already in place at the airport. Surveillance at the Barstow-Daggett Airport was the FBI's only play out here. The army was cooperating. It took me a while to reach Sam.

"What's up, Sam?" I asked when we made contact. "We've got to work the case harder at this end. We know these jerks are still out here."

"It may not matter," he said. "My boss, the honorable Sheriff of San Bernardino County, has talked to the Attorney General for the state of North Carolina, who happens to be a friend of William Giles, and is offering his full advice and assistance in this matter. The West Coast Director of Operations for the FBI also is involved. You get the picture, or do I need to spell it out?"

"No need. It's an elephant fuck, the big shots stomping around. Is there any press or television yet?"

"Thankfully no, but somebody's going to notice things at Cable Airport tomorrow."

"Do you want us to stand down out here?"

"Give me some options. What do you want to do?"

"First, I don't think the kidnappers are flying out of the Barstow-Daggett airport tomorrow. The pilot, Sherwood, almost certainly is a drug smuggler for hire. He's going to fly out from someplace way more private; just as if he had a big load of dope. How are your contacts at the DEA?"

"I know the second-in-command DEA man for Southern California. Why?"

"There is substantial military activity out here, Sam. The Marines and the Army are here for certain since they have visible bases. Maybe the CIA operates out here too. It's a perfect spot. Regardless, I'm sure that none of them care much about any two-bit marijuana or cocaine smugglers. They're all still dealing with the Vietnam troop withdrawals and all that chaos. However, this is their turf and for sure they'd want to know what the hell is going on, so they don't shoot down the wrong planes."

"Go on," Sam said.

"I believe the local DEA guys here, and maybe the local sheriff's deputies, will have a better sense of which private airstrips the smugglers prefer to use. They can't bust them all, but maybe they have snitches involved to try to get at the bigger fish, possibly even the Mexican bosses. I'm guessing loads of cocaine might be subject to more scrutiny, but marijuana is big business too."

"You're making a pile of assumptions, Jimmy. You don't know any of this."

"Correct, but I do know that hanging around the Barstow Airport tomorrow waiting for kidnappers that won't show up is a waste of our time. Or if I'm wrong the operative orders of the FBI and Mr. Giles are to stand down. There's already a team there to wave good-bye in that case.

They don't need JK or me for that."

"Don't forget that I'm part of those stand-down orders too. We don't want Pete Giles and this unfortunate Monk Tanner to get killed or harmed in any way. Assuming, for a moment, that you are correct about some or all of your suppositions, what exactly do you want to do with this information?" Sam asked. "The official Federal, North Carolina, and William Giles position, and probably my boss' position too, assuming he ever has one, is to allow the plane to take off from Barstow and then take all appropriate action at Cable Airport."

"Sam, all I want you to do for me tonight is put me together with somebody who will direct me to the best airstrips for the dope smugglers out here. Somebody knows. Beyond that, maybe you shouldn't ask me what I'm going to do with it."

"Christ, Jimmy. That smartass answer won't wash for one minute, and are you planning to drag JK down with you? This isn't a time for cowboy heroics."

"Just hear me out a little. Both Johnny Rolland and Sherwood appear to be drug users. As Agent Jensen said today, they have no idea what they are doing when it comes to a sophisticated kidnapping operation. Rolland's not dumb, but he's feral. He's the kind that wins small and loses big. He's also the kind that kills people. I'm not optimistic about Pete Giles's chances."

Sam paused. "I'm going to meet you about a quarter of the way for now. I will have a discussion with DEA personnel, assuming I can reach them tonight. It sounds like information we should know more about, if your assumptions are halfway correct. Hell, it's our county. DEA might tell me to take a hike. You know that."

"Thanks, I—"

"Wait, I'm not done," Sam barked. "Assuming you obtain any information that may lead to Rolland, Sherwood, Pete Giles, and/or Monk Tanner, you are ordered to take no action without my express consent. It will be strictly surveillance unless I say differently. You've got my operational phone number for this work. Hook it up somehow out there. JK, did you get all this?" Sam yelled into the phone. "Surveillance only if you even find these characters."

"Yes sir," JK said with emphasis.

"All right," Sam said and hung up.

"You'll like living on the edge, buddy," I told my partner. "Sam gave us just barely enough rope to hang ourselves. He's good at that."

JK grinned. "My parents want me back home in Portland anyway. I could join the family nursery business. Maybe you could learn to plant trees too."

I went to find Lieutenant Ortega. I told him that I'd like two of his best deputies for the next twenty-four hours or until the kidnappers' plane took off for Cable Airport. One of them needed to be a communication specialist who could hook us to Sam Fuller's closely guarded operational phone number. I gave him the number and asked for walkie-talkies. He agreed. Ortega was smart. He asked no questions because he had no particular desire to know what I was up to. I was outside his chain of command, thus not his problem.

CHAPTER TWENTY-EIGHT

May 15

ORTEGA'S TWO DEPUTIES ARRIVED. WE worked out the communication hook-up. Then JK volunteered to brief them. I found the small room where our cots had been put and crashed on one of them without even thinking about it. Was it just last night that I'd been with Tammy? Was that even possible? It seemed like a week ago. Plus drinking with Hank Phillips wasn't helping matters. Christ, I needed a quick nap to get my wits about me. I wasn't twenty-one anymore.

I had no idea how long I'd been asleep before a screeching noise woke me up, This scary-looking long haired biker dude was dragging my cot to the center of the room. My first impulse was to reach for my revolver on a nearby table. The biker's dark eyes noticed my move. "Easy now, sleeping beauty. I'm Miller, DEA, one of the good guys. I hear you want to know my secrets."

"A good guy? Christ, you could have fooled me," I said, still wary of him. "Maybe you're just a bad dream."

"No. I'm very real, sweetheart," Miller replied, blowing me an exaggerated kiss, More polite ways of waking you weren't working. I told your partner I was going to roust you."

"Good, otherwise he would have shot you. As you seem to know, I'm Sergeant Jimmy Sommes, I'm a homicide investigator for San Bernardino County. You can keep all your secrets unless they pertain to private airstrips. Let's go get some coffee."

We moved to the main room. The local deputies knew

Miller and vice versa. I sensed some tension. "Come on, fellas, let's eat some donuts like good cops," I said, "and figure out this detail."

JK, who could be naïve on occasion, asked Miller if he was undercover, given his obviously rough appearance. That drew a laugh from the locals. "This is the desert, man," Miller said. "I look this way because I want to. As long as I do my job, nobody gives a shit. Next question?"

"I got one," I said. "Is Willie Sherwood one of your snitches?"

"No way. I barely know the guy. He pals around with other ex- and maybe current Army spooks. You familiar with Air America out of Saigon, Cambodia, and other beauty spots?"

"Not very," I said, "but I get the idea."

Miller lit a Marlboro and continued. "Well, for one thing these pilots are very macho. Public airports bore them. Asking anybody's permission to take off or land is not their thing. Most of these fellows have no interest in using drugs. The thrill for them is the risk and reward of illegal flying and heavy loads, not to mention making lots of dough. They tend to get the bigger jobs. Second-stringers like Sherwood, who do enjoy sampling the product, take what they can get."

"Okay, here's what we know," I said. "Sherwood and another hood named Johnny Rolland are in the middle of this half-assed kidnapping operation. JK and I have very limited authority to do anything about it. But I at least want to find out where they might take off. Their destination is Cable Airport in western San Bernardino County, and the ETA is 1 p.m. tomorrow. All other air traffic to Cable is to be grounded."

"And you figure Sherwood will treat it like a drug run, correct?"

"That's my best guess."

"And you and your partner want to be there to wave good-bye, right?"

"Well, it might—"

Miller interrupted me with a loud guffaw. "Bullshit, absolute bullshit. You want to stop the fucking plane, man, shoot off the wings with an AR-15. My DEA buddies in Ontario know all about you, Sommes. I checked you out. You're not a spectator; you're an action star."

I'd had enough of this guy. "Okay, Miller, you've shown you can piss the highest on the tree. How about we settle down and figure this goddamn kidnapping out. Time is short." I stared at him.

"Okay, okay" Miller said. "I get it. But blowing up the plane sounds like fun to me. I've got too many assignments where all I do is wave good-bye to these assholes. Be nice to kick some butt."

JK stepped in, looking a little panicked. "Whoa, whoa, it's not that simple," he said. "Everybody, including Jimmy and me, is committed to the safety of the hostage, Pete Giles. And I don't want to get fired. Plus there's this other young man, Monk Tanner, who seems to be some weird mix of kidnap victim and willing crime participant."

"Sounds like Patricia Hearst," one of the locals said.

I hadn't thought of it like that. It fit.

Miller held up his hands in mock surrender. "It's JK, right? Well put, man. Maybe I'm only partly right," he said, looking at me.

The young FBI man had heard Miller yelling. He stuck his head in the door. "Everything okay here?" he asked.

"Just groovy, man, we're fine," Miller said. "I suggest you go back to your Boy Scout meeting." The FBI man shook his head and disappeared. "Fucking FBI," Miller muttered.

I burst out laughing. It was as if Dennis Hopper from *Easy Rider* was playing a DEA man. Except in that case he'd fire up a joint instead of the Marlboro cigarettes Miller was going through fast. "Are you always like this?" I asked him.

"Hell, you should see me when I get mad."

I took a deep breath. "You did a good job of calling my bluff. I would love to stop this plane from taking off. But, like JK said, we're under strict orders, and I don't plan to get fired either. However, this Johnny Rolland guy is a stick of dynamite ready to blow up. Sounds like Sherwood might not be too far behind him. So, even if it's only to verify that Pete Giles and Monk Tanner make it on the plane safely, that's still reason enough to find these guys."

"We gonna divide up or stick together?" Miller asked.

I looked at JK. "My gut feeling is that we stick together," I said. JK nodded. "You guys okay with that?" I asked the local deputies.

"Sure," one of them said. "I want to see if Miller knows what he's talking about."

"That means I can't cover my ass and give you three possibles," Miller said. "So you're going to get my best shot, which is Mrs. Orcutt's Driveway."

"Wow," one of the locals said. "It's a perfect drag racing road. Why not a plane?"

Miller filled us in with the local deputies chipping in. The "Driveway" was famous out here. In the mid-1960s the Federal Highway Administration designed and then constructed I-40, but they'd inadvertently landlocked this old lady (Mrs. Orcutt) from her driveway access to Route 66. She raised holy hell and the feds offered her lots of money for her land. She said no and wrote letters of protest to everybody she could think of, including President Lyndon Johnson and his wife, Lady Bird. She told some lies in the letters, saying she ran businesses out of her house that were critical to the economic health of the desert town of Newberry Springs. But her campaign worked. The closest planned on-ramp and off-ramp to I-40 was four miles to the west of her house and driveway. Higher-ups in the government ordered the contractor to build a perfect two-lane asphalt road covering this stretch so Mrs. Orcutt could either get on I-40 or more typically drive under it to get on her beloved Route 66 in order to reach Newberry Springs.

"Think about it," Miller said, enjoying the story. "A perfectly paved, flat and straight four-mile road that is lightly patrolled, if at all, by the local authorities or by you fellas," he said, gesturing to the sheriff's deputies. "When it was completed about five years ago, it didn't take long for some very fast cars and drivers from all over the West to discover it. Now Mrs. Orcutt has been known to wave her shotgun at these drag racers, but so far nobody has gotten shot."

I thought about my 1970 Dodge Charger and Carol's 1958 cherry red Chevy Bel Air coupe. We could have an absolute blast on this Driveway. It would make a better track than pitted old Route 66, not to mention the dips.

"Good things don't stay secret," Miller continued. "We at DEA now have reliable information—"

"That you haven't acted on," one of the locals interrupted.

"Patience, gentlemen, we are building the cases," Miller said. "As I was saying, reliable information has it that enterprising dope smugglers have also discovered the Driveway, usually for night flights on account of its proximity to I-40. Pilots can use the lights of the interstate to help them take off and land. Rumor has it that one of the small warehouse buildings behind the gas stations at the western end of the Driveway can be used on occasion to store small planes."

"All the kidnappers will care about tomorrow is an unimpeded takeoff," JK said, "so daylight doesn't matter. Their destination is known."

I had envisioned a hard-to-reach air strip tucked away in the desert far from prying eyes. But that would make it hard on the planes, the pilots, and those who unloaded all the cargo. I hadn't worked much in this desert stretch of San Bernardino County. Things were different out here. Not necessarily crooked, but perhaps there was a greater sense of constraints. Los Angeles County had more money, more people, more everything. San Bernardino County, especially here in the east, was more hard-scrabble. Miller, for all his bravado, was likely an office of one. He had to pick his battles. The sheriff's station in Barstow had hundreds of miles to patrol and police. Cars drag racing on a perfect road in an empty desert, or even an occasional small plane appearing on the same road at night, was not likely to get the authorities excited.

"Okay, Miller, let's go with Mrs. Orcutt's Driveway," I said. "When should we set up out there? We need to put a plan together first." It was after midnight. I'd slept longer than I thought.

"I'm bringing my rottweiler, too," Miller said. "That makes a team of six counting Butch. He's a mean son-of-a-bitch. We should be in position on the Driveway before sunrise. We'll need lots of ice and water and maybe some camo gear. I figure you city boys are fine with scorpions and rattlesnakes, and maybe a nosy coyote or two."

A deputy stuck his head in. "There's a Carol Loomis calling for you," he said to me. I took the call in another room.

"How's William Giles holding up?"

"As well as can be expected," Carol said. "At least he's here. His wife is doing worse. She and her brother are arriving soon at LAX. They'll all be at Cable Airport tomorrow in time for her to greet her son. Are you making any progress out there?"

I froze, realizing that I didn't want to talk to her, my best friend. I was a cop. She was not. I'd asked her to call me, because we always figured out crime problems together. Not now. Despite my orders, I knew that a part of me wanted to stop the plane by force. Miller figured that out in an instant. Carol would never forgive me if anything happened to Pete Giles on account of my actions.

"No," I said to her, "we're not really getting anywhere. Sam ordered JK and me to allow the plane to take off no matter what, so that's pretty much it."

"Okay." Carol hesitated. "I gotta go to LAX and meet Mrs. Giles. It's going to be a long day. Hang in there, Jimmy." She hung up. Man, that was weird, I thought, and I knew Carol felt it too. But it helped me reach a decision, namely no rough stuff out here.

I rejoined JK, Miller, and the rest of the team. They had a large map of Mrs. Orcutt's Driveway out on the table and were determining where to deploy. The two local deputies, in a beat-up old pickup truck, were going to set up relatively close to Mrs. Orcutt's house toward the east end of the Driveway. They knew of a dirt road running north toward the railroad track where they could hide the truck. Miller, his dog, JK, and I were going to deploy at the west end of the Driveway near the I-40 off-ramp. Miller filled us in. There was more activity there, including a gas station and an auto junkyard of sorts, which made for good cover. It also had a clear view of the possible hangar. I figured Miller had staked it out before.

"Meet you back here at 5 a.m.," Miller said. "I suggest we use my old Range Rover for the op. It's got a workable radio phone so you can do a hook-up with your boss in San Bernardino."

The two local deputies took off. Miller was leaving when I stopped him. "Listen, you figured me out pretty fast. I'd love to intervene, stop the damn plane, and maybe that had been my plan, but I can't. There's too much at stake. It's the order from my boss, but I've got some other reasons too."

"I'm cool with that, brother," Miller said, "but I'm really hoping I'm right about the Orcutt Driveway. I'd like to shut it down. Too many dope smugglers are getting a free ride on it. See ya soon."

JK had heard this exchange. He gave me a look after Miller left. "Carol?" he asked.

"Yeah, but Sam too. Let's just do our job out here and leave the crazy-ass stuff to the FBI at Cable. It's their case and their call. You've got time for a couple of hours of sleep. The cots are in the next room."

I poured myself some coffee, not wanting any more sleep. This wasn't like the Claremont bombing case of two years before. That became personal due to the relationships I'd formed with two women: Allie of course, but also with the bomber's mother, Melody. The latter had been abused by the murderers in order to shut her up. Melody, who'd be a hippie until her dying day, and I were still friends, sharing an affinity for countrified Grateful Dead tunes. Avenging

Melody became part of that case. In fact, it still was. One of the bad guys who'd abused her remained free. I continued to shadow him on my private time. Nobody knew about this.

This murder/kidnapping investigation was different. I didn't have a stake in it. It was my job to arrest Johnny Rolland for killing those two thugs at Mister Louie's last week, and to arrest Monk Tanner for helping him. The kidnapping added a twist. It also added a new criminal to the mix, Willie Sherwood, and put an innocent victim, Pete Giles, in extreme danger. The relationship I needed most to preserve was with Carol. I got this weird urge to call her back and apologize for holding out on her. But I knew she was on her way to Los Angeles.

I wished I knew where Allie was at this exact moment. Somewhere chasing after Patricia Hearst and the SLA was all I knew. Had I been unfaithful to her with Tammy? By sleeping with her even though I managed to keep it at that, just barely. Not according to Allie. She had made it clear to me that the two of us were free agents, not bound to one another by what she viewed as meaningless old moral codes. It was a new world, man, she'd told me, and a better one. We were liberated, she'd said. Then why did I sometimes imagine her with another man—some glamorous reporter in a trench coat, them drinking champagne at midnight and having the time of their lives—and then go white-hot with rage, wanting to beat the shit out of the guy? My anger also was directed at Allie, but mostly toward myself for being a world-class sucker, for falling for her. I didn't buy this "new world" moral code crap. Which meant I had cheated on her, without even having the fun. Jeez, I could go down this rabbit hole forever.

What saved me, what kept me bound to her, was my conviction she didn't fully believe all this righteous new world stuff either. Sure, the feminist in Allie was real and forever. She'd always be a working woman and never be beholden to any man, including me. But the love part? By my primitive reckoning, I wasn't sure how much that had changed over the years, over the centuries. For now, I chose to believe that she loved me. She'd said so, sort of. And that was enough for me to grab onto in order to get through all the nights without her. Maybe it was changing me too, for the better. I wasn't planning to shoot down an airplane tomorrow, not if it cost me my friendship with Carol, and my job.

Perhaps I wasn't the "action figure" that Miller had heard about from his DEA buddies. *Man, oh man.* What I really wanted was a shot or two of tequila. That would have to wait. I settled for one more hour of sleep.

CHAPTER TWENTY-NINE

May 16 – Mojave Desert

PETE AWOKE TO AN UNRULY commotion. Willie and Rolland were yelling at each other. "We're blown, you motherfucker," Willie yelled. "The FBI and the Sheriff's Department are out here looking for us. I heard it from a guard at the Barstow Jail. I give him free meth sometimes in exchange for information. Nothing's a secret in that place. Somewhere along the line, you messed this up, Johnny. I might just bail on this gig. Fifty grand ain't worth going back to the joint."

"Settle down. Did they find us? No." It was odd to hear Johnny Rolland acting as the voice of reason. He'd used less drugs than usual last night while Willie had snorted through a pile of cocaine. Could he even fly a plane in this condition? Pete was beginning to think that drugs dictated the entire personalities of these two twisted souls. Monk was quiet, also listening.

"This is it, man," I said to him, as quietly as I could.

"No whispering, college boy," Rolland yelled at me. "Get the hell away from him, Monk. He's ancient history to you now."

Those words wounded Monk. Pete could see it. Rolland might be pushing his luck. Pete hoped so. In any case, the gang would soon be on the move again. Apparently, Rolland had prevailed in the argument. This time Pete was gagged, blindfolded, handcuffed, and dumped into some sort of van. He heard the doors slam shut sideways. An evil-smelling rag was placed over his nose.

"Have a nice little nap, college boy," Rolland said. Pete

drifted off into a strange sleep.

***

Monk was driving. He'd been straight since yesterday, no pot, no coke. His mind was a jumble; he was feeling a terrible mix of conflicting loyalties. But one thing was clear. Rolland, his half-brother, was using him, nothing more. Ever since this Willie asshole had arrived, Monk was relegated to a flunky role. He also knew he'd fucked everything up. Were Johnny and Willie going to kill Pete after they got their money? Were they going to kill *him* too? He'd heard some whispered conversations about flying to Mexicali, then driving to someplace else. Willie knew the right guys, he'd said. Some bullshit like that.

Monk had no idea where Mexicali was. He cursed his own ignorance, not for the first time. He touched his light vest. He'd placed his buck knife—it had been in his marijuana stash bag the entire trip—into one of its zippered pockets, along with a sharp pin he'd found in Willie's trailer bathroom. He didn't have a plan for these items yet—and had no idea if he had the guts to use them—but they provided him with a measure of comfort. Monk knew he should be at the furniture factory in Drexel, North Carolina, driving his forklift, doing his job, minding his own business. That seemed impossible now, his old life. He'd crossed too many lines. The country music station on the radio was playing barroom songs. The drunken laments matched his mood.

"Take the next off-ramp and then turn left, Monk my man," Rolland said. They'd been traveling east on I-40, heading deeper into the desert. "You'll see a warehouse across the road from the Mobil gas station, maybe a hundred yards away. Park next to it."

Monk did as he was told. Rolland, ever alert, was eyeing him. "You okay, buddy? This is payday, man."

"Just a little nervous, I guess," Monk said.

"Understandable, but it's like baseball. It's the ninth inning, game on the line. I'm at the plate, Monk, and you know there's nobody better than me in this spot."

Monk nodded in agreement and smiled. Johnny could be smooth when he wanted to be, Monk thought. But this wasn't damn baseball, it was his life. He wanted to save Pete, and hopefully himself. That was his job. But he didn't know how.

***

Pete awoke with a terrible headache from whatever it was they'd drugged him with. They were still driving. He could hear Rolland and Monk talking but couldn't make out any words. He didn't know where Willie was. He tested the inevitable handcuffs. They seemed to be flimsy to him and maybe loosening some, but not enough. He felt like he was dying of thirst. He started to make noises through his gag. He couldn't see a goddamned thing through the blindfold. Somebody jerked the gag out.

"What do you want?" It was Willie.

"Water," Pete croaked. "And a cheeseburger." He had no idea why he'd asked for a burger. That weird drug was still affecting him.

That got a laugh out of Willie. "Yes to water, no to cheeseburger. Open your mouth."

Pete almost choked as the water was poured down his throat. The gag was jammed back into his mouth. The van had come to a stop. Then it started up again and drove into someplace that was darker and cooler.

CHAPTER THIRTY

May 16

"WE'VE GOT SOME ACTION, BOYS," Miller said, watching through a camera lens. "A white cargo van went into the warehouse, then closed the bay door." He'd snapped some photos. "I got the plate before it went in. California Blue and Gold, number 783 PLT."

I checked my watch. It was 11:30 a.m. We'd been set up for hours. Finally, something was happening. I called it in to Ortega in Barstow. Miller did the same to his DEA office. Even with the air-conditioning running full blast, it was hot in the Range Rover. The vehicle was tucked behind two semi-demolished old Chevies in an auto graveyard. JK and I had taken our shirts off.

Miller's information came in faster than the Barstow sheriff's station. He gave a little crowing laugh. "We got 'em. Van registered to Mr. William Sherwood. My guess is they've got a sweet little Cessna parked in that building. Sherwood will be starting his pre-flight routine. Man, I wish I had a bazooka."

That made me laugh in spite of myself, but alarmed JK. "Remember," he started, his voice concerned.

Miller laughed. "Just fucking with you, boys," he said, throwing a dog biscuit to his quiet but menacing rottweiler. "Ain't that right, Butch?"

JK alerted the two deputies set up further along Mrs. Orcutt's Driveway. Miller handed me the radio phone headset, "Your boss," he said.

Sam already knew we were set up near I-40 along the access road. "Well, it looks like Miller the DEA man got it right, boss," I said. "A van registered to William Sherwood just pulled into a warehouse visible from our location. They likely have a plane in there."

Sam whistled. "Tell Miller that was damn good work. In fact, kudos to all of you. Your instincts were right. Do you need additional personnel?"

I thought about it.

"Given our assignment is not to interfere with the aircraft, we don't want to spook them. Maybe two additional sheriff's vehicles on the south side of this interchange, along Route 66, in case things go haywire, but out of sight. I'm sure you'll want to alert Jensen and the FBI team, and William Giles."

"No fucking FBI Boy Scouts anywhere near us," Miller yelled, loud enough for Sam to hear. "Or choppers."

That got a chuckle out of Sam. "Tell him I got the message. I'll be at this number." He hung up.

"My suggestion is that we move the local deputies near Orcutt's house at least a mile toward us," Miller said. "There's no wind to speak of. I anticipate Sherwood will take off to the east and then cut south to avoid military air space, all of which is north of here. Then he's got a clean run to Cable Airport. Not the most direct route, but the safest. He'll likely need an hour in the air, especially if there's four people in the aircraft."

JK relayed the message to our local deputy team. It made sense to us. The waiting game continued. Ten minutes later the FBI called me. "We have a team heading your way, Sergeant Sommes, arriving shortly," Jensen said. "We need eyes on this." I mouthed *FBI* to Miller.

"Oh fuck," was his loud response.

"Who's that, Sommes?"

"It doesn't matter. Have the car pull in south of the Mobil gas station. We'll meet them there, but don't make a goddamned show of it." Jensen hung up without replying.

Miller shrugged and backed his Range Rover past some other abandoned vehicles, careful to stay out of sight of the warehouse. “I may have a guy in there, by the way,” he said.

“In the warehouse?” JK asked. “Why didn’t you tell us?”

“I was thinking about it, but the guy ducked me last night, wouldn’t return my call, the asshole. He’s a grease monkey, works on planes, and a sometime snitch of mine, unreliable but better than nothing. I pay him for information. Sherwood must have paid him more to shut his mouth. We’ll see if he comes through.”

“Not much help now, anyway,” JK said, obviously miffed. He and Miller didn’t connect too well.

A Crown Victoria that screamed *Federal Agents* drove up the road from the direction of Route 66 and turned right toward the gas station. At least there was only one. I couldn’t see any windows in the warehouse. “Don’t yell at these guys, Miller. It won’t help.”

He lit another Marlboro. “Better tell Butch not to bite off their nuts either,” was all he said.

“Vehicle driving away from the warehouse, heading north on a dirt road,” JK noted.

“That might be my guy,” Miller said. “He’ll call in soon.” JK just shook his head. I stayed out of it.

A fed in a blue golf shirt appeared. “I’m Agent Andrews. Please report.” Jesus, what was it with these guys?

“We believe that Johnny Rolland, Willie Sherwood, Monk Tanner, and their hostage, Pete Giles, will exit that warehouse to the north of us in a small plane and begin their flight to Cable Airport. Our orders are the same as yours, namely, let them depart.”

“It would have been nice to know this sooner, Sergeant Sommes,” Agent Andrews said.

“We just found out, pal,” I spat out the words to Andrews, “no thanks to you guys, so how about you shove it.” The FBI man didn’t say anything.

“Why do you need to know Agent Andrews, so you can fuck it up?” asked Miller in a quiet voice. He smiled at Andrews when he said it.

JK saved the day. “Okay, let’s just cut the meaningless

conversation. Our job is to conduct surveillance and report to our bosses, correct?" All nodded their heads, cutting the tension. That's when we all heard two loud gunshots ring out from the direction of the warehouse, changing the entire dynamic.

"Shots fired, shots fired." JK called it in. "We are advancing on the target location." The Range Rover, followed by the Crown Victoria, headed straight toward the warehouse.

CHAPTER THIRTY-ONE

May 16 – Mojave Desert

"***MAKE A TIGHT LEFT HERE*** and park in the corner," Rolland directed Monk as the van entered the warehouse. "Man, this plane is a beauty," he yelled out to Willie.

"Yes, it is," Willie answered, "and it flies like a dream. You'll see."

Monk noted that Willie sounded prideful and fairly sober for a change. The pilot in him was getting down to business. A small man with a long blond ponytail approached Willie. He was wearing grease-stained overalls, a white T-shirt, and desert boots. "I'm just about done with my pre-flight work here. The plane's gassed up and will be ready to go in about five minutes," he said.

"Fine. Hurry up with it," Willie said.

Pete was dragged out of the van. He needed to urinate and was straining at his gag to say so. It was Rolland who volunteered to take him, even taking off his blindfold "Don't want you pissing on yourself, or our airplane, college boy." As Pete passed by Monk on his way to the bathroom, he felt a sharp object thrust into the front pocket of his jeans. It was a nail, or a long pin, or maybe a key. He'd find out when he could. Rolland released the handcuffs to let Pete do his business, snapped them on again in front at Pete's waist afterwards, and then marched him back to the main room. Except for a headache from the ether, Pete felt alert. Neither Rolland nor Willie were paying much attention to him or even basic security.

The grease monkey was finished with his prep work.

Willie handed him a wad of cash. "Get out now. You were never here." The man scurried off through a north facing door.

There were cans of Coca-Cola on a work table and some potato chips. Monk grabbed a Coke and brought it over to Pete. "Can he drink this?" Monk asked. Willie, busy inspecting his plane, said, "Sure, why not." Rolland wasn't paying attention either, instead watching the guy in the overalls drive away in a Jeep. "I hope he can keep his mouth shut," he muttered to himself.

"Use the pin on the handcuffs. It should work. I'm going to stop Johnny from leaving here if I can," Monk whispered to Pete and then moved away. Pete slurped at the drink as best he could with the cuffs on, spilling some of it. spilling much of it on the floor.

"Jesus," said Rolland, "what a slob." He unlocked the cuffs again. "Eat and drink fast, both of you. We've got a plane to catch." Rolland cackled like he'd told a brilliant joke. He'd also cleaned up and was wearing a leather jacket and a Chicago Cubs baseball hat. Pete noticed that Rolland was watching Monk carefully. There was a different dynamic in play. Pete downed the rest of his drink and ate some chips. Monk did likewise, but Pete noticed he had a tortured look on his face.

Willie came over and roughly gagged and re-cuffed Pete, again in front, not noticing that Pete twisted his right hand as the cuffs clicked. Pete had transferred the sharp pin from his pocket to his right hand.

Rolland grabbed a Coke, gulped it down, and then looked at his watch. "It's game time, fellas, we're due at Cable in about an hour for payday. Let's roll. Willie, I suggest you escort Giles to that goddamn great plane of yours and get him secured," he said. "I'll join him presently after I do a little further business out here." He gathered up his big satchel, almost empty now. They'd used up most of the cocaine.

Pete had been looking at the plane. He knew it was a Cessna 172. He'd mostly trained in Piper Cubs but had flown a Cessna with an instructor a couple of times, He was struggling to remember the basics. Willie escorted Pete to the passenger door and pushed him inside, then roughly maneuvered him into the right back seat of the plane. He then pulled the seat belt tight and clipped in shut. His voice went deadly cold as he pulled out a gun. "Don't move a muscle now, or you'll be in serious trouble with me. In just a minute Johnny's going to sit back here and keep you company." He put Pete's blindfold back on. "Too bad you'll miss all the beautiful views, buddy boy," he said.

Willie moved into the pilot's seat, not realizing he'd failed to properly tie the blindfold. Pete could see out of one eye. Maybe it was all the drugs, but Willie had done a piss poor job of securing Pete, assuming Rolland was about to get on the plane. Pete knew it was giving him an opportunity. He managed to insert the pin into the lock and was straining his now bloody wrists to free up his right hand to turn the pin, hoping it would work like a key for the old cuffs. Willie had started the plane's engine. Pete knew his time to slip the cuffs was limited. A thought of the family's True Giles Test flashed through his mind. *Christ! There's no time for that now.*

Johnny Rolland was strutting around like a rooster. He flipped a switch and the warehouse door opened, engulfing them in hot desert sunlight. Monk was shoveling potato chips into his mouth with his left hand, trying his best to look like a stupid and forgettable young man. The buck knife was cradled in his right hand. It was now or never. He advanced on Rolland with a dumb smile on his face, like he was going to ask a question.

Rolland stepped back and flashed a knowing grin at Monk. "You think you can fool me for one minute, you stupid redneck? You've decided to throw in with your pal, Giles. Isn't that sweet? The truth is, I don't need you anymore, *brother*." Rolland reached into his satchel for his .44 Magnum, but he was one second too slow.

Monk sprang at him and thrust the knife into Rolland's

stomach all the way to the hilt and then twisted it violently upward toward Rolland's chest like he was gutting a deer. Blood started to pour out. "*Fuck you, brother,*" Monk choked out the words.

Rolland, gravely injured, still managed to pull away from Monk as the knife, slippery with blood, fell to the floor. He had his gun in his hand and fired two shots as he fell to the ground. One shot missed. The other didn't.

Monk felt a punch to his right upper chest that almost knocked him over. He knew he was shot. It didn't hurt yet, but it was bad. He'd also cut his hand on the knife during the stabbing. He wondered why only the small wound hurt as he staggered back. Monk turned to look toward the plane, to look for Pete, but couldn't see anything through his dimming eyes. Then he fell backwards to the floor and lay still.

"Jesus, fucking, Christ," Willie yelled. He'd watched the attack from the pilot's seat. "These crazy North Carolina assholes deserved each other. Now what? Two dead guys in the warehouse." He made his first executive decision. "To hell with this kidnapping plan, we're going to Mexicali, pardner," he announced to Pete Giles. "I'll sell you to the cartel instead."

He pointed his Colt revolver at Pete. "Like I said before, don't move one muscle or I'll shoot your kneecap off." Willie turned his attention back to flying the airplane, first exiting the warehouse, narrowly skirting Monk Tanner's motionless body in the process.

Pete felt the soft click of the handcuffs releasing their grasp. His hands were free. He released the seat belt and adjusted the blindfold. He saw two cars advancing toward the warehouse.

Willie began to taxi down the Orcutt Driveway, heading east, but he saw the cars too. Definitely cops. The operation had been blown. Shit! He needed to get airborne, fast. One of the vehicles, the Range Rover, was tearing after him, trying to catch up. It would be no contest. The car was much faster than the Cessna on the ground. Willie had a fifty-yard head start, but he needed much more than that to take off. He grabbed the radio, set it to an open police network, and said, "Attention, this is Firebird heading east adjacent to I-40. My aircraft is going to take off. Pete Giles is on this plane. Do not approach. Repeat: Pete Giles is on this plane. Do not approach."

Pete remained motionless yet tense. He was determined to stop the plane before they were airborne. His minimal flying lessons weren't worth the risk of a crash. He'd already selected a fire extinguisher as the weapon to subdue Willie. It was mounted vertically directly behind the pilot's seat. He stuffed the cuffs in his pocket and removed the blindfold. Pete felt a strange calm, and a sense of confidence, as he contemplated his attack. He knew he could do it.

The Range Rover kept coming, eating up the distance between the car and the plane. Then, with almost no time to spare, the Range Rover slowed down.

"Yippee!" crowed Willie. "We're good to—"

That's when Pete, using his best linebacker burst of speed, jumped to his left, grabbed the fire extinguisher, and in one motion smashed it to the back of Willie's head. Pete quickly hit him a second time, as hard as he could. It made a satisfying thud. The next task was to slow down the damn plane. He jumped into the front passenger seat, feeling for the throttle and finding it. He pulled it back to reduce the plane's speed. The Cessna was already veering to the left toward the scrubby desert. He'd started to straighten the plane when he felt a gun barrel stuck to his side.

"Nice try, asshole," Willie declared, blood dripping down his face.

Pete slammed his foot on the left rudder while pulling the yoke sharply to the left, propelling the plane to the left of the road down a steep embankment into a stand of creosote bushes. It flung both men to the left jammed against the pilot's seat.

Willie lost control of the gun as he hit the window. Pete grabbed him and pounded his head against the window three times. Taking no chances this time, he grabbed the handcuffs—that had for so long been his enemy—out of his pocket and used them to cuff Willie's right hand to the plane's glove box. The unconscious pilot was secure. Pete found his gun on the floor and kept it.

The engine was still running. Pete turned it off and put the key in his pocket, wondering if the plane's full gas tank might explode. Or was that only in the movies? The plane was pitched at an awkward angle. He opened the passenger door and threw the gun out. Then he balanced himself and jumped off into the sandy desert. He felt a sense of pure dizzying exhilaration. He'd vanquished his enemy. It lasted until he remembered Monk. His tormented, confused friend had redeemed himself at the last minute in the most fundamental way possible. Was Monk dead? Pete didn't know. He knew Rolland was dead. He'd seen the massive pool of blood.

The pursuing Range Rover pulled up to the edge of the road. A rottweiler jumped out followed by three men, weapons in hand. Pete knew they were on his side. "It's okay," he told them. "I guess it's just me now." All the emotion swept out of him, and he slumped to the ground, blood from his stitches—he'd torn them somehow—beginning to seep through his shirt. The dog licked his hand.

"You're Giles, right? Are you wounded?" one of the men asked as he jumped down to reach Pete.

"Where's the pilot?" the one with the long hair asked.

"In the plane," Pete said. "He's secure. He pointed to the gun in the sand. "That's his. Yeah, I'm Giles."

As to whether he was wounded, Pete realized that question might reside with him for the rest of his life, and the answer may change over time. He didn't answer it.

"Is Monk Tanner alive?" he asked instead.

CHAPTER THIRTY-TWO

May 16

THE FBI TEAM PROVED THEMSELVES useful as we wrapped up the preliminary Orcutt crime scene. They had quickly summoned a chopper from Barstow-Daggett to airlift the seriously injured Monk Tanner to the Barstow Hospital. A collapsed lung, blood loss, and shock were working against him, but the doctors seemed confident he would pull through. A second chopper took the concussed Willie Sherwood to the same hospital. Both men were being held under guard by a team of Barstow Sheriff's deputies. Johnny Rolland's destination was different, namely, the hospital's morgue.

In the warehouse, I took Pete Giles's initial statement. A medical tech had rebandaged his shoulder, but he would need further medical attention. He was exhausted and subdued. However, in his telling, Monk Tanner had behaved in heroic fashion, a man who killed the despicable gangster, Johnny Rolland, in self-defense in order to save his own life and Pete's. In so doing, he'd also thwarted Rolland's kidnapping plan. The story was okay with me for now, but Monk was going to require some serious factual rehabilitation to cover his preceding actions. I figured a good lawyer could accomplish this, given how the story ended.

As for Willie Sherwood, he was too concussed to be questioned. The FBI was going to take the lead role in his case. Based on Pete's story, it was lucky that Sherwood hadn't killed him. Not every hardened criminal knows to simply kill, not talk to his victim about it.

"You beat the bad guys, Pete," I told the young man.

Pete's telling of this remarkable episode was matter of fact. He needed to subdue the pilot and bashing his head in with the fire extinguisher offered the best approach. The fact that Monk had slipped Pete the pin that allowed him to unlock the handcuffs was crucial to the tale. We agreed to talk again the next day in San Bernardino regarding the entire Johnny Rolland adventure. He did tell me that his stitches were required on account of his getting shot at Mister Louie's on May 9. That answered that question. My gut feeling from the beginning that Pete Giles was an entirely admirable young man had been vindicated in spades.

The FBI arranged a helicopter to fly Pete to Ontario Airport to meet up with his parents and Carol. During my first call to them from the crime scene, there had been tears of joy and relief when they learned their son was safe. I noted that William Giles seemed especially excited about Pete's apprehension of the pilot under very dangerous circumstances. Our press office was fielding requests from North Carolina news organizations as well as those from all over California for information about the daring young man.

My happy boss already had Beth Bolling hard at work telling the story. I said to give all the credit to Pete Giles and, if needed, throw more credit to JK than me regarding the actions of the Sheriff's Department. I had my reasons. As for Miller, my new DEA friend, he just said to keep his name out of it altogether. He had too many other irons in the fire. I planned to look for opportunities to work with him again.

I felt fantastic about the case. The Mister Louie's homicide case was cleared from the books—Pete Giles had identified Johnny Rolland as the killer—and I'd managed to get law enforcement in the right place in order to assist Pete Giles and Monk Tanner in stopping the kidnapping plan. The lion's share of the credit for this belonged to the two brave young men, but after some months of lazy, distracted police work, I believed that I was back in the game and making the right decisions.

As for Carol and me, a small residue of mistrust remained. She congratulated me on a job well done, said all the right words, but the realization that we now occupied different roles relative to each other had been confirmed. However, in my excellent frame of mind, I believed that time and tequila surely would heal this subtle breach. In addition, William Giles insisted that Carol keep the entire $5,000 retainer for the case, no hourly accounting required. Hell, Giles could afford to be generous. He didn't have to pay the $150,000 ransom.

"I'm not sure I ever want a kidnap victim's family as a client again," Carol said. "Especially because I didn't do much to help Mr. and Mrs. Giles. I was a babysitter, not my best attribute. This was your show, Jimmy, along with those two North Carolina young men. Well done."

"The money's in the bank, right?"

"Oh yeah. Drinks on me at Marie Callender's sometime soon."

"You got it." We hung up. I asked JK to contact Monk Tanner's mother with the news. After some hesitation, she agreed to fly out to be with her son.

It took much of the afternoon to wrap up the scene. The local deputies and the FBI could take it from this point.

JK and I had a party to go to. Sam Fuller was springing for a pizza and beer shindig at headquarters to celebrate this clear victory for our department. I'd been told on more than one occasion that I was something of a "glory hog" who enjoyed press attention after a successful exploit. My reaction was that those saying this rarely had any successful exploits of their own to crow about, so screw them. Pete Giles's heroics in subduing the pilot and then stopping the plane might become a national story. It was a hell of a lot more interesting than all the dreary Watergate stuff dominating the news.

The party was in full swing by the time JK and I arrived back from the desert. Sam gave a rip-roaring speech of thanks to the two of us and did a superb job of singling out JK for his brilliant police work.

"What are you, chopped liver?" Beth Bolling asked me in

a quiet voice. "You were there too, right?"

"Ask me in three days," I said. "We've got some other stuff going on." She gave me a quizzical look but didn't push it.

I then found Hank Phillips and proceeded to some serious beer drinking. "It was kind of a zoo out there in the desert," I told him. "But having a good partner solves some problems. Now maybe Sam will get off my ass and let me do my job in peace." The Shakey's pizza was hot and crisp. Even grumpy old Hank was loosening up a little.

"Yeah, I know what you mean about fucking Sam Fuller and the top brass around here. In fact, I've got a big week coming up," Hank said.

I was about to ask him about it when somebody yelled for everybody to be quiet so we could hear the TV. An excited news reporter announced that at least three members of the infamous Symbionese Liberation Army, the SLA, had been involved in a shoot-out at a sporting goods store in Inglewood late this afternoon. Nobody had been injured, but the store had been sprayed with bullets from an automatic weapon. The criminals had escaped and were at large. We were warned by the reporter that this group of SLA members was armed and extremely dangerous and to call the FBI or the Los Angeles Police Department with any information regarding their whereabouts.

So, the SLA *was* here in SoCal. Those rumors that had brought Allie to LA were true. The radical gang that had kidnapped newspaper heiress Patricia Hearst, and then turned her into "Tania," the machine-gun-toting bank robber, had made it to LA after all. At least three of them. She must know about this. I slipped into a side room and called her apartment in San Jose. No answer. From past experience, I knew it would be futile to try to reach her at the paper. But one thing was certain. Allie was on her way to Mel's Sporting Goods store in Inglewood. The SLA and Patricia Hearst/Tania story was both her beat and her obsession.

I rejoined Hank Phillips and started in on another Budweiser. "You know about these guys, right, the SLA?" I asked him.

"Just what I read in the papers. They've been running the FBI and local cops crazy up in SF, hiding from them after they nabbed rich girl Hearst," he replied. "Then robbing banks and stuff." I noticed that he looked away from me when he mentioned robbing banks.

"It's going to be a different story down here, if they're really in LA," I said.

Hank nodded his head in agreement. "LAPD, that SWAT Unit gonna find them and kick their ass in no time, either arrest them or kill them."

"You got that right, pal." I'd just watched the FBI in action out in Barstow. It was no surprise to me that they couldn't find the SLA. The SWAT team in LA was entirely different, a new, practically military unit. The SLA's days were numbered. I had mixed feelings about the SWAT Unit. I was still a small-town cop at heart who liked to administer justice up close and personal, not hiding behind helmets and firing automatic weapons from armored attack vehicles. But these guys were the wave of the future. I wondered if Patty Hearst was going to survive the weekend.

Sam Fuller went to the front of the room. "Well, folks, I believe the party is over. I just talked to the LA Sheriff's Department. Everybody is on alert, looking for these characters. Every one of our units should have those FBI photos of the nine members of the SLA, including Patricia Hearst, handy. We've got no indication that they are headed toward San Bernardino County, but please be on the lookout. Full duty tomorrow, no time off."

"How do they know they're SLA, Sam?" a deputy asked.

Sam smiled. "Our LA colleagues in blue are playing it close to the vest as to their information. I heard a rumor it might have something to do with a parking ticket."

I flashed on our 1972 bomber/hitman case. Carol had found a parking ticket near the Claremont murder scene that eventually led us to the contract killer.

"Man, I'd like to smoke these fuckers, maybe even Tania," Phillips said to me.

"You and about a hundred LA cops with AR-15's," I said. "See ya tomorrow, man. I need some sleep." Barely keeping my eyes open, I managed to drive home to my cabin, where I slept for eight glorious hours. Finding the SLA crazies was not my case.

CHAPTER THIRTY-THREE

May 16 – Ontario, California

PETE GILES' THOUGHTS WERE A complex jumble, but he was happy to be free and alive. The doctor who'd restitched his shoulder had given him some sleeping pills and sent him on his way. He planned to take one or two tonight if needed. He'd been told that Monk was going to survive his gunshot wound. Rolling out of the warehouse in the airplane today, he'd thought Monk was dead, so this good news lightened his heart. Pete knew it was hopeless to even try to understand his complex feelings toward Monk, and hoped that time would work its magic.

It was obvious that his mother and father remained utterly baffled by the crazy road trip to "save" Johnny Rolland. His mother was exhausted. She'd arrived earlier that day, planning to be at Cable Airport for the now unnecessary resolution of the kidnapping. Pete and his parents had just returned from an attempt at a festive dinner. They'd bought him a huge steak at a restaurant near Ontario Airport and avoided sensitive topics as best they could. The evening felt eerily like a graduation dinner of sorts, but what degree or honor had he earned? His father and mother clearly were proud of him while appalled by the senseless risks that he'd taken.

They had tickets to fly home on Saturday. Pete needed to appear at the San Bernardino Sheriff's headquarters tomorrow, Friday, to answer additional questions about the entire ordeal. His father had retained a lawyer to attend the meeting, along with Carol Loomis, the private investigator who had been involved for several days. He noticed that his father was relying upon her to help him navigate the confusing ways of this foreign non-Southern place. Pete had lost the ability to figure out how many days had passed since the shooting at the club, or since driving out of Glen Alpine in Monk's silver Mustang. He was eager to go home.

Just before bed, his father came into Pete's room. "Look, I know this is not your favorite topic, but when the Giles men gather to discuss our ancestor's True Giles Test, you've earned yourself a seat at the table that dwarfs what others have done, including me. Congratulations. Maybe you'll be at the head of the table." With that his dad made a quick spin and exited. He never was much for sharing his feelings.

It made Pete shake his head. His verdict was that the entire trip had been a terrible mistake, even though he imagined the deluded Monk still thought differently, if he was able to think at all. Johnny Rolland, their high school baseball superstar hero, had become a truly evil man. He'd played Monk for a fool. Pete tried to identify any redeeming qualities that Rolland still possessed and couldn't find any. Monk's father was a small-time crook, but not a killer. Still, he could see now that Rolland and Monk were related; there was something in their eyes, some commonality in the way they responded to each other. It didn't matter now. Cain and Abel? Monk and Johnny? He knew his own mother, a regular Bible reader, would make the connection, if she hadn't already.

Pete was thrilled that Monk had come to his senses and prevailed over Rolland, battling to the death in that sandy desert warehouse. In fact, if anybody had met the ridiculous True Giles Test, essentially displaying extraordinary bravery after making critical mistakes, it was Monk Tanner, not Pete.

I'm just a football player, Pete thought with a grin. *I know how to knock the hell out of my opponents.* He took a sleeping pill. It kicked in quickly and Pete enjoyed a blessed deep and dreamless sleep.

***

To the obvious irritation of the San Bernardino Sheriff's deputies, one of them was the same one he'd talked to the day before, Pete's new lawyer dominated the Friday meeting. It seemed totally unnecessary, but the man was an experienced criminal lawyer. These people are not your friends, the lawyer told him on the way into the interview. In any case, it was over in several hours, and Pete began to contemplate the trip home. His idea of a trip to visit the seriously injured Monk had been vetoed by his parents and his lawyer. Their work done, Carol, the lawyer, his parents, and Pete walked toward their cars in the San Bernardino Sheriff's parking lot.

Pete wanted to return to Appalachian State as soon as possible. His coaches and fellow football players would help to protect him from too many reporters or interviews. He didn't mind being something of a hero, but he wanted it to be on his terms. He got a sense that Carol Loomis, the private investigator who he learned had also survived serious wounds at the hands of a cold-blooded killer, seemed to understand how he was feeling better than anybody else in the room. She gave him a quick hug as they parted. "You'll get through this," she said. Pete believed that he would. But he needed to do something first.

"Stop," Pete practically yelled at Carol as she started to open her car door. "Please, I would like you to drive me to Barstow right now. I need to see the old friend who saved my life. You can come or not." He gestured to his parents.

The lawyer started to talk. "Not you," Pete said. "I'm done with you."

The lawyer shrugged his shoulders and departed. Just another day at the office for him. William Giles started to caution Pete, but his mother stepped in. "Let our son go, Bill. He needs to do this." Addressing Pete, she said, "We'll be at the hotel. Be back there by tonight. We leave early tomorrow." She gave Pete a hug. His dad looked away. Pete didn't care.

"Nobody asked, but I'm free," Carol said with a smile.

She called somebody on her radio phone.

"Hey, Jimmy, Pete Giles and I are driving to Barstow to visit Monk Tanner. Could you make sure whoever is guarding the prisoner will allow us to visit with him?"

***

Pete could tell he was well regarded in Barstow for having subdued Willie Sherwood in that moving airplane. There were two deputies guarding Monk Tanner's hospital room, one outside, one inside. They made a point of thanking him for his efforts. As for Monk, his entire right chest area was bandaged, his right arm was in a sling, and his right hand was bandaged. He was asleep. "I'm no doctor," one of the deputies said, "but I was in the service overseas. I believe blood loss and infection were the main concerns. They've pumped lots of blood into him. He's doing much better. I'll give you some time with him. We'll be right outside."

Pete sat down in a chair near the bed. He was suddenly overcome with emotion. He waited for a spell, letting his heart rate settle. "Well, buddy, we had one hell of a time out here," he said. "I know what you had to do was really hard, but you knew it was you or him."

Monk stirred. He'd been listening. "I'll go to hell for sure, killing my brother." His eyes were still closed.

"Man, I'm no expert in any of this but your mother raised you, nobody else," Pete said. "Blood only goes so far. Johnny Rolland tricked us and used us, especially you with the 'brother' routine. It wasn't real, no matter the blood. And I was no help. I should have stopped both of us somewhere along the line. I didn't do it. Anyway, I'm going to ask my father to find you a really good lawyer and pay for it. You can beat any charges they bring."

Monk opened his eyes. "I'm so ashamed for dragging you into this. I'm not even going to ask you to forgive me. Better to forget me."

"No way in hell, man. That's not in the cards. Who else am I going to talk to when I go home on vacation? Just concentrate on getting well." It all sounded lame to Pete's ears but what else could either of them say? A nurse came in with some meds for Monk. Pete wanted to give Monk a hug goodbye but was afraid he'd hurt him. He gave his left shoulder a squeeze instead, and said, "Take care, buddy, you know where I'll be," and left the room.

Carol was waiting for him. "Glad you came?" she asked.

"Absolutely, but it was hard to know what to say. He screwed up about as badly as he possibly could and dragged me into it. But I let him; maybe part of me wanted all this crazy stuff too."

"I hear from your father it's a family tradition."

"Christ, he told you about that, the True Giles Test? It's a trap, looking for trouble in order to get out of it with a story to tell. Southern men are still fighting the damn Civil War. Maybe I'll escape out here to sunny California, become a lawyer, and learn how to surf."

She clapped Pete on the back. "Not a bad plan. You ready to head back?"

"More than ready."

Pete watched Barstow disappear behind them as they drove away, glad he didn't have a pillowcase over his head. It was time to go home.

CHAPTER THIRTY-FOUR

May 17

CRIMINAL DEFENSE LAWYERS ARE A *pain in the ass*, I reflected upon leaving the interview room at 1 p.m. on Friday. I've never liked them, never will. Our second interview with Pete Giles took twice as long as it needed to because the lawyer couldn't stop talking. Carol and I exchanged a number of pained glances. It wasn't as if young Giles faced any legal jeopardy. Frustrated, I finally turned the questioning over to the more patient JK. Pete's answers did incriminate Monk Tanner for various actions he took. He served as Johnny Rolland's getaway driver after the Mister Louie's shootings, and brand new to us, a liquor store robbery near Barstow. Then there was the matter of kidnapping Pete Giles. It was a mess.

During a break, Carol told me that Pete was going to ask his father to find a top-notch defense attorney for Monk Tanner, using some of the ransom money he'd saved. Not this turkey, of course, but Carol knew some good ones. Given all the circumstances, Monk might get off clean.

For the past several months, TV commentators, armchair psychologists, and even some cops had been speculating about Patricia Hearst/Tania and her relationship with the SLA. She'd started as a full-blown victim and had seemingly become a committed radical. In a much less complicated fashion, Monk had decided to "save" his friend and half-brother Johnny Rolland from a life of crime and instead had jumped right into Rolland's criminal activities. Until the end, that is, when he'd risked his life and taken Rolland down. It made for a fine story when presented correctly.

After wishing JK a happy rest of the weekend, I made my way to Sam Fuller's office. It was decked out as I'd never seen it. He had two police scanners on, one for LA County, one for San Bernardino County, and two small televisions turned on, but with the volume turned down. He was like a kid in a candy store. It was all about Patty Hearst and the SLA. "This is amazing stuff," he said. "The FBI raided a house in South Central LA this morning, just missed this SLA gang. There are not that many of them, you know."

"Any new leads?"

"Something new is going on," Sam said. "But the radio traffic has gone quiet. There might be a new house in play, still South Central but closer to Compton."

"Anything on Hearst?"

"Nothing. Nobody knows. You saw that San Francisco bank robbery picture of her. She's real skinny and wears a wig. But all these white people, except for the ringleader DeFreeze, who's black, wandering around South Central LA. The cops are going to find them."

Sam gave his world globe a spin, as if to turn the page. "What's up with you?"

"We finished our second interview of Pete Giles, got the info we needed, and can close those cases, both the homicides and the abortive kidnapping, with the biggest loose end being Monk Tanner. I see him as something of a victim in all this."

Sam was less sympathetic. "The DA's office can sort that out. You did fine work on these cases, Jimmy. Your instincts are damn good."

"Thanks, boss. Moving ahead, I'm going drinking with Hank Phillips at 4:30. Aside from me drinking too much, I'm not sure these sessions will turn up his mob connection. Not a whisper yet."

Sam grinned. "Well, I have a confession to make. And I owe you an apology. While you were out there raising hell in the desert, I wrecked your credit. You're pretty close to bankrupt."

I was so stunned I didn't know what to say. "What the hell," was the best I could do.

Sam raised his hands in mock surrender. "This is very, very temporary. I know a guy, he's some sort of computer genius. He and I met with your Claremont banker and figured out how to make this work. I don't understand it, but as of Wednesday, May 22nd, it all goes away, and your credit is fine. None of this happened."

The LA County scanner fired up. Something about East 54th Street. That must be the new house Sam was talking about. At the moment I didn't care. I was pissed at Sam. "I still don't get it. Wrecking my finances, my life? Jesus, Sam."

"You said it yourself. No matter how much you drink with Hank Phillips and complain about me, he still thinks you're a straight cop just letting off steam. No way is he gonna fill you in on his plans. So let's say you buy a round today for Hank and his buddies, paying with your regular Master Charge credit card. Five minutes later, the bartender—it's Red, isn't it? I've been there—comes back and says your card is declined. This computer whiz even got your credit card put in the latest bad card book."

Sam pulled out a new BankAmericard in the name of James Sommes. "Use this for the next week. It's on the department. But not around Hank."

"Maybe I'll go have a party in Tijuana instead," I groused at him.

"We should have talked, I know," Sam said. "But we're running out of time. Good luck with Phillips today."

I wandered away, still confused but beginning to understand the elegance of this sneaky play. Some people underestimated Sam Fuller, seeing a graying old cop who'd run the office for years. I knew better. When on the job, on the chase, he possessed a ruthlessness that few lawmen could match.

"You okay, Jimmy?" one of his secretaries asked. I stopped dead right in front of her desk, not even realizing where I was.

I laughed and said, "Yeah, I'm just fine. Hand me one of

those cookies, will ya, and have a good weekend."

My next stop was a drinking session with Hank Phillips and his buddies. I'd likely need more than a chocolate chip cookie in my stomach, but it was a start.

CHAPTER THIRTY-FIVE

May 17

I MET HANK PHILLIPS AND his buddies at the Mission Boulevard cop bar in Pomona to continue our boozy examination of the world around us. There was a buzz in the air. Two televisions were on. Normally they'd be turned off unless the Dodgers or Angels were on. Not today. It was all SLA/Patty Hearst. One of the greatest manhunts in history continued, and all of us felt like the cops were going to win.

Even Phillips abandoned his usual litany of complaints. I'd never claim to like the guy but felt that I understood him a little better. I imagine his childhood didn't amount to much. I was so grateful for mine. Both of us were rednecks on some level, or at least a generation or two removed. No fancy-ass English lords in our family trees. Nevertheless, my goal of busting him never changed. There was no room in my world for dirty cops.

"I think you're full of shit," Phillips said to me as we began on our first pitcher of Pabst Blue Ribbon. "Sam Fuller gave all the credit to your greenhorn partner last night. I know some DEA guys. They said you figured that whole thing out, along with their DEA desert rat, Miller."

I smiled. "First of all, Miller was great. He figured it out, not me. But I'm not quite sure you get it, Hank. Sam Fuller is out to get me, to get me reassigned back to Yucaipa. And he has the power to do it, to completely wreck my career, no questions asked. I'm pretty much fucked."

"What'd you do to him, man? I thought you were his fair-haired boy."

"Well, it's not personal. It's something on the job I can't

figure out. If I knew, I'd tell you. And it's been going on for two years now, when we broke up that Baseline Road dentist's drug ring. My big moment. Since then, no raises, no promotions, and my money's getting tight. Hell, maybe Sam's jealous. Like I told you, everybody thinks he can do no wrong. Not so. He's gotten too old for the job."

"Screw him. Let's eat," Phillips said. The mood was festive. Yesterday had been a big day for our unit. Fried chicken, French fries, and pitchers of beer were laid out, buffet style. Hank's cop friends were not a bad group, but there was this tinge of racism they couldn't shake. Not that I'm some kind of saint, but I was taught—there's my upbringing again—to view people on their merits. It worked well for me. But now came the moment of truth. I signaled Red the bartender. "Let me get these first three pitchers of Pabst. We'll figure out the food later." I handed him my Master Charge card, the old one. Red didn't really like people paying with cards, but he took it. It was just like a damn movie. I bet Sam had called him, leaving nothing to chance.

Sure enough, minutes later, the bartender returned with my card. "Card was denied," he said, not happy about it. Amidst the noise and hubbub, only Hank Phillips noticed. In an act of kindness, he quickly slipped a $20 bill to Red, telling him to keep the change. I could only imagine how I would have reacted if Sam hadn't told me. Even so, it felt a little strange. Had Sam needed to do this? I made a plate of food and started in on the chicken with my head down. The entire charade felt both cruel and perfect. I went up to the bar and asked Red for a shot of tequila. He hesitated. I put a five-dollar bill on the bar. "Real money. Does that buy two?"

Red nodded. "Then pour two." I downed mine on the spot, then took the other one to Hank. I handed it to him with a slight bow. "Like I said, I'm pretty much fucked in this town."

Then, like the night before, all of our attention went to the television. "Turn up the volume," somebody yelled. The Channel 2 announcer was blabbing away, but behind him was a small, yellow house. He gave the address: 1466 East 54th Street in South Central Los Angeles. "It's a war zone down there," somebody at our table said. "Welcome back to Vietnam, boys." Calls for surrender were being made via megaphones. A few civilians staggered out of the house.

I saw the shirts on the cops. Unlike earlier in the day, the Los Angeles Special Weapons and Tactics (SWAT) team was in charge now, not the FBI. I found myself rooting for them, even though this group was not for the timid. Some of them were less than twenty feet from the front door. "So long, fucking SLA," one of our guys said. "This ain't like those pussy San Francisco cops. Welcome to the big time."

Somebody shot tear gas canisters into the house. Often, that was all it took to finally force a surrender. Instead, a massive fusillade of shots rang out from the house. The SLA was taking it to the cops. *Jesus Christ!* I looked at my watch. It was almost 6 p.m. What followed for the next hour transfixed all of us in the bar. More folks drifted in. Sometimes there were cheers, often it was quiet. The two sides were each firing thousands of automatic rifle rounds at the other. I was amazed, pretty sure that nothing like this had happened in peacetime, if you could call it that, in our country. And where was Patty Hearst? Most likely in that house.

The camera was live, reporters dodging bullets, not just pretty faces talking in a studio. We could see civilians running away from the battle, terrified, but some journalists running toward the chaos. I thought of Allie. Of course, she'd be getting as close as she could... heedless of danger. Then the house ignited, likely from tear gas canisters, and began to burn, the flames reaching high in the sky, catching date palms on fire. Incredibly, shots from the house continued.

"Can you believe it," somebody at our table said, "they're getting burned to a crisp and still firing." Finally, the firing stopped. It was clear that everybody in the house was dead.

A simple Friday night at the cops' favorite bar had turned us all into witnesses of a battle that likely would never be forgotten. Red said that all drinks were on the house. He didn't want money. It was half celebration, half wake. The reporter said the SWAT team reported no police fatalities or civilian deaths. That drew a round of applause. Hard to believe. Thank God for that. I wanted to get into my car and drive to the battle scene and look for Allie, but knew that was dumb. The police, medical, and morgue personnel didn't need any more rubberneckers, even lawmen, and I'd never find her, anyway. But I needed to get out of the bar.

Hank saw me about to split. "Meet me tomorrow at noon at Bob's Big Boy in Pomona," he said, then left too. Nobody wanted to stick around. It was as if the bar had been part of the battle. I drove home, then called Carol. No answer. Then I called my mother. She was her usual chipper self, although she had watched the shoot-out. "I'm glad you weren't there, son," she said.

"Me too." We talked about unimportant matters for a while then ended the call. She helped me to remember that normal life was not about darkness, death, and crime.

Still restless and torn, I grabbed a Budweiser and sat on my deck in the quiet darkness. Then the phone rang. It was ominous from the start. "Is this Jimmy Sommes?" an official voice asked. I said yes.

"This is Nurse Dominguez from LA General Hospital's Emergency Room. We have a patient, Allessandra D'Amico. We found your name and phone number in her purse. She listed you as a person to contact."

"Is she okay?" I managed to ask.

"She's sleeping now. She suffered some sort of fall at that terrible shoot-out, and then later a fainting spell. That's all the information I have." Her voice was businesslike, neither consoling nor rude. She likely did this all the time, creating terror in the hearts of the recipients of her calls. Just another day at the emergency room. *Wait, goddammit, Jimmy, it's not her fault.* I thanked her and hung up.

I tried to park my brain in neutral as I sped down the freeway. I'd made a trip in this same direction five days ago, excited to be meeting my lady at the Biltmore. The destination this time was the massive hospital that most sought to avoid. LA General. It simply was too big. Patients got lost. The staff was overworked. It was a place for drug overdoses, gunshot wounds, and all the diseases that went with poverty. Did her newspaper know? They must. Then why wasn't she at Cedars-Sinai in West LA, where all the movie stars went, or some other swank hospital?

Her injury sounded like a concussion. Knowing Allie, she'd probably tried to work through it, hence the fainting spell. They had good doctors at LA General, the salt of the earth. Helping people who needed it the most. Think on the bright side: I was sober tonight. Nobody in the bar watching that crazy war movie had been drinking that much.

There was little traffic on the freeway. I made good time and parked next to the emergency room entrance in a restricted zone, so I secured my blue light on the roof of my Charger and placed my San Bernardino County Sheriff's Department placard on the dashboard to avoid being towed or stolen. I recalled that I'd been here fairly recently, checking on a prisoner.

The emergency room was busy. I imagined it always was. I identified myself at the reception desk and said I was there to see Allessandra D'Amico, electing not to play the cop card yet. I had no official business here. I was told to wait. It gave me an opportunity to think about my time with Allie, from the very beginning at Acid Bill Dixon's compound on Mt. Baldy two years ago to last week at the Biltmore. The intensity was what got to me. Together, we were always the stars in our own color movie while the rest of the world became blurred black-and-white images. I knew it was ridiculous to think our love was different from anybody else's romance, but that never stopped me. It also remained my secret. Nobody, not even Allie, knew the depth of my feelings for her. It didn't fit with my bullshit, macho image of myself, so I just shut up about it. Probably Carol came the closest to sensing it, since she saw through most of my nonsense.

In any case, here I was, wondering what had happened

to her. What had smashed her brain? Was it a ricochet from an SLA bullet? Had Allie gotten too close as she chased the ghost of Patricia Hearst, a rich girl who'd taken up with outlaws? Allie was a rich girl too, who'd chosen her own path that for a time included radicals. But she was nobody's patsy. Perhaps, however, she felt a sense of kinship with a woman who wanted no part of a newspaper heiress' privileged life. Hell, I didn't know. Allie might tell me—as soon as she woke up.

A hand awoke me from a shallow sleep. "Mr. Sommes. Miss D'Amico is awake and asked to see you." I followed the nurse through a maze of small rooms. Allie's was private.

"My newspaper editor insisted," she said with a sheepish smile. There was a bandage covering part of her head. "You like this look?" She was self-conscious. There was no need for that. The nurse cautioned me not to stay long and left us alone.

I went to her bedside and kissed her gently. She laughed and put her arms around me. "You can do better than that, Jimmy," and gave me a proper, deep kiss.

"I'm glad you're okay. Now, tell me what the hell happened to you," I said.

"Here's the short version. She told me we have five minutes. You know about the shoot-out, right?"

"Yeah, I watched the whole thing on TV."

"Toward the very end of it," Allie continued, "other houses near the SLA house were catching fire. The LA SWAT team had switched to more flammable tear gas. God knows why. I was in one of those houses behind the SLA house, and I saw," Allie's voice caught, "two of the SLA members come out the back door, guns blazing, and get blown apart by police bullets. Then the house I was in caught fire. I ran to get out, tripped, and hit my head hard on a concrete walkway. That's me, always clumsy. It started to bleed. I used my shirt to stop it." I handed Allie a cup of water, wanting to slow her down.

"Anyway, I got to a safer spot. I was with a stringer for

our paper who'd driven us down there. He got me a towel. I felt weird, but mostly okay. The shooting finally stopped. I'd written half the story already. We hung around the command post, learned that no cops or civilians had been shot, were told, off the record, that no one was alive in the house, which was obvious, and that Patty Hearst may or may not have been in there. Nobody will know until the coroner comes and identifies the bodies.

"We left that awful scene. I called in the rest of the story from a pay phone near City Hall to a rewrite man at the paper and told him I'd polish it later at the Biltmore. I hung up, then got very shaky, threw up violently, and must have passed out."

"It's okay. Don't overdo it," I said.

"But wait." She smiled, grabbing my hand. "You're missing the best part. There were two moments tonight, first when I hit my head, and then later when I started to faint or whatever it was, when all I thought about was you. Wondering if I was going to die, and never see you again." Tears clouded her eyes.

"That just can't happen, Jimmy," she whispered to me. "Because I love you."

"I love you, too. More than you know."

The nurse came back. Perfect timing. I pulled away from her. It was difficult.

"Tomorrow my paper is flying me back to a hospital in San Jose. They must like me."

"I'll come visit soon."

"You do that, cowboy, but I'm fine, really fine. See you soon." Allie closed her eyes. She was exhausted.

I walked out with the nurse. "Is she okay?"

"I'm not really supposed to say," she said, "but I can see how you feel about each other. The doctors think yes. She got a concussion, was likely dehydrated, and then kept working in a high-stress situation instead of taking care of herself. That led to the fainting spell. They'll run more tests up in San Jose. Are you a reporter too?"

"No, I'm a deputy sheriff. I catch bad guys for a living."

"Well then, you two make a lovely pair." I thought so too.

I barely remember the drive home. My heart was bursting with a combination of sheer joy and absolute exhaustion.

CHAPTER THIRTY-SIX

May 18

THE PLEASURES OF THE BOB'S Big Boy Combo beckoned. With Allie safe, my big case closed, and progress being made at this very moment regarding my lunch pal Hank Phillips's fate, it was time to enjoy the plate of food before me. It sounded simple, and boring, the Combo, namely a burger, fries, and a wedge of lettuce covered with thousand island dressing. But somehow, in the hands of this restaurant chain, it approached perfection, with one important modification: I always substituted onion rings for the mediocre fries.

It was slightly alarming that I continued to find commonalities with Hank Phillips, the man I was stalking. He loved the Combo too but stuck with the fries. Millions of other people loved Bob's Big Boy, so I was going to enjoy my meal free from any nagging worries about our shared taste in food. The onion rings were too hot so I attacked the burger first. It was delightful. After three bites or so, I ate some of the salad, which always made me feel virtuous. Then back to the burger. I left some and went after the first onion ring. It was now just right. Hank and I ate silently, which also suited me.

Toward the end of the meal, to make conversation, we talked about the SLA shoot-out. Patricia Hearst/Tania was not one of the dead bodies found at the burned-out house. Noguchi, the coroner, had announced it. He loved the spotlight. The waitress cleared away our plates and refilled our coffee cups.

"Are you wearing a wire?"

His question shocked me. "Jesus! Where did that come from? Of course not. You want to search me?" I stood up.

Hank waved for me to sit down. "I believe you. It's just... it's hard for me to figure out what's going on with you. I didn't like you before, Sam Fuller's favorite hot shot deputy who thought I was dirt. But at least it made sense. Now this. Are you trying to trap me?"

I signaled the waitress for the check. "I'll pay this, Hank. I've got cash." I wasn't much of a fisherman but knew this was a crucial moment. If I pull too hard, the fish slips the hook. "Look, I wish I wasn't dead broke with blown credit and was still Sam's favorite deputy, but shit happens. I don't believe in shrinks, never will, but sometimes you just do something too long, and think you have to perform a certain way, and it begins to fade, the reason we're doing this job. As recently as two days ago, I had these crazy guys out in Barstow ready to blow my head off with a twelve-gauge. For what, a crummy pension someday? I'll have lost my house by then and moved in with my mother." Was it too much? I wasn't sure.

Hank nodded. "Jesus, that's just how I feel sometimes." He hesitated. "Okay, fuck it. What I'm going to say now, I never said. You know the drill. Anyway, there's this guy on the other side of the law who I help from time to time, under very strict rules. No violence is one of them. Also I believe I actually can make things safer by helping him out. I get paid for this. Not a fortune, but it keeps me going."

"Wow. I never figured you for—"

"Me neither," Hank said. "I could mention you to this guy. You've heard of him. His name is Izzy Weiss."

I got up fast, almost knocking over my coffee cup. "Better that you don't do that, Hank. I'd have to think about that pretty hard. A gangster? But look, we all have to do what we have to do. I get it. See ya later, man." I walked up to the register and paid for our lunch, feeling his eyes on me. I went to my office in Alta Loma and called Carol, needing her brain and her guts.

***

"Sorry to intrude on your Saturday," I said to Carol. We were sitting in my kitchen because the deck was too hot.

"Annie's working anyway, her normal half-day on Saturday afternoons," Carol said. "We're planning a long weekend up in Santa Barbara soon, a house on the beach with no telephone."

Carol and I were drinking Dos Equis with limes. I'd used my new BankAmericard at Wolfe's Market to pick up two six-packs, along with some snacks.

"What's up with Sam?" Carol said. "In the last two weeks, he's managed to wreck your reputation and now your credit. Is he pissed at you?"

"Maybe. He knew I was slacking off on the job. He hates that in general, maybe especially so in me. But Sam can be ruthless. He's determined to reel in Hank Phillips for being a dirty cop and thinks I'm the best tool to accomplish that."

Carol munched on tortilla chips and then took a swig of her beer. "With all due respect, I think this palsy-walsy thing with Hank Phillips is borderline insane."

I laughed. "Tell me what you really think."

"Okay, I've heard two objectives so far: one, bust Hank Phillips; and two, thwart a bank robbery at an unknown Bank of America location. And the plan is for you to get close enough to Phillips to allow him to cut you in on the deal, or at least tell you the location. Is that right?"

"Yeah, that's pretty much it, and it's kind of working."

"Emphasis is on kinda, but also at terrible risk to you, Jimmy. Hank Phillips can't just decide stuff like that, even if he's smart, which he's not. Izzy Weiss or somebody even higher up in the organization would have to approve it. He may already have mentioned you to Weiss. We don't know. I hope not. And Weiss, from what I hear, is smart. Which means you might expect a knock on your door, a blow to your head, and a blindfolded trip to an undisclosed location, where Mr. Weiss can have a little chat with you about your real intentions."

"That's a little melodramatic, isn't it?"

She shrugged her shoulders. "Maybe, but I don't think you or Sam have thought this through."

"Okay, give me another approach."

Carol flashed me a devilish grin. "I think I should break into Hank Phillips's apartment and see what I can find. PIs do it all the time. I'm not a cop anymore. It's Saturday, the bank robbery is scheduled for next Tuesday, the twenty-first. That's not much time, and it takes planning. Maybe Phillips knows the location."

"When?"

"Tonight. Doesn't he always drink down at that scuzzy bar on Mission? Go keep him company."

"Wow. This PI thing is different, isn't it. He lives in Upland someplace."

Carol pulled open my Greater Ontario phone book. "Let's see if this is going to be easy." She leafed through it. "Yup. Easy. 1539 West 7th Street in Upland, Apartment 14."

I knew it. It was a mediocre apartment complex, close to the San Bernardino Freeway and Montclair Plaza. And not too far from Hank's favorite cop bar on Mission. All the comforts of home.

"Let's do a drive-by in my Chevy," Carol said. "He won't recognize it. Wear your Angels hat and shades."

"Yes, ma'am."

She drove fast as usual, going south on Padua, east on Baseline, and then turning right on Benson Avenue. We went from cute Upland to light industrial blah Upland the closer we got to the freeway. Carol turned left into the sprawling rental project and cruised around the six buildings, like a prospective tenant. There was no security. The cement swimming pool was drained. We easily found number 14. I kept my head down. It was a ground-floor unit facing away from the rental office and busy Benson Avenue.

"Piece of cake," Carol said.

"Let's go," I said, nervous to be near the place. Hank was a cop, after all, and might be more observant than Carol was giving him credit for. There was a taco stand across the street. We parked behind it and got tacos. Typical of many of the little Mexican joints, their food was excellent.

"May 18th," mused Carol. "When does it get pitch-dark, must be about 9 p.m.?"

"Make it ten. We'll be doing some serious drinking at the cop bar by then. Maybe you're right about Sam. He's turning me into a drunk."

"The door locks looked flimsy, but Hank might have a deadbolt too," Carol said.

"I doubt it. He's not a careful guy."

"I'll be prepared in any case. Louvered windows are easy too."

"You do this all the time, commit burglaries?"

Carol laughed. "Only when I have to, in order to get the goods, so to speak. Your job is not to let Hank out of your sight from nine to eleven tonight."

CHAPTER THIRTY-SEVEN

May 18

I BEGGED OFF FROM ANOTHER round of drinks around 11:30, eager to find out how Carol had got on. Phillips and I managed to avoid any further serious conversation about his other line of work. I drove to the Claremont Howard Johnson's restaurant on Indian Hill near the freeway, our planned rendezvous location. Carol was there already at a corner table with a pot of coffee, two cups, and some maps spread out. She gave me a grin. The black bag job had gone off without a hitch. She obviously loved this work. We were back to normal with the Giles family gone.

She wrinkled her nose. "You smell like a dive bar."

"Hey, this is serious undercover work. I dump as many as I drink. Any luck?"

"I think so. Let me tell you what I didn't find, namely a piece of paper clearly identifying which bank the Weiss gang is planning to rob next Tuesday. Even Hank Phillips is not stupid enough to do that. But," Carol smiled, "I found a bunch of stuff in his bedroom trash can."

She put some crumpled, stained, and mangled receipts on top of the maps. "Hank loves his cheeseburgers and fries with lots of ketchup. Yuck."

"And his beef and bean burritos," I added.

"Willie's Burgers on Arrow Boulevard in Fontana has been Hank's favorite eating spot the last three days," Carol said. "And there was a wrapper that definitely held a burrito. I wore gloves to organize this stuff."

"He's pretty gross. Is he going to miss any of this mess?"

"Nah. Like so many of you poor, pathetic men, Mr.

Phillips enjoys his dirty magazines. They were scattered all over his unmade bed. He'd miss those. But not this garbage. His food receipts in the trash can were mixed in with all the other stuff, including used tissues, candy wrappers, and soda cans. I'm a careful detective so I crumpled up some toilet paper to keep the weight the same."

"I do the same thing, stuff receipts in my jeans and dump them later. I hope the tissues were, well, not too used if you get my meaning."

"Let's not talk about that, ever," Carol said. "I washed my hands twice." She unfolded a Fontana street map and pointed to the corner of Sierra Avenue and Arrow Blvd. She first circled the Willie's Burgers location in pencil and then circled a building directly across the street.

I knew the second building but let Carol say it. "That's the downtown Fontana branch of the Bank of America, with an Arrow Blvd address. Any operational reason for Hank to be in Fontana?"

"He's been assigned to Rialto for the last three months, says it's been boring. It's one of the things he complains about all the time. But he's been assigned to Fontana at times in the past. Our Fontana Station is a short drive on Arrow to that Bank of America branch."

Carol paused. "Okay, let's play devil's advocate for a moment. He's been working in Rialto, lives in south Upland, and drinks at a cop bar in Pomona. The receipts don't show any times on them. It could be that he stops at Willie's Burgers on his way home from work because it's his favorite."

"One of the few things that Hank is serious about is food," I said. "He's always saying that In-N-Out Burger on Towne Avenue in Pomona is his number one choice, not counting Bob's Big Boy since it's more of a sit-down type restaurant."

"Okay. We need to stake out Willie's Burgers both tomorrow and especially Monday, and I know just the guy to do it: my boss, Gideon Pitts. Since I've been working out of his office to get my required PI hours for the license, we've become pretty good friends. Gideon's very good at blending in since nobody notices an old guy like him. He'll bring his portable chess set."

"The bank's closed tomorrow since it's Sunday so we don't want Phillips to show up."

"Correct, because that would mean he only goes there because he loves the food. Have you ever been there?"

"No. It's pretty new and I heard it was just another ho-hum burger joint, no big deal. Did you find anything else at the apartment?"

"I saw two phone numbers scribbled on a note pad near his phone. I can check them on my crisscross directory at the office. I don't want to call them, in case they're unlisted."

"Well done, detective lady. Are you going to pay Gideon to stake out Willie's Burgers?"

"No need. I'm bringing in all the cash these days at the agency, especially with that five grand from William Giles. Gideon will enjoy the challenge. You know, I hope the kid, Pete Giles, will be okay."

I nodded. "I was very impressed with him out in the desert. He'd just disarmed and subdued a dangerous criminal while the Cessna was rolling down that goofy road, and he seemed cool as ice about it. Might make a good cop if he's interested."

"He mentioned law school to me," Carol said.

"The kid has a bright future. Let's call it a night and talk in the morning. Thanks, Carol. You're the best."

***

It was close to 1 a.m. when I turned left on Palmer Canyon Road. My cabin was a quarter of a mile in. It faced south and was elevated above the road. The neighborhood was quiet tonight, no big Saturday night parties. I parked my Charger in front like always and prepared to start up my wooden steps. It was good to be home.

Then I heard an engine rev up to my left. Two men in a dark late-model sedan. Both the driver and the passenger gave me long looks as they slowly drove past. The inside light in the car was on, so I could see their faces. The men didn't belong in this "blue jeans and boots" locale. These hoods belonged in a Las Vegas casino or at the Santa Anita Racetrack. There was no fear in their eyes. After checking me out with their blank, fish-eye stares, the driver sped up and the sedan headed east toward Padua. It had no rear license plate.

Christ! Had I been tailed since leaving Howard Johnson's? I didn't think so. Oddly, it felt more like these characters were putting me to bed for the night. And reporting to Izzy Weiss. In other words, I was in play.

I had questions, but no answers. Had Hank Phillips blabbed about me to Izzy Weiss after I asked him not to? I wasn't going to find out tonight. The cabin was undisturbed, unless the invaders happened to be very, very good at B&E, like Carol.

The night had turned chilly. So had my mood. I took a blanket out on the deck and slept in one of the chairs, a loaded shotgun on the table. Nobody showed up. Maybe I was getting paranoid. Maybe not.

***

I drove to Carol's in the morning, a sleepy Sunday in sleepy Claremont. It was about 10 a.m. There were no dark sedans tailing me. Nevertheless, I parked on Harvard Avenue across from Sycamore School and strolled the four blocks to Carol's College Avenue bungalow. Not another soul was walking around, typical for Southern California. I knocked on her back door. Annie Hoover, Carol's partner, let me in. Max the pug greeted me. I smelled freshly baked banana bread and better coffee than I ever made. It was their bungalow now, which made me happy for both women.

"Hi, stranger. Would you like some breakfast?" Annie asked, leading me toward the kitchen. I made a plate of eggs and banana bread and poured a cup of coffee. Carol was in their comfortable living room, surrounded by all the sections of both the Sunday *New York Times* and the *LA Times*. It was a reader's feast. I headed in, automatically looking for the sports pages.

"Good morning," Carol said, immediately noticing the serious expression on my face. "Not a social call?" Annie had not followed me in. She knew it was business.

"Well, it's always a pleasure, but that little scenario you laid out last night about Izzy Weiss might be happening." I filled her in about the dark strangers in the dark car.

"I didn't see anything at Howard Johnson's last night," Carol said.

"Me neither, which is important. It's weird. It felt almost friendly last night, in a hoodlum sort of way. I'm just not sure how to manage the next two days. I also have extra incentive not to risk my life," I added and told her about Allie, her injury at the SLA shoot-out, and that the two of us might be trying to get more serious and less "modern" in our relationship. Max the pug had his head in Carol's lap.

"Good for you," Carol said. "It's about time. Take two weeks' vacation and spend it with Allie."

"I wish I could, but I've got to help Sam reel Hank Phillips in and stop a bank robbery first. It's my assignment. You'd do the same, no matter what you say."

"Yeah, you're probably right, although my time with Annie might be teaching me differently too. Anyway, Gideon Pitts is on board for today and tomorrow, and even Tuesday if we need him. There's a Moose Lodge right next to the bank, whatever the hell that is, and Gideon's got some buddies there. He'll keep watch on Willie's Burgers. I don't expect anything today. Neither do you, I know. The restaurant opens at noon, and I said two hours is enough. It'll be longer tomorrow."

"That sounds good. I'm meeting with Sam and JK this afternoon at headquarters. I'm going to tell them it might be the Fontana Bank of America, so preparations can start. I'm saying it's a hunch at this point, but Sam generally respects my hunches. I'll tell JK the whole story. He'll be impressed with your black bag job."

"Sure. Just not to Sam Fuller, lawman. I don't want him to arrest me."

CHAPTER THIRTY-EIGHT

MAY 19

"***THERE'S SOMETHING YOU'RE NOT TELLING*** me," Sam groused, "but if it's not material I'll let it slide."

"There's all kinds of stuff you haven't been telling me either, like messing up my credit," I retorted. Sometimes the best defense is a good offense.

I'd invented a different version of reality, indicating that I knew Hank Phillips had recently started hanging out at Willie's Burgers, but not saying how I knew. In any case, it got the Fontana branch of the Bank of America onto our collective radar screen. It made sense to me. Kaiser Steel, which was easily the biggest employer in Fontana, used the facility for its entire payroll expenditures. The plant had lost some business over the years but still was a major San Bernardino County economic force. My band's gifted lead guitar player, Dave Sokoloski, worked there as a welder and made good money.

"Does the bank have security cameras?" JK asked. My recollection was yes, but of a cheap quality. I cashed checks there sometimes, since I had my checking and savings accounts at the Claremont branch.

"What's your level of certainty on this?" Sam asked.

"Maybe fifty percent. I wish it was more, but Hank's not likely to tell me anything else, unless I sign up for Izzy Weiss's gang."

"Even then, the actual crooks might not buy it," Sam said. "I know the branch manager. I'll tell him we'll put a couple of plainclothes officers in the bank, maybe say they're outside auditors. I'll let him figure that out." Sam gave the world globe he kept on his desk a spin, a sign that he was deep in his planning phase. He trailed one finger on the globe, and it came to rest on Algeria. I had no idea if that was a good or bad result.

"And no FBI right now," Sam said, talking mainly to himself. "They continue to be up to their necks in dead SLA bodies, none of them is Patricia Hearst. What else?"

"We're going to watch Hank Phillips tomorrow to see if he's continuing to case the Fontana bank," JK said. I'd already told him how Carol got her Willie's Burger information.

Sam paused and gave me a suspicious look. "I'm betting that a certain Carol Loomis might be assisting law enforcement in this matter. Now it all makes more sense. Okay, let's roll with it. Given that there are potential leaks at our Fontana Station and its soon to be retiring commander is a big mouth, we won't use it as the command post. We've got to be close to the bank, though. What's up on Foothill near there?"

"There's a county social services building just above Foothill," I said. Sam made a call. The second floor was vacant. His secretary arranged for telephone services to be installed by the end of the day. A technical assistant would ensure radio communications. Office windows faced south and had a good view of the Sierra Avenue and Foothill Blvd intersection. Del Taco, McDonald's, and Burger King were nearby. We wouldn't starve.

"My initial thinking is that we arrest the robbers after they exit the bank," Sam said. I agreed, saying that one alley and two driveways needed to be blocked.

"The getaway car will be a logistical problem," JK said, "assuming they use one or even two of them." He was right. We didn't know where they'd be.

"Fortunately, the LA County Sheriff's Department has a small team that specializes in bank jobs," Sam said. "One of them will meet with us tomorrow morning at the command post. I'm staying away from San Bernardino tomorrow I've got a speaking engagement if anybody asks. That'll give me the entire day to work on this. I don't like the fact that Izzy Weiss is choosing to piss on our turf. It's as much about the power as the money for him."

I felt compelled to bring something up. "What if my information, or my assumptions about it, are dead wrong?"

"Then you're fired," Sam said with a big smile on his face. "Joking. We're going to put a very good surveillance team on Hank Phillips, starting tomorrow night. It's not ideal, but if he drives to a different bank on Tuesday, we'll scramble our forces accordingly. And we'll make sure that team has big glossy photos of your buddy, a PI named Carol Loomis, in case she's around. Try to keep her clear, Sergeant Sommes. Let's meet at eight tomorrow morning at the command center."

"One last thing, Sam," I said. "Izzy Weiss might be tailing me." I'd already filled him in on Hank Phillips's tentative offer to me. But he didn't know about last night's drive-by outside my cabin.

"Does it feel dangerous?"

"Anything with gangsters has that aspect to it, but it felt more like an approach. Maybe Izzy wants to see if I'm interested. I've told Hank it's no sale, at least not now, but he believes I'm not ratting him out, either. Carol thinks Weiss and his boys might grab me for a little chat, whether I want to or not."

That got Sam's interest. "We can pull you out of this, you know. Do you want backup?"

"I'm available," JK said.

"Okay, I appreciate all this. Let's play this out for now. Those goons could have made a move on me last night."

"Yes and no," Sam said. "JK, I want you and Officer Gutierrez to park one block away from the cop bar tonight." He grinned. "You can be making out or something. Two people attract less attention. If Jimmy comes out and there's no tail, your shift is over. Take a personal car that Phillips won't recognize."

"What do I tell Gutierrez?"

"Just that we're following an Izzy Weiss lead, and that she shouldn't talk to Phillips about it. I doubt she's eager to talk to Hank Phillips about much of anything. And, JK, call me tonight with a report. I don't care how late. I'm a light sleeper." The meeting broke up.

I called Carol to keep her up to date. She told me that Hank Phillips did not show up at Willie's Burgers today. We agreed that was good news.

"And we've been getting more confirmation on Phillips," she said. "One of those scribbled phone numbers I saw at his place is an unlisted number for Dave's Market in Ontario."

"That's Izzy's hangout."

"Yes indeed. You need me tonight?"

I told her no, that JK had my back. "Sam's going to put a team of trackers on Hank starting tomorrow night. Tell Gideon to be careful tomorrow. We're dealing with some nasty characters."

"He may be old, but he's dealt with his fair share of nasty characters." She signed off.

***

I drove home, detouring first to In-N-Out Burger in Pomona on the way. All this focus on Willie's Burgers made me crave the real thing. Drinking with Hank Phillips required food in my stomach. At least that was my excuse. I ate inside, thought about calling Allie but changed my mind. That was one of our weird rules. It always worked better when she contacted me. There were no tails when I pulled out onto Foothill. Maybe those two guys last night were just lost in Palmer Canyon. *Yeah, right.*

I soon got my answer. My parking spot outside my cabin was taken. An elegant late-model black Mercedes sedan was occupying it. I pulled in beside the car, checked to make sure that my revolver was loaded and easily available, and then turned off the engine. It was too early to take the gun out. I needed more information. I walked around the front of the Mercedes. There was a note tucked underneath the driver's side windshield wiper. It read:

Sergeant Sommes,

I took the liberty of walking up to your deck. I'm unarmed. This struck me as an excellent time for us to talk like the civilized men we are.

Regards,

IZZY WEISS

Well, I'll be damned. Notwithstanding the note, I checked for anything unusual in my surroundings. There were no goons hiding behind rocks. I heard the sounds of a baseball game on a neighbor's television. All seemed normal, except for a certain gangster on my deck. I believed him. I believed that Izzy Weiss was alone and unarmed. I felt a certain sense of kinship with my guest. Cops and robbers were not friends—were enemies—but we often understood each other in a way that civilians could never fathom.

I stamped up the stairs, making sure to be noisy. Never surprise wildlife. The man on the deck stood up to greet me. He was fiftyish, fit, and looked like he'd just left a country club golf course. Streaks of gray were visible in his thick head of black hair. "Hi, I'm Izzy. Nice place you've got here."

"Jimmy Sommes, thanks, I like it." We shook hands. I elected not to offer him a beer. This may turn out to be a cordial visit, but we certainly were not two pals hanging out.

"No, I really mean it, Serg—"

"Call me Jimmy."

"Sure, anyway, I was sitting here, relaxing, enjoying the mountain air on this deck, thinking I should do this more often."

"You could retire."

That drew a belly laugh from Izzy. "Retirement. That's a rather complex concept in my world. It needs to be distinguished from being buried in a hole in the desert."

I liked that he was making no pretense about what he did for a living. "What can I do for you, Izzy? Is it okay to call you Izzy?"

"Call me Izzy. What can you do for me? That's what I'm trying to figure out, Jimmy. Hank Phillips is a bum. I need to work with bums on many occasions. Just like I need to work with compulsive gamblers, junkies, hard-core criminals like Johnny Rolland, and beautiful women who take their clothes off in movies, or get paid for having sex. I won't bore you with all the appropriate biblical references, since you know well the forbidden fruit that comes with the territory we traverse." Fancy language.

"Hank Phillips also is a very sloppy eater," I said. "He spills on his clothes, but I'm finding that I like him a little better than I thought I would. We both like to drink." Trying to live my cover, even with Izzy.

"But you, Jimmy Sommes, are not a bum. You're also a person who can be very dangerous to people like me."

"That's true when I feel like it, Izzy, which doesn't seem to be all the time these days. I have a lady friend who got hurt at that crazy SLA shoot-out on Friday night, not gravely injured, but enough to make me want to permanently avoid bullets."

Izzy shrugged. "Nevertheless, in my opinion, there will never be enough filthy lucre or other inducements, even women, that will even come close to tempting you to cross the line, to change team jerseys, so to speak. It's not in your nature." Jesus, had he talked to Tammy about me? What did he know?

This was a moment of truth. I decided against faking it. "Yeah, you're probably right. Your side of the fence strikes me as uncomfortable. It's not really a moral thing, more a matter of complexity, or not always knowing where I'm at or what I'm doing."

Izzy nodded. "Bob Dylan said 'to live outside the law, you must be honest.'"

"And '*Where are you tonight, Sweet Marie*,'" I answered.

"Of course," Izzy said, "you're a musician. I won't be able to out-Dylan you, even though I'm a huge fan. The ultimate question remains: Do I need to harm you?"

"Or vice versa," I said. "But the thing is, I deal with specific criminal acts. I'm not a mastermind. Sam Fuller told me he got along fairly well with Joe Donatella back in the day. For one thing, unlike you, Joe Don stayed away from dope dealing."

"Which is a nostalgic and strategic impossibility in this market. The cartels will step right in and kill lots of people in the process."

"Maybe. The thing is, somebody is going to be running the mob out here. It can be you or Joe Blow as far as I'm concerned, but the less violence the better. I get that. I'm not in the moral failings business. I just want to arrest the murderers, and rapists, and other bad guys. It's my job, my calling if you will, and that includes nailing the big shots who call the shots."

"As a Cucamonga, hopefully someday to be Rancho Cucamonga, taxpayer, I appreciate that. Keep up the good work, Sergeant Sommes."

I smiled at Izzy. "I'd wish you the same, but that would be a lie."

"I'll let myself out." Izzy walked down my steps, climbed into his Mercedes, and drove off, not looking back.

I got myself a beer, reflecting on this unusual encounter with a Dylan-quoting, astrology respecting gangster. He'd brought something out in me. I sounded like a politician just then, talking to him. Sam would be proud of me. On the other hand, there were serious warning bells going off in my head. How had he known I was heading home? There must be a multi-car, expert surveillance team on me. His men were good at their jobs.

Izzy and I would certainly cross paths again, possibly soon. I tried to summon up some guilt for enjoying our conversation, and failed. I realized that only Sam was going to know about this meeting, not Carol or JK. It was private and oddly personal. It didn't change any plans. On Tuesday, we'd take down dirty cop Hank Phillips and thwart a bank robbery. That was the job. Between now and then, I believed that Izzy and his boys were not going to shoot me in the back. That could change in the near future, but even then, I figured Izzy would prefer a fair fight, not an ambush.

After a shower, I headed out to meet Hank Phillips at our favorite cop bar, hoping this was the last night of it.

CHAPTER THIRTY-NINE

MAY 20

SAM CHUCKLED AFTER I DESCRIBED my meeting with Mr. Weiss. "He's identified you as someone he wants to know on our side of the fence," Sam said. "Now you have no choice. You have to take the job promotion that I'm offering you." I knew he meant it, and that he was right.

We were drinking coffee in Upland on Monday morning before proceeding to the new temporary command post being set up in the county building at Foothill and Sierra Avenue. I'd told Sam that I was keeping the Izzy Weiss meeting to myself for now, since it didn't change our plans. He agreed, saying it had no operational value to the team, but to be ready to reconsider if JK or other officers needed to know of it for their safety.

One other item occurred to me. "Sometime tonight or maybe tomorrow morning, Tammy Bottomly's main contact should bring her in." It was difficult to say her name with a straight face, but I managed. "She should be in North Hollywood now. When all this goes down on Tuesday, Izzy's going to know that his plans got leaked. His first choice might be Hank Phillips, but Tammy figures to be in the mix." Sam made a note of this, and we left for the command center meeting at 10 a.m.

The attendees were Sam, JK, Gutierrez, me, the LA County bank job expert, and my old buddy Al Sevilla from the San Dimas office of the LA Sheriff's Department. He'd played a major role in taking down the gang responsible for the Claremont bombing case two years before. "You guys need all the help you can get," he said. I was glad to see him.

Sam had made a decision to bring Laura Gutierrez fully on board. Hank Phillips had requested a vacation day, saying he had family matters to attend to, so she was free to attend this meeting. Did Phillips even have a family? He seemed like such a loner. In any case, his vacation day fit perfectly for us. Gutierrez would be partnered with Hank tomorrow, so her role could be vital. My drinking session with Hank the night before had been uneventful and relatively short. Maybe we both were getting tired of the routine. He didn't tip off any of his plans.

The LA bank robbery expert was named Jerry Esposito. He looked and talked like a New Yorker. He was focused on the armored car schedule for the Fontana Bank of America. Joe told us something that we already knew, namely that bank robberies were becoming an inefficient way for professionals to steal money unless they could get at the vault. And these schmucks, whoever they were, were not getting to the vault. Still, there'd be lots of cash floating around among the tellers before the 1 p.m. armored car pickup. Joe figured a 12:30 hit on the bank. The robbers would be armed, certainly with handguns and possibly AR-15 automatic rifles or some other variation. How to avoid a blood bath, including civilian casualties, was a major focus of the meeting. Everybody was still affected by the level of fire power that had occurred at the SLA shoot-out.

"Two thousand to three thousand rounds fired at the SWAT team and nobody on our side got killed," JK said. "No civilians either," he added. We all agreed that it was something of a miracle, or maybe those idiots were simply terrible shots. We'd never know, since all of those inside the house were dead.

Joe did not think we should wait until the bank robbery was completed before arresting them. "Hit 'em right as they enter," was his advice. "Their focus will be on controlling the scene and the crowd."

"Does that present an evidence problem?" Sam asked. "Apprehending them before they ask for money?"

"If several armed men enter the bank wearing masks and yell 'this is a robbery' I figure your DA's office can get convictions," Joe said.

"As some of you have heard me say, I believe this is more of a power move by Izzy Weiss than anything else," Sam said. "They can make more money over lunch through their gambling and loan sharking."

"Any estimates of how much the tellers will have?" Sevilla asked.

"The bank manager says around fifteen grand on a normal weekday," Sam said. "Friday would be more."

The team worked out all the details. The head teller would be briefed in advance, but not the others. The tellers' protocol was to pay up in any case and not resist.

"What about my partner, Hank Phillips?" Officer Gutierrez asked.

"According to our information, his role is supposed to be the first lawman on the scene. He will get hit in the head or beat up for his trouble, but his presence is intended to keep others from hitting alarms or otherwise messing things up. When he shows up at the bank will be critical."

Sam checked his notes. "Your regular shift with Phillips starts at eight tomorrow morning in San Bernardino, correct? We'll have plenty of gang reports for the two of you to review. At some point, I'm guessing that he's going to suggest a journey to Fontana for a work-related reason. We'll have eyes on your vehicle. Once you arrive at or near the bank, I'm again guessing he'll tell you to stay in the car," Sam said. "If so, stay clear of the bank's front door. If not, go in the bank, but be alert."

I wasn't certain that involving Gutierrez to this degree was wise. If she acted nervous tomorrow morning, she could alert Phillips that something was up. Obviously, Sam believed in her. So be it.

As if reading my mind, Sam asked her, "Are you up for this, Officer Gutierrez? It's a tricky job."

"I'm fine. This is a little scary. I'll admit it," she said.

Sam smiled at her. "A little scary has served me very well for many years."

The trickiest issue was deciding who in law enforcement would be in the bank.

Expert Joe was emphatic on this point. "Who are your best unarmed combat instructors? This is a ninja warrior type of deal. It's likely that one of the robbers will jump up on a table, wave a gun, and declare that this is a bank robbery, or something similar. Let's assume three robbers enter the bank and start yelling at people. All three need to be disabled at lightning speed, and not by shooting at them."

I was guessing, to my disappointment, that JK and I were not going to be in the bank. I was no ninja warrior. "I've had about five years of martial arts training," Sevilla said. "I'd like to put it to use."

"I'll need to clear that with your supervisor, Al," Sam said, "since you are volunteering for this outside of your jurisdiction."

"Sure, he'll be fine with it."

"Jimmy, I want you and JK on Hank Phillips," Sam said. "We'll have eyes on him, plus Officer Gutierrez's report. So nail his ass when the deal goes down. He never has to make it through the bank's door as far as I'm concerned."

We took a break to allow Sam and his administrative staff to contact the unarmed combat instructors. I hoped they'd say yes, like Al, but there was no guarantee. This was not classroom stuff. I used the time to call my Alta Loma station. I'd spent almost no time there recently. My only message was to call Carol, which I did. It was just after noon.

"Phillips is at Willie's Burgers, right on schedule," she said. "Gideon is two tables away, playing chess with some old geezer he met, so his cover is perfect."

"Hank took a vacation day today, still went to the burger joint. Looks like it's showtime tomorrow. We're getting ready here." I filled her in on the basic approach.

"I guess I better stay clear," she said with obvious reluctance. I had an idea.

"Why don't you and your cherry red Chevy Bel Air form an outer perimeter." I thought about it. "Let's say the corner of Foothill and Haven. Probably won't mean anything, but you never know. This operation could go sideways. Lots of moving parts. Nothing ever goes as planned."

"Better than nothing, I guess. Do you need to clear this with Sam?"

"No. You're a private citizen and entitled to drink coffee or eat food in that shopping center."

"What time?"

"The expert thinks they'll hit the bank around noon so go early. And keep your illegal scanner on, or whatever you use. I suggest you release Gideon from further duty. All kinds of spooky surveillance personnel will be descending soon." We signed off. I was getting excited. Big operations are a kick in the ass. Carol was feeling it too.

The main room was buzzing when I returned. Two unarmed combat instructors were coming aboard. Another said no, something that I knew Sam, rightly or wrongly, would tuck away in his mind. That guy might not be invited to the next Christmas party. Continuing to use expert Joe's three-robber assumption, Sevilla was assigned the robber nearest to the door, likely a pure crowd control guy. Both of the combat instructors had served in Vietnam, battled with the Viet Cong, and lived to tell about it. We were confident they could take down a couple of bank robbers.

That left one thorny issue, something that could mess up the entire plan. We were blind as to the getaway car or cars. Crooks watched television just like everybody did. No good bank robbery is complete without some souped-up vehicle screeching to a halt in front of the bank as the robbers emerge with their bags of cash.

"We'll have a surveillance unit in that Moose Lodge building north of the bank," Sam said.

Joe was studying the street map. "That union hall on Arrow Boulevard will have a good vantage point, and then you need something on Sierra Avenue. The key is not to tip off the robbers."

I looked at the map. "How about the Chamber of Commerce building on Sierra?"

Heads nodded. We had our surveillance locations. Sam got up to start arranging the teams. "I suggest that all of you take some time away from this the rest of the day, unless you have specific assignments. Stay clear of other lawmen. Loose lips sink ships and so forth. Go to a movie or something. We reconvene here at seven tomorrow morning."

As JK and I got up to leave, Sam gestured for the two of us to stay back. "Once we secure the scene in the bank, your job is to arrest Hank Phillips. He may have a trick or two up his sleeve. Don't drive your Charger, Jimmy. Everybody knows it. What's your vehicle, JK?" I knew the answer. It was a Datsun sedan but not the tiny one. It had some juice. Sam said fine. The meeting was over.

I headed for home, checking for any tails. I didn't see any, but I hadn't seen one yesterday either. I'd recently bought a Gram Parsons record titled *Grievous Angel* that got released after his death last year. I put it on the turntable. I'd heard from our dipshit singer's girlfriend that his anger management therapy had concluded. Great. It was time for Salton Sea, our band, to get rolling again. I'd never forget asking Allie, the tough radical woman, to come to one of our gigs, hoping but not expecting that she'd show up. She had. I'd never been the same since, in a good if crazy-ass way. I decided to call her tomorrow night, after we arrested the bad guys. I missed her, and knew that Parsons's bittersweet music would intensify the feelings.

I was changing. A year ago, I'd have been champing at the bit, wanting to be inside the bank going toe to toe with the robbers. I still loved the action, but I wanted to pick my spots. I was going to accept that job promotion that Sam had put on the table and give it my best shot. That meeting with Izzy Weiss had cemented that. I was finally ready to accept and take on the more complex, and even ambiguous, elements of the cops-and-robbers business.

I might take one more run at trying to hire Carol to help me run the shop. San Bernardino was a goddamn big county. No matter what she said, chasing philandering husbands and all the other PI stuff would get boring. She loved the action too. I could see it in her eyes.

CHAPTER FORTY

May 21

THE NEXT DAY STARTED BADLY. Sam informed me before our meeting started that Tammy had disappeared. Her Sheriff's Department contact had arranged for a meeting with her at 10 p.m. the previous evening to discuss the logistics of safely bringing her in. She didn't show up at the North Hollywood rendezvous location. He later checked her apartment. She was gone. Her car was gone. Sam shrugged his shoulders. "Informants get jumpy when it's game day," was all he said. We both hoped it was nothing more than that, and that she hadn't blown the operation. We'd know soon enough. Since her role was still confidential, we'd keep this information to ourselves.

She wasn't the only missing person. Sam opened the morning meeting at the new Foothill command center with the news that Hank Phillips was missing. He'd managed to leave his apartment during the night, unobserved by the surveillance team, and vanished. His dirty old Oldsmobile, which he used on the job, was parked in his stall. We contacted Officer Gutierrez, who was scheduled to ride with him this morning, and told her to stand by at San Bernardino headquarters.

"Damn, I hope Izzy Weiss hasn't pulled the plug on the job," JK said.

"Let's assume not," Sam said. "Phillips's role is somewhat secondary." Regardless, he was a compromised lawman. Phillips's career was over, no matter what happened today. I was glad that Officer Gutierrez was going to be spared the job of hanging with him today. It was one too many complications. We'd had two quick strikes thrown against us already today, but the fundamental task of thwarting the bank robbery remained front and center.

We settled into business, discussing the various assignments for the day. Sam and two technicians, plus Joe Esposito, were going to remain at the command center and communicate with all of us.

"Sommes and JK will operate out of the Moose Lodge next to the bank and coordinate matters on the ground. Al," Sam gestured to Deputy Sevilla, "you, Max, and Phil will enter the bank when it opens. The bank manager will put you in a conference room where you can push paper around for a while and look busy." Max and Phil were the tough-looking unarmed combat instructors brought in to disable the bank robbers. They were wearing slacks and golf shirts.

JK said what I was thinking. "None of you look like accountants auditing bank statements to me, but what do I know." That drew a laugh.

"Hey, I went to college," Sevilla responded.

I couldn't resist. "And ran track if I recall. You were fast as hell."

"Okay, okay. Let's roll, team," Sam said. "Only critical information on the radio feed. No chitchat. This frequency is secure, but you never can tell."

***

The morning was all about positioning, getting the pieces in the right places. It went smoothly, and the sense of anticipation was building. Soon, it was rewarded. Just after noon, a white cargo van with Nevada plates was observed traveling east on Arrow Blvd. It turned into the Bank of America parking lot, cut its engine, and waited. It looked out of place. We all sensed it. I breathed a sigh of relief.

"Looks like it's going down," I said. "Watch for getaway vehicles." Shortly after that, a San Bernardino County Sheriff's patrol vehicle pulled up next to the van. That wasn't part of the plan. "Whose car is that?" somebody in the Moose

Lodge yelled out. "Christ! Don't give them a goddamned ticket."

That's always a risk with closely held assignments, an unwanted volunteer. As if listening to our excited observer, the patrol car moved away, turned right on Arrow Blvd, and parked. It was impossible to observe the officers through the tinted windows. "Keep track of that car," Sam said.

Soon thereafter, the white cargo van started its engine and moved to a location directly in front of the bank's door. This was it! The bank robbers, wearing hats and masks, exited the vehicle and started toward the bank. There were three of them, just as Joe had predicted, and they were armed, pistols but no rifles.

"They're coming in," I alerted our men inside the bank, and then a thought hit me. "Sam, check with motor pool at headquarters, see if a patrol car was checked out this morning. That might be Phillips."

"On it," he said.

The bank robbers calmly entered the bank. After that, it was silence for what felt like an eternity. No word as to what was happening inside the bank. "This is taking too long," JK muttered. Had we missed something? Maybe the robbers had disabled our ninja warriors? Then two gunshots rang out from inside the bank.

"Shots fired," I barked out to Sam and the rest of the team. "Be prepared to move."

"Not yet," Sam cautioned. Another tense minute later, Sevilla's calm voice was music to our ears. "Suspects in custody," he said, "no injuries. Our scene is secure." A swarm of officers descended on the Bank of America from outside the building. I learned later that one of the robbers managed to raise and fire his weapon as he was announcing the robbery. Only the ceiling tiles were damaged. It had been a textbook operation.

Sam's voice came on the radio. "Phillips checked out a patrol car at ten this morning, saying his car had a dead battery. Officer Gutierrez, confirm your whereabouts."

"At the San Bernardino station. Never saw him today," she answered. Good. Phillips likely was alone.

It appeared Phillips was the getaway driver, using a Sheriff's Department patrol car. Just as Sevilla announced the all-clear, somebody inside the bank mistakenly pushed the silent alarm button. All of us heard the alert. It went out to all police vehicles on all frequencies. Our observation team at the union hall saw the phantom patrol car accelerate and head west on Arrow Blvd toward Ontario. Phillips had gotten the alert and knew, with dozens of officers about to descend on the bank, that he had to get out of there pronto.

"Sam, how do we identify that patrol car?"

Sam read off the license plate to the confidential radio feed.

"Put out a BOLO on the car on this closed frequency only," he said. "He may think he's in the clear. Let's get this son-of-a bitch. Meanwhile, to those in the bank: Read the bank robbery suspects their rights and transport them to the Fontana Station ASAP. Good work, Joe and the rest of the team. I'll notify the FBI."

Meanwhile, it was up to JK and me, along with the other officers, to find Phillips the old-fashioned way. I hoped that Carol had been listening on her scanner.

"Come on, JK, let's roll." We ran out of the Moose Lodge and jumped into his Datsun. It was rigged with a siren and blue light. Where the hell to go? Phillips would ditch the police car somewhere, but maybe not right away. Unless we'd blown it somewhere, we had time to find him.

Sam came on the radio. "We have about seven patrol cars on this feed. Let's fan out. He'll likely head for the San Bernardino Freeway. There's an on-ramp at Citrus Avenue. He'll want to create some distance. I will contact the Highway Patrol separately."

It made sense, which was why I thought Hank Phillips wouldn't do it. In his mind, somebody was working backwards from his withdrawal of a patrol car this morning, including his partner, Gutierrez. "Sam, JK and I are heading north, just to hedge our bets."

"Roger that," he said and signed off.

JK was skeptical. "Man, I'd get on the freeway and haul ass for thirty minutes toward the desert, and then ditch the car."

"I've spent more time drinking with this guy than I ever want to again. He knows he's screwed, one way or another. He loves the mountains, says it's the only place he feels free. Maybe he'll head up there." After I said it, I realized the irony that Phillips and I had another commonality. We both breathed easier north of Foothill.

"Where's he going to dump the patrol car?" JK asked.

"I have no idea about that, so we're running blind. Not the first time for me."

"Me neither," said JK, gunning the car north up Sierra Avenue toward Foothill.

Five minutes later we got our answer. Sam came on the radio. "Tell JK to switch to his CB radio frequency."

JK was more of a gearhead than I was. He pulled over to the curb and relieved me from fumbling around with his radio. "This is JK on Foothill signing in."

"Subject vehicle just passed the corner of Haven and Foothill heading north toward Baseline. I'm in soft pursuit." It was Carol. She'd found him!

"Ten-four, we're about five minutes behind you."

Sam redirected the other vehicles toward us but we were in the lead. As long as Phillips stayed in the patrol car, we had him.

"He's turning left on Baseline, increasing his speed," Carol said.

I was thinking Mt. Baldy Road. Phillips was heading up the mountain like a trapped animal climbing a tree. I put JK's blue light on his hood. "Hit the siren. We need to make up time. He won't hear us from here."

Carol's voice stayed steady and calm. "He's driving just above the speed limit, not attracting attention."

JK and I were quiet, intent on our quarry. I started to

think about weapons. "Do you have your shotgun?" I asked JK. He nodded. I had a brief flashback to our first journey together, that dark night in Portland chasing an ice-cold killer with Carol's life hanging in the balance.

"He just passed Euclid," Carol said. "I'm slowing a little, don't want him to spot me."

"Okay, I'm figuring he'll stay on Baseline until he hits Padua and then turn right," I told her. "But you tell me. I figure he's going up to Baldy."

I knew Sam was directing traffic, tightening the net. JK was hauling ass, the siren blaring. We made the turn onto Baseline, going about sixty, dodging in and out of cars. "Kill the siren at Benson," I said. "I'll keep the blue light on until we get closer." JK nodded again, concentrating on the road.

After several more tense minutes, Carol briefed us. "The patrol car is turning north on Padua." Bingo! Padua led directly to Mt. Baldy Road.

Sam got out ahead of me, sending two patrol units up Glendora Ridge Road to the west. That was the only other way out of Mt. Baldy. Phillips was driving into what amounted to a box canyon.

I took down our blue light when we made the right turn on Padua. I soon saw Carol's Bel Air ahead of us.

"Behind you now, in JK's silver Datsun," I told her. I saw the rogue patrol car now, as Phillips's quixotic journey continued. If we weren't here, and if he stole a car in Baldy Village, who knew? Next stop, Mexico. No chance now. He was ours now, dead or alive. I very much wanted it to be alive.

The traffic had thinned. "Hang back now," I said to Carol.

I remembered one other option. "Sam, he could cut down toward San Antonio Heights at that sharp turn after the dam." Sam redirected one of the chase cars. I figured Phillips would only do that if he made us and was trying to escape. We drove past the big nursery on the left. I saw Phillips's patrol car climbing the big hill that took the road past the Baldy Dam. The sky was bright blue. No smog up here today. There were three cars between Phillips and

Carol's Chevy. That was perfect. I saw a marked sheriff's vehicle in my rearview mirror.

"Keep that car behind us another fifty yards back," I said. Our procession continued past the dam. Phillips slowed down, an old pickup truck in front of him. He passed by the San Antonio Heights escape road. We were clean. Next were the two tunnels.

Baldy Village was a mile in front of him along the dry twisty road. "I'd steal a car in the village," JK said. I nodded, taking my service revolver out of the holster.

"Carol, if he parks in the village, continue past him and then do a U-turn, blocking him. Are you armed?"

"Damn straight," she said.

"Careful now," Sam cautioned.

We drove past the strange gingerbread house at the entrance to Baldy Village. As a kid, it always made me think of the witch's house in "Hansel and Gretel."

"He's signaling a left turn," Carol said. We could see it too. There was a parking lot directly across the road from the Mount Baldy Lodge restaurant. That looked to be his destination.

"Pull over," I directed JK as we got closer. "I'll drive. Go flank him." JK jumped out of the barely stopped car, retrieved his shotgun from the trunk, and ran to the left. He knew what to do. I took the driver's seat and got back in the slow chase. The entire maneuver took about thirty seconds. Hank Phillips pulled into the parking lot. Carol drove past him. I cruised to a slow stop, blocking the parking lot entrance, slid over to the passenger door, and got out that side, using the car as cover. Phillips, dressed in camo like a hunter, had left the patrol car and was scanning the five or six cars in the parking lot, trying to figure out which one to steal. He turned to his right, saw me, yelled something, and then fired a quick shot at me as I ducked down. The bullet pinged off the silver Datsun.

"It's over, Hank, drop the gun," I yelled. "We've got you covered from every angle." It was an overstatement.

"I knew it. I always knew you were an asshole, Sommes, running some sort of game on me. But I played anyway," he yelled. "Why the hell not? I'm finished."

"Drop the gun, man, and you're a whole lot less finished." I could see JK now, about twenty yards behind him, using a boulder as cover, his shotgun trained on Phillips.

Phillips relaxed. "This is like a damn cowboy movie," he said. "But I'm no cop killer."

Relieved, I thought he might drop his gun, but he had something else in mind. He slowly raised his revolver toward his face. JK ran toward him. The rest of the scene was frozen. I stood up, allowing myself to be a target, trying to distract him, sensing what he was going to do. "Don't do it, Hank," I yelled.

"Why the hell not? Let me do this, Sommes," he said, starting to put the pistol in his mouth, still hesitating. Not easy to kill yourself.

Those seconds made all the difference. JK hit him from behind with a hard tackle, using his left arm to pull Phillips's gun hand away from him. The pistol flew into the air as JK and Phillips fell onto the gravel, complete with a satisfying grunt from our captive. JK had knocked the air out of him, I cuffed Phillips as he lay there gasping.

"You should play for the Rams, JK. That was perfect."

"You should have let me, Sommes," Phillips said.

"No way, pal. You don't get the easy way out." JK read Phillips his rights.

"I know my fucking rights, kid. I'm a cop, remember."

"Not much of one, and not anymore," JK said, escorting him to one of the patrol cars. It was manned by two of Sam's best officers.

"Take him to San Bernardino and book him," I told the sergeant. "JK and I will meet you there."

I saw Carol appear, looking a little tentative among all the sheriff's personnel. I gave her a hug. "You did good, Madam Detective, great, in fact. Maybe you have a future in this business."

CHAPTER FORTY-ONE

May 21

JK AND I WERE PREPARING to talk to Hank Phillips in one of the San Bernardino interrogation rooms. The police union sent him a lawyer. We knew the interview was a formality. Phillips was at least smart enough to say absolutely nothing, and had a lawyer to help him. Then we got some stunning news from Sam Fuller.

At 1:30 this same afternoon an attractive woman in a silver mini-dress, high heels, a Marilyn Monroe face mask, and a platinum blonde wig robbed the Claremont branch of the Bank of America of about $10,000. She politely displayed a small Beretta handgun and asked the head teller to quietly and quickly collect from each of the six tellers. Giving her weapon a slight wave, she calmly cautioned the tellers to avoid setting off any of the alarms. The branch manager was attending a Rotary Club golf fundraiser, and the assistant manager was on the phone with his back turned, feet on his desk, paying no attention to the floor. The few customers in the bank were likewise oblivious to the event since the woman had kept her head down, mask hidden, until she reached the counter. One man later admitted to being fixated on the woman's chest as opposed to her actions.

The robbery took five minutes. The security camera caught Marilyn Monroe robbing the bank and nothing else. The lady robber exited the bank through the Yale Avenue front door and disappeared into the sunlit day.

Sam was quiet after delivering the news. "What about Phillips?" JK asked. "Should we interview him now?"

"Let him stew for a while. No harm done." Sam had a

sheet of paper in front of him. "Tammy Lee Bottomly," he mused, "what a name. Her police contact called me, saying the Claremont bank robber fits her description."

Did it ever. I even remembered that dress. It all fit just as tightly as that dress. Tammy had disappeared from her apartment at exactly the right time. She had a well-developed sense of irony, among other things. All I could do was shake my head. "Who the hell knows," I said. I figured it had to be her. Was she forced to do it? I doubted that. She hadn't blown the Fontana operation. She could have. Tammy was happily playing both sides of the fence. Unlike Phillips, she was smart enough to pull it off.

"Do you think the Fontana job was just a diversion?" JK asked Sam.

"No. Joe told me that the three men we arrested in Fontana are experienced and respected men in the business. LA County wants them for several robberies. That makes this bust even better. Izzy Weiss likely rented them, but his colleagues in the LA mob wouldn't have tolerated them being wasted as a diversion. As it is, Izzy will have some explaining to do to his fellow mobsters. It will test his leadership, especially as a Jew up against all those Italian 'made men.' They will never fully trust him. The FBI is questioning the robbers now, just for the record. They won't talk."

"It was a perfect double-header, Claremont in LA County and Fontana in our county," I said. "Izzy means business."

"Just between us, I'm glad we stopped the San Bernardino County robbery, our jurisdiction," Sam said. "The team did a fine job, starting with you two. LA County can deal with the Claremont thing. It's their problem. Now, go talk to that dirty cop, just for the record."

As expected, the interrogation was a waste of time. His lawyer advised Hank to say nothing, and he followed orders. I stared at him the entire time that JK questioned him. Phillips kept his head down, wouldn't meet my eyes. To hell with him. We were done until the trial. Time to call it a good day. I was tempted to call Carol to see if she wanted to have a drink, but decided against it. I couldn't talk to her about Tammy so better to let things settle down. It was great to be working with her again, though.

I went home instead, thinking I might listen to more of those new Gram Parsons tunes and then try and reach Allie. I'd barely entered my cabin when the telephone rang. I picked up and a voice I knew began to speak. Izzy Weiss.

"I'd say each of us went one for two today, Jimmy. That's a five hundred average in baseball, better than Ted Williams ever did." He wanted to gloat, to get the last laugh.

"Yeah, but two at-bats mean nothing in baseball. Let's see what the future holds." I didn't even bother to ask how he got my unlisted phone number. "I hear it was quite a looker that pulled off the Claremont job. Anybody I know?"

"A gentleman never divulges such secrets. You, of all people, should know that when it comes to certain ladies." There was a sharp edge to his voice. He knew something about Tammy and me, whatever set of lies she'd chosen to tell him.

"Yeah, but you're no gentleman, Izzy." I hung up. I'd had enough of him and his schemes for one day. But I knew, with absolute certainty, that he and I were now engaged in a long-term match, one in which somebody was going to lose big. I reserved the last laugh for me and put it on the proverbial shelf for safe keeping. Then I shook him off me the way a dog shakes off water. I had happier things in mind.

My telephone had a long cord. I grabbed a Budweiser from the refrigerator and took it out to the deck along with the telephone. I called a number in San Jose. Allie wasn't there, but she'd just installed one of those new-fangled answering machines. She needed it for her work, never wanting to miss a story. And maybe for me too, I hoped. After the beep, I left a message: "I'm going to be in the bar at the Sycamore Inn this coming Saturday, May 25th, at 7 p.m. in one of those secluded corner booths. I sure hope you show up wearing one of those sexy black dresses of yours."

CHAPTER FORTY-TWO

May 25

I ***GOT THERE FIRST, FEELING*** nervous. We'd been lovers for two years, shared and kept secrets, endured separation and heartbreak, but somehow survived it all. Tonight, however, felt different, almost like a first date. My armor, and hopefully hers, had been set aside. Allie had called and told me she was coming, but I was never really sure. Previously, if she'd gotten a Patricia Hearst tip, it was game over. Now, after her scare in Los Angeles, her trip to the hospital, her seeing my face in her mind before passing out, I sensed a transformation. I'd told Pedro the bartender to bring us a bottle of champagne the second she arrived.

Allie entered the bar, needing a moment for her eyes to adjust to the darkness. She saw me and smiled, a little shyly for such a self-assured woman. The sexy black dress was in place. Her injuries had healed. The champagne arrived. I poured two glasses. We talked about nothing of consequence, both needing a break from our work, and ordered steaks. I must have eaten it. Mostly I remember looking into her dark eyes and studying her Italian Renaissance face. I never tired of it. We drank a bottle of red wine. Allie loved red wine, and it went better with the food. After dinner we drank cognac. The alcohol tonight was a far cry from my usual beer and tequila, and it had me seeing double. At some point, she moved to sit next to me in the booth. I could feel the heat of her thighs through her stockings and her wandering hand on my thigh.

"Does this joint have any bungalows?" she whispered in my ear, her cognac gone. "I want to spend the night here.

You're a cop. Make it happen."

It was worth a try. In the earlier "Route 66" days, movie stars used to stay here. I paid the bill and then talked to Pedro, still not expecting much. To my amazement, he said yes. There was a party house out back, reserved as an amenity for their VIP customers. We were lucky. It was available tonight. I emptied my wallet. I think it held fifty bucks. He tried to say no, but I insisted.

We walked up the dark gravel path toward the cabin, both of us giddy, trying our best to avoid the century plants that ran alongside. I may have even muttered something about it, saying I didn't want to fall on my ass into the cactus. "Don't worry about that, or anything else, cowboy," she said. "We've got all the time in the world."

On impulse, I threw open the door, picked her up, and carried her across the threshold. She started to complain, then her face melted into my neck. I felt tears. We found the bed. We made love in candlelight. Time no longer existed. After long, solitary journeys, we were home at last.

In the morning, as sunlight began to filter through the shutters, Allie turned to me sleepily and asked, "Where are we, Jimmy?" I knew it was rhetorical. Allessandra D'Amico always knew exactly where she was.

Yet, I loved the question. It was filled to the brim with a rich multitude of possible answers. I kept it simple. "Just north of Foothill, babe, right where we belong."

Acknowledgements

My thanks to veteran newshound, David Allen, for providing a Forward to this novel. His expanded turf now covers all of the Inland Empire plus portions of Los Angeles County, and David's columns chronicle the events and people of the region with his customary blend of humor and heart.

I also want to thank my teachers, my fellow students and friends, and even the dreaded vice-principals at Sycamore School, El Roble Intermediate School, and Claremont High School (one year) for providing me with a wonderful Claremont, California education. After a frolic and detour to Illinois, I returned and attended Claremont Men's (now McKenna) College, where, despite myself, I grew up and benefited from a classic CMC liberal arts education. All these years provided me with a rich treasure trove of experiences and memories that I plan to continue to explore and channel through my protagonists, Jimmy Sommes and Carol Loomis who, like me, are true Claremonters.

About the Author

Orlando Davidson graduated from Claremont Men's (now McKenna) College and UCLA School of Law in the 1970's and headed west to the Hawaiian Islands. After a thirty-five-year career in Hawaii working as an attorney, planner, lobbyist, and public official, Orlando relocated to western North Carolina and began to write fiction. *Baseline Road*, his first novel, and now *North of Foothill* were shaped by his student days in California during the tumultuous 1970's. He now resides in Oregon.